HELLO AMERICA

J·G·BALLARD
HELLO AMERICA

Carroll & Graf Publishers, Inc.
New York

First published in the United States of America by Carroll & Graf
Publishers, Inc. 1988

Carroll & Graf Publishers, Inc.
260 Fifth Avenue
New York, NY 10001

Library of Congress Cataloging-in-Publication Data

Ballard, J. G., 1930–
  Hello America.

  I. Title.
PR6052.A46H4   1988   823′.914   88-20251
ISBN 0-88184-455-1

Manufactured in the United States of America

Contents

1 | The Golden Coast

'There's gold, Wayne, gold dust everywhere! Wake up! The streets of America *are* paved with gold!'

Later, when they beached the SS *Apollo* against the derelict Cunard pier at the lower tip of Manhattan, Wayne was to remember with some amusement how excited McNair had been as he burst into the sail locker. The chief engineer gesticulated wildly, his beard glowing like an overlit lantern.

'Wayne, it's everything we've dreamed of! Look at it just once, even if it blinds you!'

He almost tipped Wayne from his hammock. Steadying himself against the metal ceiling, Wayne gazed at McNair's inflamed beard. An eerie copper light filled the sail locker, surrounding him with bales of golden carpets, as if they had steamed into the eye of a radioactive hurricane.

'McNair, wait! See Dr Ricci! You may be − !'

But McNair had gone, ready to rouse the ship. Wayne listened to him shouting at the two startled stokers in the coal bunker. While he slept through the afternoon − he had come off the long night watch at eight that morning − the *Apollo* had anchored half a mile from the Brooklyn shore, presumably to give Professor Summers and the scientific members of the expedition time to test the atmosphere. Now they were ready to make way again and enter New York harbour, their first landfall after the voyage from Plymouth.

Winches wheezed and grunted, the anchor chains dragged at the rusty bow plates. Wayne climbed from his hammock and dressed quickly, glancing into the cracked mirror that swung from the door. A golden face stared back at him, startled eyes under the blond thatch like a gawky angel's. As he reached the deck a cloud of soot-flakes fell from the funnel and covered the glowing fore-sail with hundreds of fireflies. Crew and passengers crowded the rail, waiting impatiently while the antique engines of the *Apollo*, clearly exhausted by the seven-week voyage across the Atlantic, laboured against the slack coastal water.

Annoyed with himself — already he was trembling with excitement like a child — Wayne looked out at the magnetic coast. An immense golden sheen lay over the Brooklyn shoreline, reflected from the silent quays and warehouses. The afternoon sun hung above the deserted Manhattan streets, adding its light to the glittering field below. For a moment Wayne almost believed that these long-silent avenues and expressways had carpeted themselves with the rarest treasures in preparation for just his visit.

Behind the *Apollo* was the massive span of the Verrazano Narrows suspension bridge, long familiar to Wayne from the ancient slides in the Geographical Society library in Dublin. He had gazed for hours at the photographs, as he had at a thousand other images of America, but he was unprepared for the spectacular size and mysterious form of the bridge. In some way it had managed to exaggerate itself during the long century it had been forgotten by everyone else. Many of the vertical cables had snapped, and the huge, copper-hued structure, covered with rust and verdigris, resembled a recumbent harp that had played its last song to the indifferent sea.

Wayne stared at the approaching city, again unable to reconcile the scene in front of him with the image of the Manhattan skyline he had day-dreamed over in the darkness of the library projection room. Dozens of towers rose through the afternoon light. Even at a distance of three miles the glass curtain-walling of these huge buildings glowed like bronze mirrors, as if the streets below them were stacked with bullion. Wayne could see the old Empire State Building, venerable patriarch of the city, the twin columns of the World Trade Center, and the 200-storey OPEC Tower which dominated Wall Street, its neon sign pointing towards Mecca. Together they formed the familiar skyline whose peaks and canyons Wayne knew by heart, and which now seemed transformed by this dream of gold.

He listened to McNair shouting at the stokers through the engine-room portholes below him.

'Good God, you'll need more than your shovels! It must be six inches deep, blown all the way from the Appalachians!'

Wayne laughed aloud at the golden shore, caught up by McNair's excitement. Although only twenty-five, a mere four years older than Wayne, McNair liked to affect a distracted, world-weary manner, particularly when showing anyone round his detested engine-room, with its coal-fired boilers, bizarre pistons and connecting rods straight out of the nineteenth century. Still, McNair knew his stuff, and could make anything work. Give him a lever and he would move the world, if not the SS *Apollo*. Edison and Henry Ford would have been proud of him.

And for all his strange humour, McNair had been the first to befriend Wayne after the young stowaway was found by Dr Ricci, shivering under the canvas awning of the captain's gig two days out from Plymouth. It was McNair who had interceded with Captain Steiner, and moved Wayne's hammock from the damp scullery behind the galley to the dark warmth of the sail-locker. Perhaps McNair saw in Wayne's determination to reach the United States something of his own intense need to get away from a tired and candle-lit Europe with its interminable rationing and subsistence living, its total lack of any flair and opportunity.

Nor was McNair alone in this — the *Apollo* carried an invisible cargo of dreams and private motives. As the funnel showered smuts on to their heads, the passengers on either side of Wayne were pointing silently to the golden coasts of

Manhattan, Brooklyn and the Jersey shore, awed by this glittering welcome from a long-forsaken continent.

Then Wayne heard little Orlowski, the expedition leader, calling impatiently to Captain Steiner for more steam. Orlowski's voice had temporarily lost the American accent that had snaked in over his Kiev vowels during the voyage. Through his miniature pocket megaphone he bellowed:

'Full ahead, Captain! We're all waiting for you! Don't change your mind now . . .'

But Steiner, as always, was taking his own time. He stood in the centre of his bridge beside the helmsman, legs well apart, calmly contemplating the golden shore like an experienced traveller outstaring a mirage. A stocky, compact man with curiously sensitive hands, he was now in his mid-forties, and had served in the Israeli Navy for nearly twenty years. Keen chess-player who never gave away a move, amateur mathematician and expert navigator, he had intrigued Wayne from their first meeting, as he peered up from the overturned gig into the Captain's wry gaze.

Wayne was certain that Steiner, like everyone else on board the *Apollo*, harboured secret ambitions of his own. After his discovery in the rowing-boat, the Captain had ordered Wayne down to his cabin. As Steiner locked away Dr Ricci's confiscated pistol in the safe, Wayne had glimpsed a neatly tied bundle of ancient *Time* and *Look* magazines on the shelf below the bullion box. Their brown pages were compressed like copper leaf, fossils of an America that had vanished a hundred years ago. Then, two weeks out of Plymouth, during one of the long calms, Steiner called Wayne back to his cabin after the stowaway had brought his supper from the galley.

'It's all right, Wayne . . .' Steiner smiled with some amusement at this seaborne Tom Sawyer, with his thatch of blond hair, legs like stilts, eyes lit by all kinds of strange dreams. Wayne was trembling with excitement as he faced the Captain – both Ricci and Professor Summers had been urging Orlowski to re-route the *Apollo*'s passage so that they could put Wayne ashore at the Azores.

'Wayne, calm down. You look as if you're about to take over the ship.' Could he already see Wayne's aggressiveness in his broad shoulders, in the thickening bones of his forehead and jaw? 'You'll be glad to hear we're not calling in at the Azores. But I want to show you something else.'

Leaving his supper uneaten, Steiner opened the safe and quietly unwrapped the *Time* and *Look* magazines. He turned the faded pages, showing Wayne the illustrations of the Cape Kennedy Space Center, the Space Shuttle landing at Edwards Air Force Base after a test flight, and the recovery of an Apollo capsule from the Pacific. There was a special bicentennial supplement celebrating every aspect of American life in the long-ago 1970s — the crowded streets of Washington on Carter's Inauguration Day, long queues of holiday jets on the runways of Kennedy Airport, happy vacationers lying by the swimming-pools of Miami, raking the ski-slopes of Aspen, Colorado, fitting out their yachts in a huge marina at San Diego, all the enormous vitality of this once extraordinary nation preserved in these sepia photographs.

'Well, Wayne, you want to go to America. Let's see how much you know about it.' Steiner sounded sceptical, but nodded encouragingly as Wayne moved from picture to picture:

'That's easy — the Golden Gate Bridge; Caesar's Palace in Las Vegas; LA — Mann's Chinese Theatre; Fisherman's Wharf in Frisco; Detroit — the Edsel Ford Expressway. Any more, Captain?'

'Not for now, Wayne. But that's very good, you're a stowaway with a difference. We'll have to work together . . .'

Not one in a thousand Europeans of Wayne's age would have had the faintest idea what these ancient scenic views represented. Sadly, Europe, Asia and the rest of the populated world had long since lost interest in America. But clearly Steiner had guessed that Wayne would recognise them. As he locked away the magazines he remarked:

'With luck you'll be seeing them soon. Tell me, Wayne,

from where in the United States did your family originally come?' He glanced at Wayne's long-boned figure, child-like straw hair. 'Kansas, the Midwest somewhere? You look like a Texan . . .'

'New England!' Wayne lied before stopping himself. 'Jamestown. My great-grandfather ran a hardware store.'

'Jamestown?' Steiner nodded sagely, careful not to smile as he beckoned Wayne to the door. 'Well, you're going back to the beginning, all right. Perhaps you'll start everything up again, Wayne. You could even be President. From stow-away to the White House, stranger things have happened.' He gazed thoughtfully at Wayne, his shrewd, navigator's face almost serious, set in a curious expression Wayne was to remember for ever.

'Think, Wayne — the forty-fifth President of the United States . . .'

2 | Collision Course

Why had he lied to Steiner?

Taking his eyes off the golden shore in front of him, Wayne looked up at the bridge, where Steiner stood beside the helmsman, binoculars raised to scan the flat water of the channel. Wayne angrily drummed his right hand on the rail. He could have told the truth, the Captain would have been sympathetic, he was something of an outcast himself, this sea-wandering Jew who had turned his back on his own true nation. Why hadn't he blurted out: I don't know where I came from, who my father was, let alone my grandparents. My mother died five years ago, after spending half her life as a psychiatric outpatient and the rest as a barely competent secretary at the American University in Dublin. All she left me were years of rambling fantasy and a blank space on my birth certificate. Tell me, Captain, who I am . . .

A sharp spray rose from the cutwater of the *Apollo* and stung Wayne's cheeks. Steiner was ringing down to the engine-room for more steam, and the ship gained speed across the bay, drawn towards the magnetic coast as if by the heavier gravity of this land of dreams. Remembering Steiner's words — the forty-fifth President? — Wayne thought of his mother again. During her last years in the asylum she often rambled about Wayne's real father, variously Henry Ford V; the last US President-in-Exile, President Brown (a devoutly religious nonagenarian who had died sixty years before Wayne's birth in a Zen monastery in Osaka); and a long-forgotten folk singer named Bob Dylan, one of whose records she endlessly played beside her bed on a hand-cranked gramophone.

But once, during a brief moment of lucidity while recovering from an overdose of Seconal, his mother fixed Wayne with a calm eye and told him that his father had been Dr William Fleming, Professor of Computer Sciences at the American University, who had vanished during an ill-fated expedition to the United States twenty years earlier.

Wayne had thought nothing of this odd confession. But while going through the unhappy muddle of his mother's possessions after her death — a mad antique shop of costume jewellery, newspaper clippings and drug vials — he had come across a ribbon-wrapped set of postcards, signed by Dr Fleming and postmarked 'Southampton, England', the expedition's point of departure. The tone of these brief but intimate messages, the repeated mention of being back for 'the great day', and the solicitous interest in this young secretary's pregnancy had together sown their seed in Wayne's mind.

Was his obsession with America, which his unknown ancestors had abandoned a century earlier, was his determination to return to this lost continent merely an attempt to find his true father? Or had he invented the quest for his father in order to give his obsession some kind of romantic meaning?

Did it matter now? Wayne pulled himself from his thoughts and gazed through the quickening spray at the Manhattan skyline rising towards him across the vivid water. Like his unknown ancestors centuries before him, he had come to America to forget the past, to turn his back for ever on an exhausted Europe. For the first time since he had stowed aboard the *Apollo*, Wayne felt a sudden sense of companionship, almost of commitment to his fellow passengers who had braved the long voyage with him.

On either side of him people were pressed against the rail, ignoring the spray whipped up by the rusty bows, members of the crew and the scientific expedition elbow to elbow. Even Dr Paul Ricci for once failed to annoy Wayne. The dapper, self-immersed nuclear physicist was the one member of the expedition whom Wayne disliked – a dozen times during the voyage he had strolled up behind Wayne as he worked in the log-room over the old street-maps of Manhattan and Washington, implying with a smirk that the whole of the United States was already his territory. He now stood beside Professor Summers, calling out landmarks to her.

'There's the Ford Building, Anne, and the Arab Quarter. If you look closely you can see the Lincoln Memorial . . . '

Had his grandparents ever lived in Manhattan, as he claimed? Wayne was about to correct him, but everyone had fallen silent. Orlowski, the expedition commissar, stood next to Wayne, holding the mainmast shrouds as if frightened that the increased speed of the *Apollo* might lift him off his little feet and carry him away over the topsails. Ricci had placed his arm around Professor Summers's waist, his ludicrous commentary ended, protecting himself behind her from the golden shore.

For once, Anne Summers made no effort to push him away. Despite the spray, her severe make-up remained in place, but the wind had begun to unravel the blonde hair which she kept tightly rolled in a bun. For all her efforts, Wayne reflected, the long voyage had freshened her Saxon complexion and given her toneless face and high, pale forehead an almost schoolgirlish glow. Wayne was her greatest admirer. Once, to her annoyance, he had entered the radiology lab without knocking and found her immersed in a small mirror, combing her hair to its breathtaking waist length, her face made up like a film actress of old, a screen goddess dreaming among her reaction columns and radiation counters. She had snapped out of the reverie soon enough, swearing at Wayne in a surprisingly guttural American which recalled McNair's quiet comment that she had changed her name from Sommer half an hour before the *Apollo* sailed from Plymouth.

But now the serene, far-away look had returned. She leaned against Ricci's arm, and even had time for a reassuring smile at Wayne.

'Professor Summers, is gold dust dangerous to inhale?' Wayne asked. 'It could be radioactive.'

'*Gold*, Wayne?' She laughed knowingly at the glittering shore. 'Don't worry, I think the transmutation of metals takes rather more than strong sunlight . . . '

Yet something was amiss. For no clear reason Wayne backed away from the rail. Shielding his eyes from the glare, he crossed the deck and climbed the metal ladder to the roof of the stables. Below him the twenty mules and baggage horses stirred restlessly in their stalls, whinnying to each other through the shafts of overbright sunlight. Wayne steadied himself against the ventilator, trying to identify this curious presentiment of danger. After the long journey across the Atlantic, was he losing his nerve at the prospect of actually setting foot on America? He searched the rigging and the surrounding sea, peering through the smoke at the Brooklyn and Jersey shorelines.

Conspicuously, the only composed person aboard the *Apollo* was Captain Steiner. As everyone crowded the rail, cheering on the approaching land, Steiner stood beside the helmsman, binoculars fixed on a small patch of open water a hundred yards ahead of them. Checking their speed, he glanced at Wayne in an almost conspiratorial way. The *Apollo* was now racing like a twelve-metre sloop through the choppy water, the ancient steam engines ready to burst the decks. The horses staggered in their stalls, thrown about by the surging motion of the ship. Steiner had crammed every square foot of sail on to the yards, as if this cautious ocean-navigator had decided to end his voyage with a yachtsman's flourish.

Already they were passing the first of the sunken refugee ships in the harbour. Dozens of the rusty hulks sat in the bay around the lower tip of Manhattan, masts and super-structures above the water, relics of the panic a century earlier when America had finally abandoned itself. In the

16

mosaics of flaking paint that clung to the riddled funnels Wayne could make out the livery of long-forgotten lines — Cunard, Holland-America, P & O. Even the SS *United States* was there, lying on its side below the Battery, called out of its retirement at Coney Island to ferry tens of thousands of fleeing Americans as the cities emptied and the deserts crept eastwards across the continent. The mouth of the East River was blocked by a boom of sunken freighters, the last of a mournful fleet of vessels chartered from the world's ports and then abandoned here when there was no fuel left to bunker them for the Atlantic voyage. New York harbour then had been a place of fear, exhaustion and despair. Wayne stared through the curtains of rainbowing spray that lifted off the starboard bow. The *Apollo* changed course to avoid the tilting flight-deck of the USS *Nimitz*. The huge nuclear-powered aircraft carrier had been scuttled here by its mutinous crew when they refused to fire on the thousands of small boats and makeshift rafts that jammed its harbour exit. Wayne remembered the photographs and grainy film strips of those last frantic days of the evacuation of America, when the latecomers, millions of them by then from the Middle West and the states around the Great Lakes, had arrived in New York. They moved through the streets of Manhattan, the sun and the desert only a few days behind them, to find that the last evacuation ships had left.

'Captain Steiner! We're there, Captain — you don't need to break our necks . . . . ' As a bow wave splashed across the deck Orlowski wiped his plump face on his sleeve. He called out again to the Captain, his voice lost in the drumming of the engines and the boom of the funnel, the cracking sails drenched with soot and spray.

But Steiner ignored the commissar. He swayed lightly on his sturdy legs, eyes fixed in an almost mesmerised way on the wreck-strewn water in front of them, a demented sea-captain in an opera. As the *Apollo* leapt through the spray, porpoising over the black, spit-flecked waves, Wayne clung to the ventilation shaft above the nervous horses. The after-noon sunlight glared down at them from the thousands of silent windows in the downtown office blocks, and off the almost liquid back of the gold dust gleaming in the streets. Suddenly it occurred to Wayne that perhaps the entire Fort Knox reserves lay on the quayside, abandoned there by the last army units before they could be shipped to Europe.

'Captain Steiner — three fathoms!'

As the *Apollo* ran down the last of the water there was a shout from the two seamen trying to swing a plumb-line in the bows.

'Captain — hard to port! There's a reef!'

'Astern, Captain! She'll break her keel!'

'Captain — ?'

3 | A Drowned Mermaid

Sailors were running in panic across the decks. A petty officer collided with Dr Ricci as he flinched from the rail. Professor Summers waved warningly to Steiner, while two midshipmen scrambled into the main-mast shrouds, trying to find safety in the sky.

The *Apollo* had lost momentum, its speed cut by half. The sails slackened, and in the silence Wayne heard only the smoke pounding from the hot funnel behind him. Then there was a low, jarring noise, as if an iron blade was scraping the hull. The ship gave a small shudder, leaning on its starboard side like an injured whale. Almost motionless in the water, it swung slowly in the wind as the propeller screwed a torrent of boiling foam around the stern.

Everyone rushed back to the rail. The horses staggered to their feet in the stables, and their nasal bleating rose above the noise of the engines. Wayne jumped down on to the deck and pushed between Ricci and Anne Summers. The sailors were shouting to each other and pointing to the water, but Wayne looked back at the Captain. As the helmsman picked himself off the deck, nursing his bruised knees, Steiner had matter-of-factly taken the wheel. The *Apollo* swung clockwise in the water, its sails limp in the calming air. Steiner stared at the great towers of Manhattan now less than half a mile away. It seemed to Wayne that the Captain had never looked happier. Had he made the long uncertain voyage across the Atlantic secretly determined to sink his

19

ship these few hundred yards from their goal, so that they would all perish and he could plunder alone the treasures of this waiting land?

'Wayne, lying down there, can you see?' Wayne felt Anne Summers seize his arm. 'There's a sleeping mermaid!'

Wayne peered into the water. The *Apollo*'s propeller had stopped, and the mass of churning bubbles dissolved in the water that swilled against the hull. Lying on her back beside the ship, like its drowned bride, was the statue of an immense reclining woman. Almost as long as the *Apollo*, she rested on a bed of concrete blocks, the ruins of an underwater plinth. Her classical features were only a few feet below the surface. Washed by the waves, her grey face reminded Wayne of his dead mother's when he gazed into her open coffin in the asylum mortuary.

'Wayne, who is she?' Anne Summers stared at the impassive face. A colony of lobsters had taken up residence in the woman's nostrils. As they emerged from their domain, peering up at the dripping bulk of the *Apollo*, Anne held her handsome nose. 'Wayne, she must be some kind of goddess . . .'

Paul Ricci squeezed between them. 'A local marine deity,' he suavely informed them. 'The Americans of the eastern seaboard worshipped a pantheon of underwater creatures – you'll remember Moby Dick, Hemingway's *Old Man and the Sea*, even the great white shark affectionately christened "Jaws".'

Anne Summers stared doubtfully at the statue. She moved her hand from Ricci's. 'Rather a fierce form of worship, Paul, not to mention a hazard to shipping.' She added, as an afterthought: 'I think we're sinking.'

Sure enough, a clamour of shouts had begun.

'Captain, we're holed! We're making water!' The petty officer rounded up his sailors. 'Get the forward pumps going, and put your backs into it or we'll settle here!'

Wayne struck the rail with both fists. He laughed aloud as the sailors ran past him. He realised now what had been missing from the mental picture of New York harbour he had carried with him across the Atlantic.

'Wayne, for heaven's sake . . . ' Anne Summers tried to calm him. 'You're going to have to swim, you know.'

'Liberty! Professor Summers, don't you remember?' Wayne pointed to the Jersey shore, where a rocky island stood in the main channel. Even now the remains of a classical pedestal could be seen. 'The Statue of Liberty!'

They stared into the water beside the *Apollo*. The lamp held aloft for generations of immigrants from the Old World had vanished, but the crown still remained around the figure's head. One of its radiating spikes had left a ten-yard-long gash in the *Apollo*'s hull.

'You're right, Wayne. My God, though, we're going down!' Anne Summers looked round wildly, a hand to her blonde bun. 'The equipment, Paul! What's the matter with Steiner?'

The first rusty water foamed from the fore-mast pump-heads. Orlowski was screaming at the Captain, his plump index finger raised accusingly. But Steiner strolled in a leisurely way around the helm, a satisfied light in his eyes. He ignored the commissar and the pandemonium on the deck, his mouth relaxed as he spoke to the engine-room on the brass voice tube.

Below the stern the two-bladed propeller thwacked the water. A heavy black smoke billowed from the funnel. The *Apollo* made way, dipping cumbersomely through the waves. The cold pump-water raced across the deck to the scuppers, sluicing around Wayne's ankles. Ricci and Anne Summers backed off, but Wayne stared down at the immense statue moving away from them. At the climax of the evacuation of America, under the personal control of President Brown, the Statue of Liberty had been lowered from her plinth and prepared for shipment to the new American colonies in Europe. In a sudden storm, however, the wooden lighter built to transport the statue had broken loose from its tugs, drifted free across the bay and lost its bows on the razor-sharp keel of a scuttled freighter. In the chaos that filled the final days of the evacuation the exact

21

location of the statue had never been established, and she had been left to break up in the cold waters of the next century.

So already the expedition had made its first discovery!

From that moment, as the *Apollo* limped, bow decks awash, towards New York harbour, Wayne resolved to keep a diary of the extraordinary visions he would see in the following months, led by this image of his dead mother asleep below the waves. In all good time he would present his record to Dr Fleming, the once and future father whom he, would find somewhere in America, waiting for him in the golden paradises of the west.

4 | Secret Cargoes

Landfall! At last the *Apollo* had negotiated the boom of wrecked ships in the entrance to the Hudson River and beached itself on a silt bank alongside the old Cunard pier. Lulled by the steady beat of the pumps, and the confidence that even if the *Apollo* foundered they could swim ashore, the crew and expedition members had fallen silent. When the *Apollo* buried its wounded bows in the wet silt everyone gathered at the rail, looking at the vivid quays in front of them, at the soundless city with its great towers and abandoned streets, a million empty windows lit by the afternoon sun.

Already they could see the dunes that filled the floors of these deserted canyons. The rolling sand lay ten feet deep, undisturbed by any footstep for almost a century, smoothed by the onshore winds and covered with a fine glaze of golden dust. For Wayne it seemed a magical carpet, a metallised dream from the fairy tales of his childhood. He held his breath as the ship settled into the mud under the falling tide, and prayed that the silence and calm aboard the *Apollo* would not give way to a sudden, greedy stampede.

There was more than enough for them all, gold beyond the dreams of Columbus, Cortez and the conquistadores. Wayne had a vision of the crew and passengers dressed in their coronation armour, he himself in gilded doublet and hose, Anne Summers in gleaming breastplates and skirt of gold leaf, Paul Ricci in a sinister black and gold armour,

Steiner in a golden cape at the helm of a new gold-plated *Apollo* ready for its return voyage in triumph to Plymouth and the Old World . . .

The ship's siren hooted, three long blasts that shattered Wayne's ears. The sounds echoed among the silent skyscrapers, reverberated to and fro across Central Park, and were lost miles away in uptown Manhattan. Wayne clung to the faint echoes. In some way the harsh noise marked the real moment of their arrival, releasing them all from the voyage across the Atlantic, closing the past behind them as they prepared to step ashore. Like the immigrants of old, each had brought a small, precious baggage, a clutch of hopes and ambitions to be bartered against the possibilities of this new land.

McNair was thinking of gold. He stood on the forward docking bridge by the coal bunker hatchway, and wiped the black anthracite dust from his beard. He was looking up at the Cunard wharf, and at the very different dust that lay over the sunlit dunes. The sand was now an almost liquid bronze in the late afternoon. A desert sea had flowed through Manhattan and congealed around these huge towers. The ravages of a century's hostile climate had split the Appalachians and sprung this ransom from their hidden lodes.

Already McNair was thinking hard, deciding how best they could gather in this golden crop. Rather than disturb the surface with spade and shovel or with a mechanised dragline, they needed a modified combine harvester, which they could then drive across the dunes, its specially slatted blades scooping up just the precious topsoil.

McNair stared back at the huge buildings, at the giant piers of the concrete expressways and overpasses. True, he had been surprised by the brute size of the suspension bridge across the narrows, and by the vast dimensions of the old *United States* and the *Nimitz*. But already McNair's pugnacity had returned, and he had every intention of meeting this great continent on his own terms. The years of

24

training at the marine engineering school in the Glasgow shipyards would not be wasted. The skills needed to resurrect this dormant giant, to wake its railroads, dams and bridges, its mines and industries, were very much those that lay in his own hands. The computer men and communications wizards could come later, when the basic clockwork was ticking soundly.

During the past century the small American colony in Scotland had almost been assimilated into the local community, but McNair had always known that he would one day return to the United States. He needed its size and scale to find his real talents, which he was certain were far beyond those of a mere ship's engineer. He came from a family whose roots lay in the great technologies of America's past — one of his ancestors had worked on the NASA team that put Neil Armstrong on the Moon.

When the vacancy on the *Apollo* was posted McNair had been serving as second engineer aboard a bulk coal carrier on the Murmansk–Newcastle run. No one else was interested, but McNair volunteered without thinking, even though he would not be part of the inland expedition. Now, having propelled the *Apollo* across the Atlantic, he was ready to step ashore and start things moving.

The gold was a lucky bonus, a signal to him to back his own obsessions to the end. The fossil fuels, coal, gas and oil, might have run out here, but America always had something unexpected up its sleeve. McNair cared nothing for the gold's ornamental or monetary value, except in the eyes of others. With the gold they could buy coal, bauxite, timber and iron ore from the rag-tag nations in southern Africa and South America.

McNair gazed confidently at the empty city, reminding himself that the principal mission of the *Apollo* expedition was to investigate the small but significant increase in atmospheric radioactivity which had been detected over the American continent in recent years. Perhaps the core of one of the old nuclear power stations had begun to leak dangerously, or a decaying war-head in some forgotten weapons silo had reached critical mass. Whatever the reason, the possibilities excited him. He thought of the two physicists, Ricci and Anne Summers, heads lost among their Geiger counters. But if only they could harness that dormant nuclear power they would really rouse a sleeping giant, start nothing less than a third industrial revolution . . .

For Orlowski, who was standing by the stern rail, one eye warily on Captain Steiner, this first sight of the empty skyscrapers of Manhattan prompted far more ambiguous feelings. He had never wanted to come on the expedition in the first place. After three successful but rigorous years opening up the new Arctic coalfields on Novaya Zemlya he had been looking forward to a comfortable desk at the Moscow headquarters of the Energy Resources Ministry. He remembered the post of expedition leader being circulated in the office newsletter, but had dismissed it out of hand. No one but a fool would want to spend six months wandering around the barren north American continent, a forgotten wilderness as distant as Patagonia.

There was some concern now over these leaks of radio-activity – small clouds of fall-out had recently drifted across the North Atlantic − but the few reconnaissance expeditions during the past fifty years had reported back nothing of value, a land long since stripped by a greedy nation of all its coal and oil. In fact, the Fleming expedition twenty years earlier had ended in disaster, its members perishing of thirst in the great salt wastes of Tennessee after inexplicably leaving their planned itinerary. The rescue mission four months later had found an abandoned camp outside Memphis, a trail of skeletons gnawed by lizards and gophers.

For obvious reasons it was then decreed that any future expeditions would be headed by a political leader, whose main job would be to keep a tight rein on the impulsive scientists. Anyone, Orlowski decided, other than Gregor Orlowski. But annoyingly some faceless rival at the Ministry had discovered his American antecedents. His great-grandparents had returned from Philadelphia to the original family home in the Ukraine on board the very first emigrant boat, changed their name back from Orwell to Orlowski and rapidly reassimilated themselves into Russian life.

Before he could protest, Orlowski found himself at the dockside in Plymouth, England, in charge of this apparently professional but in fact very strange team. At times, as they crossed the Atlantic, Orlowski had felt that he was supervising a crew of sleepwalkers. Like himself, every member of the expedition had American ancestry, but unlike himself none of them had made any real effort to assimilate themselves into their readopted nations. From the day they sailed he was convinced that they had each smuggled some secret cargo aboard — long experience as an expedition leader had given him a sharp nose for illicit alcohol, black market electric batteries, an overweight suitcase lined with coal briquettes.

However, it soon became clear that their reasons for joining the expedition had little to do with its scientific mission, and that the real contraband was their collective fantasy of America. The discovery of the young stowaway, Wayne, had acted as the catalyst — all these private escapees had soon come out into the open, united by their shared dream of 'freedom' (the last great illusion of the twentieth century), the same conviction that they would make a new life and fulfil themselves that must have been felt by their distant forbears when they were herded through the immigration pens of Ellis Island.

Yet what could they conceivably find in that landscape of ash and clinker, in those empty cities that required more fuel to run them in a day than the whole planet now consumed in a month? Probably none of them knew — with the single exception of Steiner, standing on the bridge of his sinking ship with his quiet, good-humoured smile. No real captain tried to sink his ship, and Orlowski was sure that Steiner had deliberately ruptured the bows of the *Apollo* across the submerged statue. The scattered American communities in Western Europe still offered a small reward for the whereabouts of the statue, but Steiner's motives would be more complex.

Orlowski thought of the hours which the Captain and his young stowaway spent going through the old *Time* and *Look* magazines, almost drugged by the lavish advertisements. Then there had been the embarrassing matter of the christening of the ship — officially *Survey Vessel 299*. Orlowski had proposed the *E. F. Schumacher*, but far from supporting him everyone had howled him down. At Steiner's prompting they unanimously accepted Wayne's suggestion, the *Apollo*. A sentimental gesture, an invitation to think big instead of small, to shoot for the moon, which Orlowski had tolerated, slightly moved himself by the thought that in a way they were duplicating Armstrong's voyage. But the terrain of America would be as desolate as the Moon's. He would have to watch everything, all kinds of psychological mischief could be hatched up here.

Yes, he decided, they would quickly establish the source of the nuclear leaks, radio the full findings to the monitoring station at Stockholm and then return to Europe at the first opportunity, leaving to a larger and better-equipped expedition the task of neutralising the danger.

Meanwhile he would make the most of the enforced time here, collect a few souvenirs (through the strange gold light over the Brooklyn shore he could actually see an old Exxon gasoline sign, worth a good few roubles) for Valentina and the girls. And travellers' tales, useful at Ministry cocktail parties. This brooding, ancient landscape with its dead cities — for a moment Orlowski imagined himself being colonial administrator of New York, pro-consul of thousands of miles of arid wilderness. The prospect steadied him as he prepared to step ashore. This was a large land, waiting for a large man to rule it . . .

As he wiped the soot from his elegant hands on to the midship's rail, Dr Paul Ricci was thinking: So this is New York — or was. Greatest city of the twentieth century, here you heard the heart-beat of international finance, industry and entertainment. Now it's as remote from the real world as Pompeii or Persepolis. It's a fossil, my God, preserved here on the edge of the desert like one of those ghost towns in the Wild West. Did my ancestors really live in these vast canyons? They came on a cattle boat from Naples in the 1890s, and a century later went back to Naples on a cattle boat. Now I'm making another stab at it.

Still, the place has possibilities, all sorts of dormant things might be lying here, waiting to be roused. Like the beautiful Professor Summers. She's standoffish now in her moody way, but once we hit the expedition trail, the dust on our bronzed bodies, the smell of horses between our thighs, the hint of danger as we track down this radiation leak (no doubt a ruptured reactor core, they were in such a hurry to get out they didn't pack enough concrete around them), she'll behave a little differently . . .

But it's hot here, all right, I can see the heat shimmering off the dunes. Better, though, than being back in Turin, that small scandal over the Institute Library Fund was about to explode. I would have had to testify at the inquiry, my own role would have been difficult to conceal . . . professional disgrace, imagine spending the next ten years as a factory chemist at the fishmeal processing plant in Trieste, a shared room in a dormitory, the stink of dried squid. No, even this empty city is preferable. Whatever else you might say about these people, they had size and style. Maybe great-grandfather Ricci did come from here. I can see him in a big car cruising down Broadway, what did they call that huge chrome beast — yes, a Cadillac.

For Professor Summers, her first impressions of Manhattan were still confused by the *Apollo*'s mad dash across the wreck-strewn bay and their collision with the submerged statue. What was Steiner playing at, this curious man with his intense, unsettling eyes, forever gazing at her? The empty metropolis now only a stone's throw away had the same disconcerting effect, it already seemed to be trying to provoke her. There was an undeniable abrasive glamour about New York even now, a whiff of the energy and enterprise of the ruthless men of affairs who had erected these skyscrapers. She had been brought up in the American ghetto in Berlin (Anna Sommer was her Germanised name, which on a strange impulse she had re-Anglicised back to Anne Summers after her first night in Plymouth), and New York occupied a special place in the expatriate memory. There was even a cocktail called a Manhattan, a confection of whiskey and vermouth. Native Europeans were always chiding their American-descended cousins for their forbears' vulgar tastes, but Anne loved the elusive flavour of the Manhattan, with its dark memories of glamorous hotels, limousines and gangsters . . .

But back to business, this 'cocktail' in front of her might contain as one of its mystery ingredients a dangerous radioactive isotope. Fortunately she had kept her scientific work up to scratch during the voyage, five hours a day in the laboratory despite Ricci's protests and seasickness. Clearly the *Apollo* would be in no position for some time to evacuate them in an emergency. The latest reports from Stockholm suggested that the fall-out vectors in the North American airstream emanated from somewhere south of the Great Lakes – Cincinnati and Cleveland. Curiously, although she had not confided this to Ricci, the isotopes involved were barium and lanthanum, those released by old-fashioned atomic weapons, the war-heads of tactical artillery shells, for example. Perhaps the corrosion of a century had cut its way into one of the old nuclear arsenals.

Meanwhile she would rigorously carry out the thrice-daily seismographic and radiation measurements, keep an eye on Ricci (far too slapdash, and clearly prepared to steal any credit), and protect her immaculate white skin from this barbarous sun. Why had she volunteered in the first place? – leaving the small but comfortable flatlet in Spandau; her attractive if earnest lover, a middle-aged pharmacologist at the State Veterinary Collective; the extra meat ration once a month. But despite all these, she needed to breathe, to extend herself, even to dream. Avoiding Steiner's eyes, she looked up at the huge, raw buildings, with their brute strength. She knew that she had come to the last place on earth, where dreams could still take wing.

As for Captain Steiner, he stood alone on his bridge, pressing his tired back against the spokes of the helm. Out of curiosity he had been watching the behaviour of his crew and passengers, trying to guess how they would react in the next few minutes. It had been a long voyage, a confidence trick of a special kind, with many risky decisions to be made. But he had beached the leaking *Apollo* as planned on the silt bank beside the Cunard pier, in the very space once occupied by the great Queens. Here she would sit long enough for him to carry out the rest of his private quest.

Steiner steadied the slight shaking in his hands, remembering the final dash across the harbour. Fortunately the submerged statue had not been moved by the currents. She lay line astern of the *Nimitz*, exactly as described by the senile survey ship captain in Genoa whom Steiner had spent so many shore-leaves patiently plying with grappa. He thought of his own long years of service in the Israeli Navy, patrolling the mill-pond Mediterranean for OPEC corsairs. Despite the steep Atlantic seas ahead, he had really been preparing himself, not for the open ocean, but for the open land. For the silent desert of the American continent, so unlike the highrise-infested landscape of Israel, Jordan and Sinai.

He began to empty his mind of everything but the terrain beyond the gates of the city, the open doors at the ends of the long avenues that led out into the deserted continent, a land as great as any ocean, on which he himself would soon navigate, this descendant of Phoenix and Pasadena physicians who had always secretly regretted not being sired by plainsmen and astronauts. Now he had returned to his own country, where he would soon ride again, one foot on the stirrup of the land, the other with luck on space itself.

5 | To the Inland Sea

Everyone was going ashore, leaving him behind! Surprised by the rush to disembark, Wayne found his hands clamped to the rail, as if Orlowski had crept up behind him with a pair of handcuffs. A sudden excitement had overtaken the crew and expedition members alike, a long-pent need to throw themselves on to American soil. One moment they were all staring at the grey skyscrapers and deserted streets, and the next there was a mad stampede for the gangway. Sailors abandoned the pumps, dashed to the fo'c'sle and emerged with duffel bags and empty suitcases, eager to ransack every store in town.

Only Orlowski turned his back to the shore. He stamped on the deck, bellowing through his pocket megaphone at the Captain. 'Steiner! Call your men back! Can't you control your crew? Captain!'

But Steiner leaned amiably against the helm, like a tolerant gondolier watching a party of easily excited tourists leave his craft.

McNair was the first ashore. He climbed the fore-mast shrouds, let out some barbarous Scots-American war-cry, and leapt on to the silt bank below. He sank to his thighs in the wet mud, struggled free and strode up the oozing slope. Everyone on the gangway watched him, waiting to see if anything happened. He reached the deck of the rusting Cunard pier, then ran towards the first of the great golden dunes that spilled over the riverside streets. Wayne saw his mud-stained arms send up a spray of gilded dust as he bent down and seized the bright sand. His golden figure disappeared over the crest of the dune, muffled voice echoing among the office blocks.

Within minutes the crew had laid a temporary catwalk of life-rafts and decking planks across the silt bank, and set off towards the city, waving their suitcases at each other. Behind them followed the expedition members, while Steiner watched from the bridge of the abandoned *Apollo*. Orlowski took the lead, solar topee protecting his bald head. Now that they had left the ship his good humour had returned, but he glanced at the Geiger counter in Paul Ricci's hand, as if he half-expected the silent streets to be ticking with radioactivity.

'Extraordinary,' he confided, 'I feel like Columbus. By rights the natives should appear now, bearing traditional gifts of hamburgers and comic books. Are we quite safe?'

Anne Summers did her best to reassure the commissar. 'Dear Orlowski, do relax. There are no natives, and no trace of radioactivity within a hundred miles. Your chief danger is colliding into a parked car.'

Ricci knelt in the fine sand. He scooped up a handful of grains, his quick eyes following the footprints which McNair had left across the dune.

'It's remarkable, Anne. Even from here it looks like gold. An analysis might be worth making − I'd like to reserve the spectrometer for an hour tonight.'

Wayne followed at their heels, eager to get away. He looked back at Steiner, who waved him ahead, pointing towards the city. The Captain's complex motives unsettled him. As Anne Summers paused to shake the sand from her shoes, he darted between her and Ricci.

'Wayne!' Orlowski caught his arm. 'Don't touch anything! You're a stowaway, remember. You've no official status in this hemisphere.'

Laughing, Wayne pulled away from him. For the first time he felt on equal terms. 'Gregor, come on! There's the whole of America here.'

He sprinted ahead to the great dunes which spilled from the riverside streets across the dock basin. The bright sand came towards him, its warm flank glittering in the sunlight, a golden breast on to which he threw himself happily.

For the next heady but confusing hours they carried out their first foray into the empty city. As Wayne trudged down the airless, dune-filled canyon that had once been Seventh Avenue, he soon discovered that if any streets in America were paved with gold it was not here in Manhattan. The golden carpet that seemed to cover the city with a treasure beyond the dreams of the conquistadores had been a complete illusion. As he listened to the distant shouts of the sailors, and the breaking plate glass of bars and stores, he realised that he was surrounded by a wilderness of sand, a harsh bronze dust heated by a relentless sun.

He was standing in the ash pit of a huge solar furnace. Wayne felt sorry for McNair, but the illusion had served its purpose, left a striking memory in all their minds of their first sighting of America. At the same time, the golden glare around him was a sharp reminder of all his own misapprehensions. Wayne had expected to find the streets lined with brightly gleaming cars, those Fords, Buicks and Chryslers whose extravagant styling he had studied in the old magazines, symbols of the speed and style of the United States and archetypal villains of the energy crisis.

But the dunes were at least ten feet deep, reaching up to the second floors of the office buildings. Half the Appalachians had been destroyed by the sun to yield this deluge of rock and dust. Street signs and traffic lights protruded from the sand, a rusty metallic flora, old telephone lines trailed waist-high, marking out a labyrinth of pedestrian catwalks. Here and there, in the hollows between the dunes, were the glass doors of bars and jewellery stores, dark grottoes like subterranean caves.

Wayne plodded along Broadway, past the silent hotels and theatre façades. In the centre of Times Square a giant saguaro cactus raised its thirty-foot arms into the overheated air, an imposing sentinel guarding the entrance to a desert nature reserve. Clumps of sage-brush hung from the rusting neon signs, as if the whole of Manhattan had been transformed into a set for the ultimate western. Prickly pear flourished in the second-floor windows of banks and finance houses, yucca and mesquite shaded the doorways of airline offices and travel agents.

At the intersection of Fifth Avenue and 57th Street, Wayne paused to catch his breath from the effort of climbing the sand-hills. As he leaned against the dusty eyes of a traffic light there was a sudden armoured flicker from the half-submerged neon display on a building twenty feet behind him. From the shadows emerged a small but plainly venomous lizard − a gila monster inspecting the blundering young man as possible prey.

Wayne kicked the fine sand into its face and set off at a run. On all sides was a secret but rich desert life. Scorpions twitched like nervous executives in the windows of the old advertising agencies. A sidewinder basking in a publisher's doorway paused to observe Wayne approach and then uncoiled itself in the shadows, waiting patiently among the desks like a merciless editor. Rattlesnakes rested in the burrow-weed on the window-sills of theatrical agents, clicking their rattles at Wayne as if dismissing him from a painful audition.

Wayne pressed on towards Central Park. Already he could see the hundreds of giant cacti that stood in ranks down the length of the park, transforming this once green rectangle into a desert replica of itself, a red ochre wilderness shipped from Arizona and lowered down from the sky. Drenched in sweat, he looked round wistfully for one of the water hydrants that were part of the folklore of summer New York. At intervals, following the routes of the subway system, the sea had seeped in through storm-drains and sewers. Groves of miniature tamarisks and creosote bushes sprang from the underground car-parks of the great hotels, salt grass and paloverde choked the sand-filled concourse of Rockefeller Plaza.

Searching for something to drink, Wayne turned back along Fifth Avenue. He climbed a shallow dune and stepped through an open window into the second floor of a huge department store. Sand lay in drifts among the suites of furniture and barbecue equipment. A tableau family of well-dressed mannequins sat around a dining-room table, gazing politely at the waxwork meal laid in front of them, oblivious of the fine sand, the dust of past time, that covered their faces and shoulders.

Deciding to return to the *Apollo*, Wayne set off down the Avenue, picking his way among the cooler hollows and saddles. Already he felt slightly disappointed, as if someone had reached New York just before him and stolen his dream. Besides, there was something macabre about this empty metropolis overrun by sand. The ancient desert cities of Egypt and Babylonia were safely distanced from them by the span of millennia. But for all its rusting neon signs, the New York around him seemed preserved in limbo, its vast buildings abandoned only the previous day.

Pausing to rest again, Wayne stepped into the second floor of a large office block, a long shadowy promenade on which hundreds of desks stood in lines, each with a telephone and typewriter, as if occupied at night by a phantom regiment of secretaries. Thinking of the Fleming expedition, he lifted one of the receivers, almost expecting to hear the warning voice of his long-lost father, urging him back to the safety of Europe.

Light flared in the street outside. As Wayne hid behind the window pillar a golden figure appeared on the crest of the nearest dune, a creature with gilded arms and blazing beard. It gazed around like a deranged animal, kicking at the dust.

'McNair!' Wayne leapt through the window and ran forward. 'McNair, it's all right!'

The engineer was covered with the bright sand. An almost metallic film had caked itself into the mud on his beard, shirt and trousers. He greeted Wayne with a weary wave.

36

'Hello, Wayne, what do you think of America? Find any gold, by the way? We were going to be rich, load the *Apollo* with a cargo of El Dorados, trade the damned stuff in for a few machine tools and a lick of paint. It's *rust*, Wayne, the rust of a hundred years . . . '

Wayne pointed to the western horizon. 'McNair, we can still find gold, and silver. There's the whole of America over there.'

'Good for you.' A cracked golden smile parted McNair's lips. 'We'll fit the *Apollo* with wheels and sail her to the Rockies.'

He gave an ironic salute to a man on horseback, braided cap over his sunglasses, who had appeared from behind the giant cactus at the street junction beside them. 'Did you hear that, Captain Steiner? Are you ready to cast off? We're setting sail for the gold coast, westwards on the first tide . . . '

With a wild lunge he kicked up a spray of sand, then nodded at the eventless blue sky and silent streets, ready to attack anything that moved.

Steiner approached at a leisurely pace, gently urging his black mare up the slope. His dark face was expressionless behind the sunglasses. Looking up at him, Wayne reflected that for all his nautical gear Steiner seemed more at home on his horse than on the bridge of the *Apollo*. The heat and the desert light, the unsettled mare churning the hot sand with a nervous hoof, the great cactus at the Captain's shoulder, together made Steiner resemble some plainsman of the Old West.

'This tide won't ebb, McNair — not for a million years, anyway. Let's get back to the ship. Help him, Wayne.'

A coiled rope hung from his saddle. Had he been stalking McNair through the dusty streets, waiting to lasso and truss the engineer like a wayward steer overexcited by its own shadow? As they returned to the *Apollo*, Wayne watched the Captain with renewed respect. Groups of sailors were making their way back, some drunk on looted whiskey, kicking their overstuffed suitcases. One man dragged by its artificial hair a fibre-glass mannequin of a naked woman, a department store dummy of a kind unknown for years in clothes-rationed Europe. Orlowski waited at the Cunard pier, amicably fanning his face with a newly acquired Stetson. Ricci was complaining in a bad-tempered way at Anne Summers, who struggled gamely through the sand, one hand on her unravelling bun, this slipping granny knot that would let loose her concealed American self.

Secure on his horse, Steiner moved behind them all, waiting until they were safely aboard, as if about to abandon them there and set off alone across the inland sea of the empty continent.

6 | The Great American Desert

At seven o'clock that evening, when the air at last began to cool, a small reconnaissance party set out through the shaded streets to the north-western perimeter of the deserted city. Steiner rode by himself in the lead, followed by Orlowski and Anne Summers, with Wayne taking up the rear on a little palomino. Ricci had stayed behind, fuming in his cabin after an altercation with the Captain, who had caught him smuggling aboard a heavy automatic pistol he had looted from a gunsmith's.

Manhattan was silent, the huge buildings withdrawing into their emptiness as the sun moved across the western land. They passed the George Washington Bridge, and then paused to look out over the mile-wide channel of the Hudson River.

In front of them was an unbroken expanse of sand strewn with sage-brush, a dusty plantation of cacti and prickly pear. A century earlier the Hudson had dried up, and was now a broad wadi filled with the desert flora that had come in from New Jersey. The harsh and glaring light of the early afternoon had given way to the red earth colours of evening. They stood silently by their horses at the edge of the half-buried expressway. Beyond the Jersey shore Wayne could see the rectangular profiles of isolated buildings, their sunset façades like mesas in Monument Valley. Already they had arrived at an authentic replica of Utah or Arizona.

Nearby was a small six-storey office block whose glass

doors had long ago been smashed by vandals. After tethering their horses, they climbed the stairway around the elevator shaft to the roof. Together they looked out over the empty land, like prospective purchasers offered a wilderness for sale.

'It's a *desert* . . . ' In a gesture of respect, Orlowski took off his Stetson and held it against his plump chest. 'Nothing but desert, probably all the way to the Pacific.'

Anne Summers shielded her eyes from the sun's disc, now bisected by the horizon. The vermilion glow gave her face a flush of animation, as if she were a convalescent already showing a marked improvement on the first day of arrival at a desert resort. Without thinking, she touched Wayne's shoulder, concerned for the young stowaway's sake.

'It's strange, and yet familiar at the same time. I feel I've been here. Gregor, we knew the climate had changed.'

'But not like this. This is like the Sahara in the twentieth century. It's going to affect the mission — we aren't equipped for this sort of terrain. What do you say, Captain?'

Steiner had removed his sunglasses and was staring out across the dried river. His deeply tanned face had become more hawk-like, his eyes had moved back into their sockets under the weathered overhang of his forehead.

'I don't agree, Commissar,' he replied calmly. 'It's all that much more of a challenge. Do you understand, Wayne?'

Wayne understood all too well. The next morning, as Orlowski and Anne Summers supervised the transfer ashore of the expedition's stores, Wayne joined the party of armed sailors who explored the area around New York. Led by Steiner, they rode ten miles out into the desert, a sunbaked wilderness that stretched as far as the Catskills and almost certainly well beyond them. Here and there, in Jonkers and the Bronx, they came across a fresh-water spring in a highway culvert, or a few shabby date palms reared from the cracked floor of a motel swimming-pool. But these small oases were clearly too few to sustain a long expedition inland.

This sight of the failed continent only served to spur Steiner on — his long-dormant resources for surviving in this arid world were now emerging. Yet all of them were strongly affected by the sight of this once powerful nation lying derelict in the dusty sunlight. They rode through the silent suburbs of uptown New York, across the precarious hulk of the Brooklyn Bridge to Long Island, and over the bleached ghost of the Hudson to the Jersey shore. The endless succession of roofless houses, deserted shopping malls and sand-covered parking lots was unsettling enough. Resting from the noon glare, Wayne and the sailors wandered through the abandoned supermarkets, whose shelves were still loaded with the canned goods no one had been able to cook. They climbed to the top floors of lavishly furnished apartment houses that had become freezing tenements in the North American winter. Everywhere the desert had moved in, cacti thrived in the shaded forecourts of fortified filling stations, creosote bushes had taken over the suburban gardens. At Kennedy Airport hundreds of abandoned airliners sat on flattened tyres, mesquite and prickly pear grew through the wings of parked Concordes and 747s.

All around them, as well, was ample evidence of the desperate attempts by the last Americans to beat the energy crisis. Within this once heroic landscape of giant highways, factories and tower blocks there existed a second shabby world of metal shanties fitted with wood-burning stoves, pathetic home-made solar-power units rigged to the roofs of modest houses like ambitious conceptual sculptures, ramshackle water-wheels whose blades were locked for ever now in sand-clogged streams. Thousands of makeshift windmills had been erected in back yards and drive-ways, their metal blades cut from the shells of refrigerators and washing machines. And even more ominously, the quiet streets of Queens and Brooklyn were filled with fortress-like gas stations, government water depots built like block-houses, gun-slits still visible among the crumbling sandbags.

And everywhere, to Wayne's relief, there were the cars. They sat nose to rear bumper in the dust, rusting shells transformed into metal bowers for the wild flowers that sprang through the broken windshields, their engine compartments a home for kangaroo rats and gophers.

It was the cars that most surprised Wayne. His childhood in Dublin had been fed by dreams of an America filled with automobiles, immense chromium mastodons with grilles like temple façades. But the vehicles he found in the streets and suburbs of New York were small and cramped, as if they had been designed for a race of dwarfs. Many of them had been fitted with gas cylinders and charcoal burners, others were antique steam-driven contraptions with grotesque pipes and compression chambers.

When Steiner and the sailors returned to the *Apollo*, Wayne dismounted outside a sand-filled automobile showroom on Park Avenue. He spent the hot afternoon digging away a huge dune that had rolled in across the display vehicles, preserving their still bright chromium and paintwork. He pulled back the door of one of these miniature vehicles, a Cadillac Seville only six feet long. He sat at the cramped controls, reading the admonitory instructions below the General Motors medallion, the warnings against excessive acceleration, speeds above thirty miles an hour, unnecessary braking.

Wayne cried out, laughing at himself. Where were the Cadillacs and Continentals of yesteryear? Into what exile had vanished the true Imperial splendour?

7 ‖ The Crisis Years

Reluctant to sleep, they sat late into the night on the deck of the *Apollo*, crew and passengers together. Under the pleasant glow of the rigging lights, Wayne listened to Orlowski, Steiner and Anne Summers discuss their revised plans for the expedition. After two days in New York, they were still laboriously trying to make sense of the vast climatic upheaval that had denuded this once powerful and fertile land.

As Orlowski pointed out, the first ominous signs of the decline and fall of America had become apparent as early as the middle years of the twentieth century. Then a few far-sighted scientists and politicians had warned that the world's energy resources – in particular, its oil, coal and natural gas – were being consumed at an ever-increasing rate that would exhaust all known reserves well within the lifetimes of their own grandchildren. Needless to say, these warnings were ignored. Despite the emergence of vocal ecology and soft technology movements, the industrialisation of the planet, and especially of the developing nations, continued apace. However, by the 1970s energy sources at last began to run out as predicted. In the 1980s there was a temporary oil glut as consumption was reduced, but the underlying trend soon reasserted itself. The price of oil, hitherto a small and static fraction in world manufacturing costs, suddenly tripled, quadrupled and by the early 1990s had risen twenty-fold. An internationally coordinated search for new oil reserves provided a brief respite, but by the late 1990s, as the industrial activity of the United States, Japan, Western Europe and the Soviet bloc continued unchecked, the first signs of an insoluble global energy crisis began to appear.

Unable to pay the vastly increased price for imported oil, a number of once thriving economies abruptly collapsed. Egypt, Ghana, Brazil and the Argentine were forced to cancel huge programmes of industrialisation. The ambitious Western Sahara irrigation project was abandoned, the Upper Amazon dam left uncompleted. The construction of the vast new port complex at Zanzibar, which would have made it the Rotterdam of Central Africa, was halted overnight. Elsewhere, too, the effects were equally unsettling. At the orders of the French and British governments, work ceased on the Cross-Channel Bridge. The approaching arms of the two immense systems of linked suspension bridges were then separated by only a single mile of open water, but since the exhaustion of the North Sea oil and gas fields in the last years of the 1990s it had become clear that the huge volume of road traffic anticipated would never materialise.

All over the world industrial production began to falter. Stock markets slumped, avalanching numerals in Wall Street, the Bourse and the City of London showed all the signs of an even greater recession than the 1929 Crash. By the late-1990s the automotive giants of the United States, Europe and Japan had cut car production by a third. As armies of workers were laid off, hundreds of component manufacturers were forced into bankruptcy, factories closed, dole queues formed in once prosperous suburbs. For the first time in more than a century, demographers noticed a small but significant drift from town and city back to the countryside.

In 1999 the last barrel of crude oil was pumped from an American well. The once huge reservoirs of petroleum which had fuelled the US economy throughout the twentieth century, and made it the greatest industrial power ever known, had at last run dry. From then on, America was forced to rely on an increasingly scarce supply of imported oil. But the planet's main reserves, in the Middle East and the Soviet Union, were themselves almost exhausted.

Every industrial nation in the world had now introduced strict fuel rationing, and government action at the highest levels was concentrated on the task of finding new energy sources. A dozen UN agencies initiated cash programmes to develop feasible systems of wave-generated power, plans were drawn up for tidal dams, windmills and solar generators of every conceivable kind. A belated attempt was made to revive the nuclear power industry, whose growth the anti-nuclear lobbies of a dozen countries had effectively suppressed in the 1980s.

However, these alternative energy sources could only meet a tenth of the needs of the United States, Japan and Europe. The price of gasoline at the American filling station had already climbed from 75¢ a gallon in 1978 to $5 in 1990, and to $25 in 1995. After the introduction of rationing in 1998, the price of bootleg gasoline on the black market rose to $100 a gallon on the Atlantic coast of the United States, and to over $250 in California.

The end came quickly. In 1999 General Motors declared itself bankrupt and went into liquidation. A few months later it was followed by Ford, Chrysler, Exxon, Mobil and Texaco. For the first time in over a hundred years no motor-cars were manufactured in the United States. In his Millennial Address to Congress in the year 2000, President Brown recited a poignant Zen tantra and then made the momentous announcement that henceforth the operation of private gasoline-driven vehicles would be illegal. Despite this emergency decree, there was a widespread sense that once again the government of the United States had been overtaken by events. Traffic had long ceased to flow along the great turnpikes and interstate highways of America. Waist-high weeds flourished in the cracked concrete of the California freeways, millions of abandoned cars rusted on flattened tyres in the garages and parking lots of the nation.

No one, however, could have antipated the rapid collapse of this once powerful industrial nation. The shortage

45

of gasoline had prepared the American public for the rationing of electric power that soon followed. People everywhere tolerated the frequent blackouts, the sudden dimming of their television screens, the failures of water supplies and food deliveries to their neighbourhoods, the long walks and cycle rides to school, office and supermarket.

But as the traffic drew finally to a halt in the first months of the year 2000, as the silent streets were disturbed only by a few municipal buses and armour-plated vehicles carrying emergency supplies, the whole nation seemed to lose its vitality, its belief in itself and its future. The sight of millions of abandoned vehicles seemed a last judgment on the failure of a people's will.

Over the next ten years, life in the United States began to run down, with endless blackouts and rationing, electricity limited to an hour a day. Everywhere industries failed, production lines slowed to a halt. Cities emptied as people drifted back to the small towns, to the safety of rural communities far away from the violence and looting of the dying metropolis.

However, with almost no sources of energy available, existence soon became untenable except at a primitive agricultural level. The freezing winters and airless summers of the American Midwest sapped the confidence of the struggling farm communities, their subsistence cropping already overburdened by refugees from the cities.

Already the first Americans had reluctantly packed their bags and set sail across the Atlantic for Europe. Here, conservationist and socialist regimes with long experience of strong centralised government were able to maintain a low-level industrial life. The light bulbs might shine dimly, but at least there was work in the small farm cooperatives and state-run coal mines, in the nationalised engineering factories and food-processing plants, and above all in the vast bureaucracies that stretched around half the globe from Portugal to Korea.

The pace of migration continued, as more and more areas of the United States were abandoned. A huge fleet of ships berthed in the harbours of New York, Boston and Baltimore, San Diego and San Francisco. Over the next twenty years virtually the entire population of the United States migrated back to its original ethnic departure points in Europe and Africa, Asia and South America, a vast reverse migration duplicating the original westward passage two hundred years earlier. White Americans emigrated back to Italy and Germany, eastern Europe, Britain and Ireland, black Americans to Africa and the West Indies, Chicanos waded south across the Rio Grande.

By the year 2030 the American continent had been totally abandoned, its once teeming cities empty and silent. With the agreement of its European partners, the President, Supreme Court and Congress set up a US Government-in-Exile in West Berlin, but its role was inevitably ceremonial rather than real. After President Brown's retreat to a Zen monastery in Japan the office of the Presidency was declared to be in abeyance, Congress dissolved itself and all future elections to federal office were postponed indefinitely. The government and nation of the United States ceased to exist.

In the years that followed, widespread measures of climatic control were carried out by the world government to feed the increased populations of Europe and Asia. These impressive feats of geo-engineering steadily transformed the landscape of the American continent. Chief among them was the damming of the shallow waters of the Bering Straits between Siberia and Alaska. By pumping the cold Arctic water south into the Pacific, so that warmer Atlantic currents would flow into the Arctic Circle through the Greenland Gap, the entire climates of northern Europe and Siberia were revitalised. For the first time, winter temperatures rose above freezing-point, permafrost melted, and millions of acres of wilderness were reclaimed for agriculture and coal-mining, summer wheat-crops were harvested well within the Arctic Circle.

Unfortunately, the consequences for the United States were calamitous. The northward flow of hot equatorial

Atlantic water drawn up into the Greenland Gap soon transformed the climate of the eastern seaboard. As the last emigrants struggled aboard the converted troopships in Boston and New York harbours, a blistering heat lay over the parched coastline, dust-clouds hung above the abandoned cities. As they looked back over the stern-rails of the convoy ships bound for Europe, the departing Americans could already see the desert moving in to take over their towns and suburbs.

Meanwhile, the Pacific coast of the American continent was ravaged by an equally extreme climatic change. The cold Arctic waters pumped southwards over the Bering Dam cut through the warm Pacific deeps like a series of icy guillotines. By the middle of the twenty-first century Japan had become a frozen wilderness, an archipelago of glaciers that turned the once fertile hillsides into terraced ice-rinks. Hundreds of cubic miles of cold water plunged south to the Equator, turning the sunny atolls and lagoons of the Marshall Islands into the freezing fishing grounds of a few hardy whale-hunters living in igloos and snow-capped cabins.

Displaced by this frozen tide, the Equatorial waters were driven towards the American coast. A hot Polynesian Current replaced the cold Humboldt and struck the beaches of California from the south. The warm, moisture-laden air blowing over the coastal mountains produced torrential rainstorms and flash-floods. The departing Americans from the sometime sunshine state who set off across the Pacific to Australia and New Zealand looked back to see the harbours of Long Beach and San Diego shrouded by immense thunderstorms that struck inland as far as the Rockies. The last reports from Las Vegas described the abandoned gambling capital sitting half-submerged in a lake of rain-lashed water, its wheels stilled, the dying lights of its hotels reflected in the meadows of the drowned desert, a violent mirror reflecting all the failure and humiliation of America.

8 | Thirstland

Ten days after the arrival of the *Apollo* in New York harbour, a small expedition set off on horseback down the eastern desert coast of the United States. Led by Captain Steiner, it crossed the sand-filled Hudson River and moved out along the wide and empty deck of what had once been the New Jersey Turnpike.

For Wayne, sitting up on the supply wagon, the reins of the mule team gripped firmly in his hands, these first miles immediately brought back all the excitement he had felt when the *Apollo* sailed into New York harbour. Shielding his eyes from the glaring sand on either side of the Turnpike, he expertly cracked the mules' dusty rumps as they lagged behind the leisurely hooves of Orlowski's sturdy pinto. The distant skyscrapers of Manhattan and the office blocks of Newark and Jersey City were at last falling behind them, and after the confused days in New York they were now entering the Great American Desert.

Although they had come across no trace of the previous Fleming expedition, Wayne felt a surge of confidence, the certainty that they would find the El Dorado he had dreamed of for so long — not the literal golden city sought by McNair, but that vision of the United States enshrined in the pages of *Time* and *Look*, and which still existed somewhere. Wayne listened to the rubber tyres of the supply wagon cut through the soft sand. Movement was what America was about, expressed all its energy, its belief in itself. He looked out over the thirstlands of New Jersey, certain that he could master and tame this wilderness, in some way make it bloom again.

Almost three hundred yards away now, Steiner rode his black mare at the head of the expedition, his dark figure shimmering in the haze that rose from the metalled road. At times the Captain would seem to disappear, leaving a leaky question mark on the quivering air, as if he were slipping away into a parallel continuum. Behind him came the baggage train of twenty horses, loaded with supplies, camping equipment and the scientific instruments — half the laboratory from the *Apollo* packed into dozens of saddlebags.

'Orlowski, can you call Steiner back? He's leading his own separate expedition again . . . ' Dr Ricci had dismounted, and was setting up the seismographic tripods and radiation counters, ready to carry out the latest in the series of five-mile measurements. Anne Summers, meanwhile, was unstrapping the radio receiver tuned to the transmitter of a gamma-ray detector mounted on the roof of the Pan Am Building in Manhattan. On the last day Wayne and a young sailor had made the heroic climb up the endless stairways to the helicopter pad, where they had set up the machine, recompensed by a breath-taking view of the American desert stretching to the Appalachians.

As usual, Ricci seemed tired and fractious, slapping the dust from his elegant leather jacket — clearly the American wilderness was not glamorous enough for him. However Anne Summers, Wayne was glad to note, looked trim and self-possessed, and worked the radio in a business-like way. Three days after their arrival in New York she had suddenly pulled the pin from the bun behind her neck, and there had emerged, like a flare of light from a grenade, the long blonde hair that now shielded her from the sun. Already, in Wayne's eyes, this white mane made her resemble some beautiful nomadic widow, endlessly crossing the desert in search of a young husband.

The baggage horses plodded along, heads down in the heat, nervous of the cactus-dotted terrain to the east of the

Turnpike. As Wayne had discovered, the animals needed to be watched all the time, and the expedition was undermanned. Orlowski had assigned two reluctant seamen to join the party, but within an hour of leaving New York they had defected, slipping away among the cars and trucks that littered the wadi of the Hudson. Naturally they preferred to stay behind in Manhattan with the rest of the *Apollo*'s crew, repairing the ship by day and carousing in the empty bars by night, looting the abandoned apartments for the treasure of exotic clothes and record players that would make each of them a millionaire when he went home.

Wayne had fully expected to be left behind with the ship, especially after Steiner's surprise insistence on joining the expedition and leaving his command in the hands of McNair. But after the defection of the sailors a bad-tempered Ricci had galloped back to collect Wayne, and he found himself in charge of the supply wagon. Fortunately, the mules responded to Wayne, though as he snapped at their ambling flanks with the dusty reins he wondered how to keep up with the rest of the party. The surface of the six-lane highway was littered with the husks of rotting suitcases and jerricans. At least, they were moving south along a relatively empty road. The north-bound lanes, towards New York and the Jersey harbour, were lined with the rusting hulks of cars and buses, bizarre charcoal-burning vehicles with gas cylinders on their roofs, left behind here when they ran out of fuel and their passengers stepped down to walk the last miles to the evacuation points.

Reassuring himself, Wayne listened to the splash and murmur in the metal tanks behind him. No one was going to leave him here, he realised, they were all dependent on the supply wagon, both for the thousand gallons of fresh water in the steel casks, and for the distillation apparatus that would supplement their rations from any damp salt pans or freshwater springs they might come across. In an emergency they could always head for the sea, fuel the still with driftwood and dried kelp and sit it out on the beach until the *Apollo* arrived. All the same, they needed Wayne. If he chose to steer the supply wagon behind one of these derelict buses, they would certainly be in something of a spot.

'Professor Summers! Would you join me? Dr Ricci!'

Wayne sat up with a guilty frown. Had Steiner read his thoughts? The Captain had stopped in the shade of a route indicator that overtopped even the giant cactus beside it. He was calling to the two scientists as they finished packing their equipment and remounted. Steiner still wore his mariner's cap, but under the narrow peak his face already had the expressionless yet wary look of the solitary sheriff or gunfighter. But Wyatt Earp, Wayne thought idiotically, had never worn sunglasses . . .

'Come on, Wayne. Don't play at being left behind. Orlowski!'

'Captain, I'm not your galley slave.' Perspiring, Orlowski dug his heels into the pinto and cantered the last few yards. With his short legs and plump chest, sweating freely in his grey Brooks Brothers lounge suit, Orlowski had already cast himself as Sancho Panza to Steiner's Quixote.

'"Trenton . . . Wilmington . . . Atlantic City . . ."' Orlowski peered up at the route indicator, wiping his face with a silk handkerchief, one of several dozen he had calmly removed from a store on Fifth Avenue. 'What a help these signs would have been to the founding fathers, they might have taken a sharp U-turn . . . May I remind you, Captain, that I am in charge of this expedition — you are here to assist in navigation.'

'And supervise the horses,' Ricci added, fidgeting in his saddle. 'This beast you picked for me, Steiner, is already lame.'

Steiner circled him on his strong black mare, nodding thoughtfully at the physicist. 'I'd rather guess it's your backside that's lame, Doctor. Could I suggest that you ride side-saddle?'

As Orlowski separated them, Steiner turned in a flurry of flinty dust. Watching him gallop ahead, Wayne had a sud-

52

den premonition: one day Steiner will ride off and leave us to die. In fact, that's his entire plan, even he probably doesn't realise that we're only here to carry his baggage. Wayne whipped the mules, trying to catch up with Anne Summers, but she was riding on ahead, annoyed with the bickering men.

Disputes and trivial irritations had filled their ten days in New York. After the first excitements of their arrival on American soil a marked sense of unease had set in; worse still, a feeling of disorientation. The huge sand dunes that reached as far as Bowery Park, the hot winds and giant cacti, and the relentless glare of the desert stretching inland as far as they could see, together made nonsense of the whole voyage. While Orlowski and Steiner argued over the future of the *Apollo*, the expedition had been in danger of breaking up. Everyone was retreating into their own dreams – it was not only the sailors who were looting the dead city. Even Anne Summers brought back her own little booty, a full-length black evening gown from Macy's Fifth Avenue. Alone with her mirror in the laboratory, she paraded up and down among the retorts and Geiger counters, inviting the bored Wayne to compliment her.

At dusk Ricci would invariably swap his lab coat for one of his selection of flashy suits. On their last evening in New York, Wayne came across him in 42nd Street, sitting in the back of an antique limousine which the desert wind had exposed between the dunes. He wore a pin-striped suit of extravagant cut with lapels like wings, and cradled a rusty Thompson gun between his knees. On the seat beside him were bundles of old greenbacks he had taken from the vaults of a nearby bank. When Wayne spoke to him he merely stared into the Manhattan dusk, a dream of gangsters in his dark eyes.

Of all the members of the crew and expedition, only Orlowski and Wayne seemed unaffected by their landfall in America; the one without any vision, the other sustained by a fantasy so potent that nothing could dent it. The solitary Steiner had undergone the most marked sea-change. As far as the *Apollo* was concerned, the Captain had abandoned ship in all senses. His lack of concern for the rusting vessel with its gashed hull, the eloquent implication in his brief shrug that they would never make the return voyage across the Atlantic, so enraged Orlowski that on the fifth day the little commissar had ordered Ricci to arrest Steiner and clap him in his own brig.

Wayne remembered the remarkable speed with which the physicist had whipped the pistol from his sleeve, then circled the cabin in the approved hoodlum manner. Steiner had watched with amusement, hands raised in mock alarm, nodding to Wayne as if to say: look out, remember this for the future. Fortunately McNair had emerged from his engine-room. Calming Orlowski, he saluted Steiner and stated that he would be happy to stay behind with the *Apollo* and supervise the repairs while the Captain accompanied the expedition down to Washington. In two months' time the *Apollo* would pick them up and sail on to Miami.

But now, as the column of riders and animals moved south along the New Jersey Turnpike, the time for self-indulgence was over. Deliberately, Wayne immersed himself in the landscape around him, the endless dusty towns separated by salt pans, the terrain of sage-brush and burrow-weed. He steered the mules past the rusting cars, his eyes already keen enough to spot the trembling scorpions, an uneasy rattler resting under a parked bus, a gila monster disturbed by the horses' hooves. Half a mile ahead, a solitary kite circled above some unwary gopher. Under a sky of hot metal, the whole of America seemed embalmed by the dust, mothballed here under the white sand, waiting for one huge puff to be blown into life again.

Already Wayne felt a sense of challenge — the five of them were effectively alone on this continent, free to behave in any way they wished. Their only loyalty was to their own dreams, and to the needs of their own nerve-endings. Adjusting himself to this new domain, Wayne watched Ricci with the hard gaze of the raptor soaring above them, and wondered how to seize his neck.

Later that day, however, as they approached the empty city of Trenton, Wayne discovered that they were by no means alone in this apparently deserted land.

9 | The Indians

An hour before dusk the expedition made camp for its first night in the American wilderness. As the weary animals and their riders plodded along the turnpike, Steiner signalled the column down the embankment towards an isolated building half a mile away − what had once been a pleasant country hotel beside a small lake and golf course. There, in the rock-strewn drive beside a silent fountain, they dismounted like travellers at a desert caravanserai.

However, at this hostelry no one emerged to greet them. A shallow dune ran up the entrance steps to the revolving doors. The glass windows looking out on to the cracked lake-bed were almost opaque with dirt. The dust of years hung in swathes, lace curtains guarding a convention of ghosts.

Without a word, Steiner strode off and began to explore the hotel, testing the doors and windows. To Wayne's annoyance, the others made no attempt to unsaddle the horses. They stood listlessly by the tired beasts, like funeral mutes in cloaks of milled bone. Wayne waited for Orlowski to take command, but for once the commissar was subdued, staring under his dusty Stetson at the arid landscape, his eyes dreaming of Moscow.

Before they could collapse, Wayne called out cheerfully: 'Right, everyone, let's unsaddle. Dr Ricci, tether the horses by the fountain, we'll water them there. You can help me back the wagon up.'

'Wayne – ?' Orlowski took off his hat, staring with suspicion at the sometime stowaway who now so clearly stood a foot taller than himself. Then he nodded approvingly. 'Right . . . Professor Summers, forget about the seismograph just for now — there won't be another earthquake in the next hour. Get the radio tuned to New York, we'll talk to McNair and see if there's any news from Stockholm. Rescue, perhaps. Ricci, you follow Wayne, he seems to know what to do.'

When they had fed the horses and set up the mess tent Wayne left them to get on with the task of preparing supper. Steiner had forced a window into the hotel and was moving around the upstairs floors, searching the bedrooms. As Wayne climbed into the hotel he looked back at the others, who were now working among the horses and piles of equipment. He realised that he had taken a small but significant step in asserting his right to be a full member of the expedition. At the same time, he needed to keep an eye on Steiner, who strode through the dusty tables in the dimly lit bar, not a sign of fatigue in his strong step. Both he and Steiner were coming into their own in America.

Ten minutes later, when they found five gallons of brackish water in the sealed boiler of the hotel's central heating unit, Wayne waited with some interest for the Captain's response.

'Wayne, there's water here, and probably all the way across America, in thousands of abandoned motels. A few gallons, but enough.'

'Enough for one man, Captain.'

'Or two. Just about . . . ' Steiner whistled a sombre tune to himself. 'I'll take you with me. Before we're through, Wayne, we'll sit together on the beach at Malibu.'

Wayne siphoned the precious fluid into a bucket, ready to carry it out to the storage tank on the distillation wagon. Could he trust Steiner? Probably not. It suddenly occurred to Wayne that if the Captain did leave them, he himself might soon take command of the expedition.

'Steiner, why did you come to America? There's

nothing here.'

'But that's why I came. Anyway, you don't believe that, Wayne. There's everything here.'

'Only for me, Steiner.'

At dusk they all rested in their canvas chairs on the terrace of the hotel, and watched the evening light fade against the cerise façades of the Trenton office blocks. These desert cities of the eastern American coast, Wayne reflected, were more beautiful than Benares or Samarkand. Where were the traders in jewels, ivory and spices, the journeymen of the peacock trail?

When they had finished their supper Steiner strode off across the cracked surface of the lake, rifle under his arm, ostensibly to look for game.

'Porcupine pie . . . Does that man never rest?' Paul Ricci dusted the lapels of his tuxedo. 'Follow him, Wayne, see what he's up to.'

'Wayne is as tired as you are, Paul.' Anne Summers held Wayne's arm. 'Steiner needs to be alone. You stay here, Wayne.'

She had become far more pleasant to Wayne since he had taken charge of the expedition's water supply, and had already charmed a few extra pints out of him. For all this, Wayne felt that she had begun to see him, not as a young stowaway, but as a man of almost her own age. Wayne was glad to be of use to her, and even encouraged it. She had done wonders with her evening ration of water, which Wayne had carried up to the bathroom of the suite she had selected on the third floor of the hotel. Wayne had presented her with an old lipstick – a vivid, greasy plug in a gilt capsule of a type not seen in Europe for fifty years – which he found in a dressing-table drawer. The exhilarating carmine bow across her mouth outshone the brilliant dusk. He decided to keep an eye open for more of these rare cosmetics.

'It's all right, Anne, I want to look at the mules.' Embarrassed by this first use of her name, Wayne ran off across the terrace. He had planned to spend the evening with his diary, but Steiner's disappearance unsettled him. After a token inspection of the two mules, now standing quietly by the temporary water trough in the ornamental fountain, Wayne set off along the shore of the drained lake. Around him the elegantly contoured desert stretched through the sunset, the sometime greens of the former golf course now crossed by the candelabra shadows of the giant cacti.

There was no sign of Steiner. Half a mile from the hotel Wayne rested on the seat of an old golf-cart embedded in a dune by the ninth hole.

It was here that he saw an extraordinary apparition, the first mirage of the Great American Desert.

Emerging from a grove of yuccas three hundred yards away was a line of six Arabian camels. Four of them carried riders on their rolling humps, dark-faced figures each wearing a long white burnouse. Even at this distance Wayne could see the wary eyes of these desert nomads, their sun-blackened hands never far from the antique rifles in their saddle holsters. Unaware of Wayne, they moved past at a steady pace, and headed towards the entrance of a ruined motel. The camels stepped cautiously between the rusting cars parked in its drive, and disappeared among the dusty date palms that leaned against a neon sign whose letters were still legible in the evening light.

Careful not to give himself away, Wayne sat motionlessly in the golf-cart. Who were these uneasy riders on their strange mounts? Were they Asiatic Arabs who had moved through the Himalayas and the Gobi Desert, and somehow crossed the land bridge of the Bering Straits? Perhaps they had been drawn with their camels across half the world by the scents of this vast new desert, the wilderness where only they were at home. For all their Bedouin appearance, their weapons and alien eyes, Wayne felt a surge of confidence at the thought that he was not alone on this barren continent.

Behind Wayne there was a quiet foot-fall. He turned to find Steiner standing beside the golf-cart, eyeing the distant green as if about to launch a shot into the dark. Lit by the last of the sunset, Steiner's face seemed as weathered as the Arabs', all the secret routes of a continent in its deep seams.

'So you're not the first American, Wayne. Never mind, where they go, others can follow. I think we should introduce ourselves.'

10 | The Starship

Flames rose from the small fire beside the diving-board. The sparks flickered in the dark air, reflected in the shallow water of the swimming-pool, and in the cartridge bandoliers of the three men and one woman eating the roast flesh of the rattlesnake. For ten minutes no one had spoken, and as the fire died they could hear the distant voices of Orlowski and Ricci calling through the night air.

Wayne listened to the camels stirring under the date palms by the motel's neon sign. Steiner sat forward over the fire, wiping the grease from his hands and casually ignoring the rifle which he had propped against the diving-board. The three nomads, their woman crouched behind them, were as nervous as birds. Their sharp desert eyes searched the darkness, unsettled by the slightest movement.

'That was good – there's nothing like ripe game.' Steiner tossed a piece of snake-skin into the fire, where it sent up a shower of embers that made the nomads flinch. 'Don't worry about our friends. We'll leave before they find us. Now tell me, Heinz, about this vision in the sky. You all saw it, hanging over the centre of Boston?'

'Weren't a vision.' The leader of the nomads nodded at his son and daughter-in-law. He was a busy little anteater of a man, with a soft tongue that teased the last of the rattler's flesh from his fingers. 'You ask GM and Xerox. Weren't a vision at all, Captain.'

'Dad's right – giant space-ship, no doubt about that,

Captain.' The son, GM, a restless youth with a scarred face, lifted his ancient M16 to the dark sky. 'Higher than the OPEC Tower and Empire State together.'

'Just hung there,' added his wife Xerox. She sat in tandem behind her husband, bright-eyed and pregnant, little more than a child. 'I thought it was coming to take us up to heaven.'

'That's it, heaven . . .' The fourth nomad, Pepsodent, a strong, solemn young negro, spoke with a deep sigh. 'It moved off to the south, like telling us to leave, get away before the big quake comes.'

Steiner flicked a stone into the shallow water in the swimming-pool. The brackish fluid leaked through the cracked walls from some underground spring, forming this palm-girt oasis. 'The quakes, yes — we know something about them, our seismographs have been picking them up. Have you ever seen a quake hit one of the cities, Heinz?'

The older man shook his head, glancing uneagerly at the ground around them, as if the mere mention of the disaster might split the seams of the night-earth. 'Didn't see it, none of us — but one of the Professors outside Boston said he saw Cincinnati go. First the star-ship came in the sky two nights before, then the whole city just blew up in a big flash. All gone in a puff of dust.'

'A strange kind of earthquake,' Steiner commented. 'What about you, GM, have you ever been to one of the quake cities?'

'That makes you sick, Captain. Really sick.' GM grimaced and touched his wife's large belly, as if wondering where in this tainted land he could find a refuge for the child. 'Water makes you sick, dust makes you sick. Even just breathing will sicken you.'

'The tribes having to move on, but they got nowhere to go.' Pepsodent rolled his large eyes. 'Can't go west, quakes hit Cincinnati and Cleveland. Now the star-ship hanging over Boston. It's the end of the world!'

'Certainly sounds like it,' Steiner agreed. He smiled reassuringly at the nomads, as if believing everything these simple souls had told him. 'What do you think, Wayne?'

Wayne made no reply, unsure what to think. The past hour, sitting beside this drained swimming-pool as the smell of the camels mingled with the odour of roasting rattlesnake, had muddled all his assumptions about the United States. These strange tales of mile-wide space-ships and mysterious earthquakes he had ignored from the start, however seriously Steiner seemed to take them. Clearly the Captain liked these guileless desert folk with their camels and their ancient rifles and their visions in the sky.

Yet these sun-wizened people were *real* Americans, direct descendants of the few thousands who had stayed behind when the rest of the United States emigrated to Europe. Heinz, Pepsodent, GM and Xerox were among the last remnants of one of the dozen tribes that roved the continent. An hour earlier, when he and Steiner had walked up to the motel, the four nomads had been dismounting from their camels. They greeted Wayne and the Captain without hostility, and obviously had been aware of the expedition's presence. Steiner they seemed unsure about, unable to place his darker features and long, desert gaze. But as they peered curiously at Wayne's blond hair and unmarked skin it was clear that they did not regard this young visitor as a true American in any sense at all.

Wayne stared back at them, annoyed that they had crossed the path of his private dream. Under their white burnouses − the most sensible costume for desert wanderers − the three men wore old grey suits of pin-striped worsted taken from the Trenton and Newark department stores, the traditional uniform of the Executives, the tribe to which they belonged. The Executives' ancestral foraging grounds were New Jersey, Long Island, and the one-time commuter areas around New York City. Heinz, his son GM, and their young friend Pepsodent − they were named after the products manufactured by the great corporations in Manhattan − all carried in their pockets a strange clutter of dry fountain pens and cracked pocket calculators, relics of the office-workers they imitated. At intervals Heinz would push a long-empty inhaler into his nostrils and snort appreciatively, Pepsodent flashed a dented cigarette case at the night sky, doors to a miniature universe, GM took out a clutch of calculators and tapped the dead buttons with a knowing smile at Xerox, as if working out the exact date of her delivery.

Together they had been visiting the homelands of a tribe to the north, the Professors of Boston, to which Xerox belonged. ('Why Xerox?' Steiner had asked, at which GM proudly patted his wife's pregnant waist and replied sensibly: 'All women called Xerox — they make good copies.') Then the premonitory visions in the sky had appeared over Boston harbour, and they set off in panic for the south, bypassing New York, fearful of the deathly quake to come.

As they roasted the rattlesnake on its spit, Heinz and GM told Steiner of the American 'nations', these tribes of new aboriginal Indians who had replaced the original redskins. Once there had been as many as a thousand members in each tribe, but they had now dwindled to fewer than a hundred, scattered by the earthquakes and the portents in the sky. All of them had been illiterate for generations, and the only words they could read were the brand names on neon signs — their friends and relatives were called Big Mac, U-drive, Texaco and 7 Up. However, the Professors, named after the great universities in the Boston area, were one of the most resourceful of the clans, distilling a crude alcoholic spirit from the chemical laboratory equipment. Were the visions in the sky a result of too much hooch? Now the Professors had been driven into the hunting grounds of less friendly tribes. Not all of them, Heinz explained, could be trusted.

'There's the Bureaucrats around Washington — had big ideas once for pulling all the tribes together, until we found they just wanted to tax us. Then there's the Astronauts down in Florida — '

'They're so crazy!' Pepsodent interjected with a hoot of friendly admiration. 'Got some kind of space-age religion, and all the hardware with it.'

'Hardware is right,' GM guffawed. 'Ever seen a camel in a tin overcoat?'

Steiner laughed agreeably. 'Could they be behind these space-ships in the sky?'

But Heinz and the others agreed that this was beyond the Astronauts' reach. Watching these sun-wizened nomads ramble away together, Wayne was in no doubt that they were capable of doing little more than steer their shabby camels from one oasis to the next. So there might well exist a technologically more advanced group, shepherding these threadbare aborigines away from the areas contaminated by the decaying nuclear generators. None of these people would ever have seen an aircraft, so even a small helicopter hovering overhead would seem like the apocalypse . . .

'Then there's the Gangsters,' Heinz was explaining. 'They used to be around Chicago and Detroit. There's the Gays from San Francisco. They moved out of the West years ago.'

'There's something funny about the Gays,' GM added, holding his wife's shoulders protectively. 'I don't know what it is, but I don't like it.'

'Better than the Divorcees,' Pepsodent rejoined. 'That's an all-woman tribe from Reno. They move around everywhere. Watch out for them, Captain, they'll promise to wed you, then steal your camel and cut your throat before the night's out. GM got caught once, didn't you . . . ?'

As Steiner and the old man chuckled together over this, Wayne spoke for the first time, trying to put an end to these reminiscences.

'Apart from the tribes — have you seen any other expeditions?'

'Expeditions?' Puzzled by the word, and by Wayne's sharp tone, the old man glanced at Steiner.

'Explorers,' Wayne tried to explain. 'From across the sea. There was a big expedition twenty years ago, led by a man with white hair —?'

GM looked up from his wife's belly. 'That sounds like the Gamblers. They used to hunt around Vegas, they had a white-haired man who came from the sea — '

Before GM could finish there was a shot from the darkness, cracking apart the desert night. Voices shouted, and glass spilled from the neon sign above the motel as a second rifle shot rang out. Wayne could hear Orlowski and Ricci arguing with each other as they blundered around in the dark.

'It's all right — we know them.' Steiner stood up, raising his hands reassuringly. But already the nomads were on their feet. They scuttled about in the dim light like fearful animals about to be trapped.

Five minutes later, when Wayne and the Captain returned to the pool with Orlowski and Ricci, the three aborigines and the woman had vanished into the night, taking their camels with them. Somewhere among the long desert shadows Wayne caught a glimpse of a beast loping through the rusty cars and date palms.

Orlowski looked down at the drained pool, at the remains of the fire and the roast snake. His small nose pricked at the smell of the camels. He shook a finger at Dr Ricci, who had fired without thinking at the reflections of the flickering embers in the neon sign. Turning to Steiner, he pointed to the imprints of bare feet in the sand.

'What's this, Captain? A whole beach of Man Fridays . . . Have you saved us from the cannibals?'

As they walked away from the motel Steiner stared back wistfully through the darkness.

'Cannibals? Those were Americans, Wayne, real Americans.'

'They're aborigines,' Wayne said. 'I wish we could help them. But I admire them, Steiner, like you do.'

'Good. Self-reliance, a proper respect for the heavens above and a healthy suspicion of the tax-man below — those are qualities your Jamestown forbears would have approved of, Wayne. Perhaps one day they'll be able to help us.'

'I doubt it.' Wayne gestured at the desert around them, at the distant spires of the empty cities. 'Captain, this isn't a huge reservation. I believe in a different kind of America. I hope there'll be room for them there.'

'I hope there'll be room for me, Wayne. Will there?'

'I think so, Steiner . . . ' Wayne joined in the banter, but he remembered Orlowski's words, and the hungry way in which the nomads had looked at his muscular body. Uneasily he noticed that Steiner was watching him with that same hard gaze, the same glint of white teeth against the dark desert.

11 | The Oval Office

For the next ten days the expedition pressed on down the New Jersey Turnpike, heading south-west towards Washington. The endless ribbon of the highway unwound into the haze, lined with mile after mile of abandoned cars and trucks. Each evening they left the road and spent the night in one of the hundreds of empty motels and country clubs along the route, resting around the drained swimming-pools that seemed to cover the entire continent. After supper Wayne and Steiner would ride out through the cool dusk air to search for damp potash lakes and salt pans, any sign of a modest river system fed by the Appalachians, the first hint of a more temperate and fertile climate.

If anything, however, the aridity of the landscape had deepened. Now and then, across the desert floor, they would see the bivouac fires of the few nomads who crossed the land, their camels tethered in the shade of the Joshua trees. But after their meeting with Heinz, Pepsodent, GM and Xerox they never again came close enough to these wandering 'Indians' to barter some part of their equipment for information about the interior of the United States.

Bypassing Trenton and Philadelphia, they moved towards Baltimore, joining the Kennedy Memorial Highway at Wilmington. The empty cities lay embalmed in the desert haze, surrounded by their silent suburbs, whose parks and tennis courts were covered by an ever-thickening dust. Each evening the long lines of office blocks would seem to rise from the eastern horizon, and there would be a brief magical glitter from thousands of windows. As they changed from a pale cyclamen to a deep vermilion the great façades were like huge billboards advertising the desert to come.

Yet despite this ambiguous welcome, and the likelihood that the Great American Desert stretched far beyond the Appalachians to the Rockies and the California coast, the spirits of the expedition never faltered. By the time they reached Washington, and rode down Route 1 towards Constitution Avenue, Wayne had reflected more than once that none of them had discussed the journey back to Europe. The possibility of leaving America and making the return voyage had ceased to exist in their minds.

Steiner, as Wayne expected, rose to the occasion.

'So this is Washington, once the most important capital city in the world, seat of its greatest nation. Think, Wayne: from here orders went out to launch armadas, win world wars, land men on the moon . . . '

Steiner let his arm drop, signalling the expedition to a halt. The column of riders and baggage animals, led by Wayne and the water-wagon, paused below the still imposing frontage of the National Art Gallery.

Wayne gazed across the Mall towards the Lincoln Memorial. Like that traveller of old standing between the ankles of Ozymandias, all he could see were the same dunes and cactus rolling up the once green sward, the same mesquite and burrow-weed. To his left, four hundred yards away, was the Capitol, one of the three most potent images, along with the White House and the Manhattan skyline, that Wayne had brought with him from the Old World. It stood in the silence, surrounded by giant cactus, its portico cracked and toppled into the sand. The great dome was holed, a segment collapsed inwards like the shell of a broken egg. At the other end of the Mall the dunes rolled towards the dry basin of the Potomac. In the Lincoln Memorial, Abraham Lincoln sat up to his knees in the sand, staring pensively at the yuccas and gophers.

Wayne looked round at his companions, waiting for them to protest at what they saw. But none of them seemed surprised, let alone dismayed, by the scene in front of them, as if this was how Washington should appear to its visitors, a lost desert city.

Orlowski cantered forward to the head of the column. Resting in the shadow of the water-wagon, he fanned himself with his Stetson. 'Well, Wayne, it all looks in remarkably good condition. Nothing seems to have changed. Right, Captain, let's move on.'

'We'll try the White House,' Steiner told him, as they set off westwards along the line of great museums, dusty hulks half-buried by the dunes. 'There may be a command post there. If not, we'll swear you in, Gregor, as head of the provisional government.'

'Why not Professor Summers?' Orlowski rejoined. 'The first woman President. Or Wayne, even?'

'I'm ready, Gregor,' Wayne called back promptly. 'I'd be even younger than John-John.'

Keeping up their spirits without too much effort, they moved through the cacti and Joshua trees towards the Washington Monument. They began to spread out again, and soon there was at least fifty yards between each of them. Wayne flicked at the flies on the mules' flanks. He knew that they were all secretly relieved that Washington was empty, and that they were alone here at the heart of their dream.

They spent their first night in the White House. As expected, the building was deserted, its great state-rooms and offices open to the evening air. The sand rolled up to the windows and spilled across the floors in a white lacework untouched by a single footprint. As Steiner sat guard on his horse outside, Wayne and Orlowski stepped through the broken bullet-proof windows into the Oval Office.

Without thinking, Orlowski removed his hat. He and Wayne stood in the ankle-deep sand, gazing at the large desk set in the bow of the windows. President Brown's? Or a store-room substitute set up here by the last evacuation commander? For some reason Wayne was convinced that Presidents had once touched the leather surface of this very desk. A small kitchen fire had been lit in one corner, blackening the white paintwork, and the walls were marked with a few half-hearted graffiti — 'Bob and Ella Tulloch, Tacoma, 2015', 'Astronauts Rule!', 'Charles Manson Lives'. But the Presidential desk remained intact, preserved by some strange power, the force of its own authority.

'It's all here, Wayne,' Orlowski remarked quietly. 'Absolutely as it was . . .'

Moved by the commissar's emotion, Wayne held his shoulder. 'It's been waiting for you all these years, Gregor.'

'Wayne, that's generous of you . . .'

They were joined by Ricci and Anne Summers, and for an hour they wandered together through the gutted offices and state-rooms, past the lines of teletypes and computer terminals, the peeling emergency bulletins and evacuation schedules, the dozens of blank television screens. Later, when the sun fell away across the cactus-filled basin of the Potomac, the expedition members made a quiet tour of the museums and monuments that surrounded the Mall.

Only Wayne stayed behind, volunteering to water the horses and unpack the equipment.

Concerned for him, Anne Summers dusted the sand from Wayne's blond hair. 'You'll be here when we get back, Wayne . . . ?'

'Of course,' Wayne assured her. 'We've reached, Washington, Anne — it's the real start of the expedition.'

Two hours later, when they returned to the Ellipse, they found that Wayne had unpacked the camp beds and carried them into the White House. He assigned himself to the Oval Office, unrolling his sleeping bag on the floor beside the desk, intending to mount his own guard over the sand-strewn room. The dignity of the Presidential office was something he intended to preserve, and he was glad that no one joked at him.

Perhaps it was the potent atmosphere that still hung over the centre of the capital, but during the next few days Wayne noticed that the expedition began to lose its momentum, or at least to change direction, its compass turning to some new internal bearing. They set up camp on the sometime front lawn of the White House, with mess tent, galley and communications office, but Ricci and Anne Summers took little interest in the scientific work. They spoke briefly by radio to McNair as the repairs to the *Apollo* neared completion, but the seismograph and radiation counters sat in a corner of the tent under a gathering layer of dust. Instead, they spent all day exploring the museums and Congress buildings, NASA headquarters, the Supreme Court and the Smithsonian Institution. As they ate supper in the mess tent they discussed the marvels and discoveries of the day like package tourists on the first leg of an unlimited continental tour.

'Gregor, have you seen the Nixon Memorial?' Ricci asked on the third evening. 'It's impressive, you have to admit. The power of the Presidency in those days . . . '

'The Imperial Presidency,' Orlowski commented sagely, gesturing at the massive buildings around the Mall. 'Just like the old Kremlin.'

'And the Jerry Brown Islamic Center,' Anne Summers added. 'An exact fibre-glass replica of the Taj Mahal, one and a half times life-size. What about you, Wayne?' she asked solicitously. 'You're being left out of everything. Why don't you go to the Air Force Museum?'

'I was there today,' Wayne lied calmly. 'I sat in Lindbergh's plane and in the Apollo 9 moonship.'

He was glad to indulge their enthusiasms. Steiner was away as usual, obsessively riding through the desert suburbs of the city, now and then honouring with his moody silhouette the skylines of the Pentagon and the Watergate building. His absence left Wayne effectively in charge. Far from being out of things, Wayne was the hinge at the centre, the pivot of that swinging compass . . . In fact, he had spent his spare time clearing up the Oval Office, shovelling the sand through the cracked windows, scraping the graffiti from the walls. Certain things had to be done, rites of passage in preparation for their real departure. The start of the expedition, he had said without thinking. Yes, but to where?

Wayne watched his companions, waiting for them to discuss their last days on American soil, the specimens and documents to be collected, the detailed photographic record to be made, the maps to be annotated for the benefit of the next expedition. But they remained silent, sitting around the mess table under the canvas awning with curiously settled expressions, not unlike the trio of mannequins he had seen in the Manhattan department store. Ricci toyed with the radio headphones, thoughts clearly a continent away from McNair, and admired the calf-length cavalry boots he had found in a military outfitters to which Wayne had steered him. Anne Summers held a set of radiation logs in one hand, while turning the pages of an old copy of *Cosmopolitan* from Wayne's haversack. Oblivious of the desert and cacti beyond the tent, of her cotton fatigues and chapped skin, she was lost in a dream of glamorous Hollywood villas. Even Orlowski seemed to have anything but the expedition on his mind. He closely examined a large road map, but when Wayne glanced across the table he saw that the commissar was tracing out the interstate highway between Kansas and Colorado.

Under the guise of crossing America, as Wayne soon discovered, they were about to begin that far longer safari across the diameters of their own skulls.

12 | Camels and A-Bombs

The clearest sign of the new direction which the expedition would take came at the end of their first week in Washington. Steiner had been away for the night, camping by himself in a pup tent on the drained bed of the Potomac, and after breakfast Orlowski strolled off to inspect the Executive Office Building. Ricci and Anne Summers rode out to see the mausoleum of the three Kennedy Presidents at Arlington, leaving Wayne to distil the casks of sea-water he had collected the previous day by mule team from the Tidal Basin.

Wayne was glad to stay behind. He had already made his own brief tour of the great museums and offices of state, he had stared with awe at the Apollo space-craft, at the Wright *Flier* and the *Spirit of St Louis*. (Curiously, the aircraft that most impressed him was a late-twentieth-century man-powered machine, the *Gossamer Albatross*, a delicate pedal-driven glider, now a dusty relic but once a poem to challenge the sun.) But there were more important things to get on with. After listening to the reassuring drip of pure water through the coils of the distillation column, he set off with his shovel for the Lincoln Memorial.

For the next two hours he worked away in the cool light, deep in the centre of the building, clearing away the sand that surrounded the statue. A vast dune had flowed in across Lincoln's knees, a white tide of dust at which his stone eyes stared pensively. After they had gone the sand would come in again, but the effort, Wayne knew, was worthwhile.

Resting with his coffee thermos on the steps of the Memorial, he was surprised to see Steiner approaching on foot along the centre of the Mall, a white burnouse flowing from his shoulders. Behind him came two camels, ropes through their fleshy noses, plodding at a leisurely pace across the sand. They reached the Ellipse, and Wayne then noticed that a small party of nomads — Bureaucrats, he guessed, from the dark ties they still wore around their shirtless necks — had pitched camp at the foot of the Washington Monument. As the dark-faced women, also wearing ties, squatted on the ground by a fire of dried cactus, the men gathered around Steiner's black mare, inspecting its flanks and hindquarters with eager eyes.

By the time Wayne reached the camp Steiner had tethered the camels to the White House railings. He wiped his sunglasses with satisfaction.

'I had the best of that one, Wayne. They're worried about something, though, they were too distracted to bargain.'

'From now on you're going to ride a camel?' Wayne was wary of Steiner's buoyant mood. The billowing white robe had given him a new sense of freedom. Was the Captain naked underneath it? In burnouse and sunglasses he looked like a modern-day Bedouin chieftain, with a degree in petrology and a merciless way with hostages.

'Of course, Wayne — we should have brought camels in the first place. These two are descended from a pair in the San Diego Zoo. They're the true ship of the desert, not the horse.'

'But why did the Indians take your mare?' Wayne asked. 'I've never seen any of them ride a horse.'

Steiner helped himself to a cup of warm water. The dark sickle of an incipient beard was sharpening the line of his jaws. 'Wayne, they're not planning to ride the mare. They're going to eat her. Horse is a rare delicacy for these people. God knows what's worrying them, though. All they want to do is eat.'

As the mare was led away behind the Monument, Steiner noticed Wayne frowning. 'Look, Wayne, I'm sorry to see her go − but we're almost out of oats. Sooner or later we'll have to trade in the whole team. These camels can survive on yucca leaves and cactus pith.'

Wayne looked at the Captain with some surprise. They had spoken by radio to McNair the previous afternoon. Seaworthy again, the *Apollo* would set sail in three days' time for Norfolk, Virginia, and rendezvous there with the expedition.

'Captain, the *Apollo* will soon be here. There's enough fodder aboard for six months.'

Steiner nodded at Wayne, his eyes focusing with an effort on the young man's by no means guileless face, as if re-engaging with some past reality which Wayne's reference to his former command had briefly touched.

'The *Apollo* − you're right, Wayne. But I wasn't really thinking of the ship . . .'

Digesting this oblique remark, Wayne squatted in the shade of the wagon, while Steiner made his first attempt to ride the camels. The huge, slow beasts had been well trained, and the Captain soon mastered the high saddle, the long rolling gait, the lurching, ungainly way to mount and dismount, the sudden buckling legs that threatened to pitch the rider on to his face.

As Steiner exercised the camels around the Ellipse, two other parties of nomads entered the Mall. Each contained half a dozen members, three dark-faced men in white robes, the rest women with small children. The first group were Bureaucrats, and pitched their tents on the steps of the Department of Agriculture building. The second Wayne easily identified as Gangsters. Riding at a slouch, they ambled aggressively past the White House entrance, the men wearing chalk-stripe suits under their white robes, the women with peroxide hair and the silver lamé jackets of gun molls. An intact caricature of old Chicago, they made a leisurely circuit of the Mall, peering in a sullen way at the great museums and office buildings. For whatever reasons, they at last decided on the Houses of Congress, and set up camp below the shattered dome of the Capitol.

Unsettled by the gathering Indians, and by the ominous smoke from the barbecue fire behind the Washington Monument, Wayne left the camp and climbed the dunes to the White House. He needed to be alone, to think over everything in the quiet sanctuary of the Oval Office.

However, as he pushed back the door he saw that someone was sitting behind the President's desk.

'Come in, Wayne,' Orlowski called out. 'I'd like to talk to you.' He had moved Wayne's sleeping bag out of his way and was relaxing in a high-backed wicker chair he had produced from somewhere. He beckoned Wayne forward with an expansive wave, wafting a powerful odour of bourbon across the room. As Wayne approached the desk he could see the neck of a bottle protruding from the bottom drawer. In the faint dust across the leather surface Orlowski had written:

PRESIDENT GREGORY ORWELL 2114–2126

Orlowski giggled, and then checked himself, assuming an owlishly serious expression. 'I've given myself three terms, Wayne, like Roosevelt and Teddy Kennedy. One of my great-grandparents was mayor of Toledo, I would certainly have gone into politics. Wayne, these talents run in the blood. But look at this.'

He pointed through the cracked windows. Several new parties of nomads had arrived, their camels ambling past the giant cacti. 'What's bringing them here? Talk to Steiner, Wayne, before he goes completely native. For all you know, a substantial part of the American population may now be in Washington. Perhaps they're looking for a leader? We could constitute an Electoral College, and vote by show of hands on the Athenian pattern. I would accept the nomination, Wayne.'

With growing irritation, Wayne watched the commissar

as his pudgy hands caressed the desk. This overweight ministry factotum knew and cared nothing for America, given half a chance he would turn the whole continent into a suburb of Siberia. Suddenly Wayne wanted Orlowski out of his chair, out of the Oval Office and out of the White House.

'It's a remarkable idea, Gregor — Gregory, that is. I'd be happy to be your campaign manager.'

'Good . . . ' Orlowski's eyes lolled contentedly as he re-traced his name in more emphatic letters. 'You can play a vital part, Wayne, in the rebirth of the American nation. Now, assume I am President. What's my first step in this historic task?'

'Destroy the Bering Straits Dam,' Wayne said promptly. When Orlowski looked up in surprise, Wayne continued, his fluent tongue masking his sarcasm: 'There must be enough nuclear missiles in Nebraska to do the job — as far as I can see they were never removed from their silos, just deactivated and sealed into the concrete. McNair's a great engineer, he'd rebuild the launch ramps, Professor Summers and Dr Ricci could renovate the war-heads and put together an arsenal in no time. We take out the dam, then reverse the flow of Arctic water into the Pacific, bring the Gulf Stream back from the African coast. The first heavy rain will turn this desert green again, America will run with rivers, Kansas and Iowa will be like your beloved steppes.'

'Wayne!' Unsure whether Wayne was wholly serious, Orlowski stood up. His feet were steady, and already he looked completely sober. With a sharp gesture, he wiped his name from the desk. 'Wayne, I'm impressed. What ambition! After my third term *you* can be President. But Moscow might not approve, all that permafrost, you know, the great Siberian wheat basin would turn into an ice-rink overnight.'

'But what could they do? Faced with an ultimatum?' Wayne pressed on, curious to see how his fantasy had intrigued the commissar. 'There are no nuclear weapons in the east, not even a real standing army — just a lot of police and union officials. It would take them years to organise a naval expedition. By then the Mall could be knee-deep in sweet corn.'

'Fascinating, Wayne . . . ' Orlowski was staring at him thoughtfully, as if seeing something in Wayne's character for the first time, his tempter in this no longer so gauche young stowaway. 'All very true, and good reason for us to rejoin the *Apollo* before we get carried away. I want Dr Ricci to establish a base camp at Norfolk, Virginia. You'll set off with him tomorrow. Meanwhile, get your things out of here — you can take over one of the secretaries' rooms. I'm moving into the Oval Office.'

'No — ' Without thinking, Wayne stepped forward to the desk. 'I'm staying here, Gregor. You move in with the secretaries.'

'What? Wayne!' As Orlowski stepped backwards Wayne picked up the commissar's hat. The two men grappled clumsily, tripping over each other's feet, too angry to hear the voice shouting in the corridor outside. Wayne felt himself pinned against the desk. Orlowski had seized his elbows in a powerful grip, and was twisting his right arm out of its socket. Panting for breath, Wayne looked down at their hand-prints in the dust, frantic smears marking this ludicrous struggle, the last two men in America indian-wrestling across the chief executive's desk.

'Wayne! For God's sake, Gregor, let him go!'

Anne Summers broke into the room, confused after running through the empty White House, like the distraught wife of a murdered President abandoned by his staff.

'Gregor! There's been another earthquake — a major tremor from the centre of Boston!' Breathless with alarm, she pointed at the cracked windows. 'We've lost contact with the *Apollo*. I think McNair and the crew are all dead!'

'Professor Summers, calm yourself . . . ' With a hard glance at Wayne, the commissar picked up his hat. 'They're in New York, more than a hundred miles away. There must be an instrument error. There's no fault line running through Boston.'

'No!' Trying to quieten Orlowski, she pulled him from the desk. 'It's not that. There's been a huge release of radio-activity. The Geiger counters on the Pan Am Building are recording a vast burst of neutrons. Don't you understand, Gregor — ? An atomic bomb has been detonated over Boston!'

13 | West

They waited in the dusk around the radio tent. At last, as the aerial's shadow stretched along the Mall to the hundred or so watching nomads, they heard McNair's voice coming in over the short wave. Calmer now, Anne Summers crouched beside the receiver, tirelessly repeating the expedition's call sign. All afternoon, while she took turns with Ricci and Orlowski, an unbroken static tone had emerged from the loudspeaker, but at seven o'clock, the agreed rendezvous hour, they heard McNair's jaunty voice.

'He's coming through!' Anne silenced them with a wave. 'But it's a tape-recording, we won't be able to talk to him. God only knows where he is!'

Wayne gripped the shaft of the aerial mast. He was still trembling with anger at Orlowski, and a confused guilt that his plan for destroying the Bering Dam had set off the Boston explosion. He listened to McNair's voice distorted by the heavy static.

' . . . it's 4 o'clock here in New York, Professor Summers. In half an hour I'm riding out to Long Island with the reconnaissance party, so I'm putting this on tape for the 7 o'clock bulletin. To bring you up to date, work has gone well on the *Apollo*'s keel, this morning we riveted down the last of the copper plates, we were all set to start the winches and pull her off the silt bank. Just after 1.30 I was on the roof of the Pan Am Building − Wayne will be impressed to hear that I got one of the elevators working. As I was putting a new battery into Dr Ricci's transmitter I felt a sudden tremor under my feet. The whole building shook, there must have been a huge ground-surge through the rocky mantle, almost a tectonic shift. You could see Manhattan tremble. Looking out to the north-east I saw an extraordinary glow over the desert. It lasted about five seconds, then faded into a luminous cloud. Down at the dock everyone stopped work. The quake must have set off an old munitions dump somewhere in Long Island, there's a cloud of debris about ten miles wide moving down the coast to New York on the south-westerly. I'll let you know what we find in the 7 o'clock bulletin tomorrow, Orlowski might want to notify Moscow . . . Give my best to the Captain, you can tell him the *Apollo* looks even more handsome than the SS *Lenin* . . .'

As the message ended, Anne Summers frowned at the receiver, like someone remembering a bad dream. With her worn nails, chapped skin and dusty blonde hair she looked ten years older than the young physicist who had stepped ashore in Manhattan – stupidly, Wayne could only think of giving her a new lipstick and a movie magazine.

Steiner stepped forward, slinging the rolled burnouse over one shoulder. He had ridden up on his camel only a few minutes before the start of the broadcast, sharp nose sniffing the dusk air as if he could smell the explosion. He embraced Anne reassuringly, then examined the numerical print-out from the Manhattan transmitter.

'These radiation readings, Anne – they're high, I take it?'

Orlowski fanned his face with his hat. He was looking at Wayne, though he had clearly forgotten their confrontation. 'This strange cloud – is there any more information, Professor? We'll have to wait for tomorrow's bulletin.'

'Gregor . . . ' With a tired flourish, Anne tore off the print-out and stuffed the paper strip into the commissar's hat. 'There won't be any more information, and there won't be a bulletin tomorrow, or any other evening. The cloud which McNair and his men were riding out to investigate consists of fall-out from an atomic explosion – I don't know how or why, perhaps released from a nuclear submarine in one of the Boston dry-docks. The radioactivity levels in Manhattan are into the amber zone. Paul?'

Ricci was stroking the lapels of his black leather jacket, as if aware that he would soon be returning the garment to its rightful owners. 'Well beyond. Gregor, Captain Steiner, look at this. 217 Fermis, 223, 235, then over 254 Fermis half an hour ago. That's three times the lethal limit. I'm afraid McNair and your men, Captain, are already as good as dead.'

Orlowski played with the paper tape inside his hat, a third-rate conjuror trying to think of a new trick. He listened to the ascending clicks from the transmitter, snapping his fingers at the same time. Steiner left the tent and walked across the evening sand, followed by Ricci and Anne Summers. Dozens of nomads squatted among the cactus trees, drawn in some way to the aerials above the radio tent, cryptic beacons of a new cargo cult. Shielding Anne from the cool air, Steiner draped his burnouse over her shoulders, a gesture by this dark-faced sea-captain that seemed to mark her as one of his own. She knelt on the cold sand, clenched hands pressing the coarse crystals away from her, staring back at Wayne as if identifying him with this poisoned land.

'Well, Wayne, we have to think.' Orlowski peered at the whiplash tracing of the seismograph, and at the radio receiver unravelling its nightmare Fermi numbers. He beckoned Wayne outside. 'We'll talk to the others – and you support me.'

As they approached the nomads Orlowski shook his hat threateningly. Turning his back on them, he said: 'Captain, we should set off for New York.'

Ricci kicked at the sand between them. His handsome face was pinched and fretful. The jagged shadow of the radio aerial marked his cheek with a flicker of black lightning. 'Gregor, didn't you listen? There's no point! By the time we get there they'll all be . . . '

'We must move on, then, to the south.' Orlowski rallied

himself. He pulled the paper print-out from his hat and let it unravel away on the night air. A Bureaucrat snatched it from the sand and began an eager, white-toothed mime of reciting the numbers. Orlowski watched him with a shudder. 'This cloud, these nuclear explosions, we weren't warned to expect them. We'll have to go south, to Miami, we can rest there and wait for a rescue ship.' Orlowski gazed round encouragingly. 'Miami, yes. Professor Summers, think of all those swimming-pools . . . '

He stopped as Steiner turned to face him, a hand raised to silence the commissar. The Captain was smiling to himself in an almost euphoric way, as if he had secretly bartered their equipment for the nomads' fermented cactus juice.

'No, Gregor, we're not going south − not for all the swimming-pools in Miami. We're not going south because that isn't an American direction. When Americans started to move south everything went wrong.' Steiner turned to Wayne and put a hand on his shoulder. 'Right, Wayne? You know the American direction . . . '

'Of course.' Pointedly, Wayne pushed the Captain's hand away.

'Go on, then. Tell Gregor.'

Wayne looked at the cracked egg-dome of the Capitol, lit by the last of the sunset, and at the circle of waiting nomads. Orlowski was watching him with the same confused but hopeful gaze, as if Wayne were a young redeemer with his planetary dreams of moving the seas and the winds.

'West,' Wayne said.

14 | Wayne's Diary: Part One

June 5. Manassas Battlefield Park

We left Washington at 6 o'clock this morning, and are resting here for the night in a Holiday Inn off Interstate 66. A long desert day, small towns almost invisible in the yellow haze, much more intense than it was near the coast. I think we're bearing up better than the camels — they must be unsettled by the way we ride, and by all the last-minute bargaining when Ricci got overexcited and tried to trade his roan stallion for the head Gangster's huge dromedary. To his surprise, the chief offered Paul one of his wives instead, an electric blonde like an angry doll. But Anne put her foot down, and Ricci rode the first five miles in a sulk.

Luckily, the harsh landscape soon sobered us all. The same endless cactus and creosote bush, eroded buttes and drained salt pans. The odd kit fox and kangaroo rat among the desert buttercups, but not a sign of any Indians. I thought a few might have followed us, but I guess they're too frightened by the earthquakes. There must have been 300 of them sheltering in the Mall, drawn there by some ancestral memory of the power of the Presidency and Congress, all that's left of a million times that number of original Americans. A curious lot, though not unfriendly, despite their talk of dragons leaping from the ground, strange wingless machines speeding through the air, all mixed up with bizarre images in the sky, everything from the familiar space-ship to a giant rodent who sounded suspiciously like

Mickey Mouse. One of the Divorcees from Reno (remarkably motherly, despite the fierce blue rinse and mascara, she pulled me into her little tent on the steps of the Supreme Court building and offered to legally adopt me!) even talked some rubbish about the 'President of the West', a weird, white-faced man with staring eyes who lives in the sky . . .

For all that, the great old USA is still here under the desert sun — all it needs is rain, a hundred-year downpour, say. Surprisingly, there's a fair amount of water around in rusty cisterns and roof tanks, brackish but almost drinkable. Steiner has just suggested that we abandon the water-wagon, and I've agreed. It was already slowing us down, and we have the portable distillation column and filter unit. He has an amazing faith that the desert will look after us. 'Only adapt, Wayne — the way you breathe, sleep, walk, think.' He embraces the desert, I'm sure he'll never be fully happy until he's the last man in America. Orlowski is quiet, still hasn't forgiven me, he makes me uneasy. Ricci is like a neurotic gangster, all aggression and small vanities. Anne is very calm, sits in her dusty armchair in the lounge of this motel like the Queen of Sheba with a slight dose of sun-stroke. I've given her a make-up set I found in the man-ageress's bedroom, she's very slowly painting her face as I write this, watching me all the while in an odd way . . .

June 9. Lexington, Virginia

Four long days, up into the Appalachians — camels are fine and it's our turn to feel weary. Down through the Shenandoah Valley into the Blue Ridge country. No mountain music here or fightin' McCoys, just blazing rock and sand. It's more like Sinai — we resemble the Lost Tribe in more senses than one (even have our Moses leading us in his white robe, half pirate chief, half old Arab navigator — Steiner certainly knows his atlas of the heavens). There was a crisis yesterday when we found we'd left behind all the batteries for the radio transmitters. This means we're totally out of touch with any rescue expedition that might reach

New York or Miami. Orlowski nearly went berserk, he didn't know whom to accuse, we were all equally suspect. He sat on his camel with his face as red as a signal lamp, and ordered us back to Washington. Not a hope. No one moved an inch. When Gregor took out his pistol Steiner calmly pointed out that the batteries had probably been broken into by the Indians. Orlowski stared at him – for a moment I was certain he didn't recognise the Captain or any of us – and then suddenly holstered the gun and waved us forward, as if nothing had happened and no one would want to get in touch with Moscow anyway.

Thinking about it, I feel that for a few minutes Orlowski was his old self, but then the desert came back and took him over again.

June 18. Louisville, Kentucky. Interstate 64

Camping in a dusty Howard Johnson on the banks of what was once the Ohio River – now a sand-filled wadi like a huge drainage ditch, yachts and power-boats embedded in shallow dunes. Everyone very tired – Orlowski was asleep on his camel for miles, Anne Summers had a nagging row with Steiner, who once again went off ahead, out of sight all day, and then came back with his hunting trophies, three dead rattlesnakes hung around his neck. The Captain would clearly like to rid himself of us all, looks at us as if we were rather tiresome guests at some huge dude ranch. For the first time I feel that he might dislike me, I make him uneasy in some way. I'm too ambitious, I want to irrigate this desert in all senses, while he prefers to think of America as just the ultimate backdrop to his fantasies of being alone.

For the first time there's a certain anxiety about the water position. As we've moved west across Kentucky the land has become more and more arid, it's getting harder to find even small amounts of water in heating pipes and cisterns. There's plenty of Scotch and Bourbon, though, in cellars and bond-stores, I'm having to distil off the alcohol to get at the 25 per cent residue of water. Takes hours to cool, we sit around sipping non-alcoholic hot toddies. Being in charge of the water supply certainly gives me a lot of authority . . .

Hard to believe that this is where they ran the Kentucky Derby, that we've just crossed the Blue Grass country. Not a sign of tobacco fields, mint juleps and green velvet pastures, only wilderness and bone-like alluvial fans. Too tired to go out and explore the city. Orlowski is wandering around the car park, like a man in a movie looking for his ignition keys. Usually Ricci picks up a new suit for the next day, but he's sitting in the empty lobby, like a small-time bookie who's arrived a century too late. Anne is relaxing in the beauty parlour, gazing at herself in the mirrors, about to put on her make-up (as I notice she does before the share-out of the evening water ration!)

An hour ago one of the lame baggage camels slipped and fell into the drained swimming-pool. Steiner calmly shot the poor beast, but the smell made us all change our rooms. No one is bothering to cook tonight.

Like the others, I'm starting to think about water all the time.

July 10. Mount Vernon, Illinois. Interstate 64

1.30 p.m. Too hot to travel in the middle of the day. While Steiner disappears into the town we're resting here in a shady hangar out at the airport. Crossing the Wabash two days ago another of the baggage camels fell into an ash-filled gulley and had to be destroyed. For the last hour we've been lying under the cool wing of a DC-8, trying to agree about what equipment to leave behind. Orlowski suggested we keep the last radio transmitter, in case we find suitable batteries somewhere, but Anne and Ricci voted him down. We all agreed that there isn't anything we'd want to say, anyway. I took their side, and that seemed to clinch it. More and more the others are listening to me. Anne really accepts now that I'm not a child, and that in some way I give the expedition its real compass bearing. I can understand how religions always started in the desert —

it's like an extension of one's mind. Far from being a wilderness, every rock and prickly pear, every gopher and grasshopper seems to be part of one's brain, a realm of magic where everything is possible. The whiteness, too, I feel close to some new truth that I'm leading the others towards.

Anyway, the radio stays here, among the dusty aircraft, even though it means we're now totally out of touch with the rest of the world. A good thing. For all the tiredness, there's a quiet determination to keep moving west.

Surprise: Steiner has come back with a bottle of Californian brandy, 'the distillation,' he says, 'of the sweet Pacific rain . . . ' He sits in the cockpit of a Cessna, drinking by himself, Elijah in his stalled chariot. Curiously, for the first time I feel that the rest of us are more at home in the desert than he is. He's still aware of himself, he's just swapped the open Atlantic for the sand-seas of Kentucky and Illinois, while we are at one with the dust.

July 28. St Louis, Missouri. Interstate 70

At last we've reached the banks of the Mississippi. Writing this on the bridge of the great *Admiral* riverboat. If and when we reach California I won't be surprised if the Pacific Ocean itself is drained dry. Delayed for three days while Orlowski recovered after a bout of fever picked up from infected water — I've been getting careless with the still, but it's hot work chopping up motel doors and fence-posts. He lay in his hotel room in Mount Vernon, going through a remarkably elaborate fantasy of being President of the USA. To encourage him I pretended to be his chief of staff, addressed him as President Orwell, said we were going to set up the Western White House in Beverly Hills, he'd be surrounded by glamorous economists and film stars. It really made him better — people's fantasies are astonishingly easy to stimulate. Steiner watched all this very disapprovingly, that pistol under his robe bothers me. He knows I'm manipulating everyone, but he doesn't know why. The first settlers to cross America were driven by their fantasies too.

Still, thanks to me, and some carefully fractionated Johnnie Walker, Orlowski pulled round. Today, as we rode into St Louis, looking up at that sagging Gateway Arch — like a sign for the ultimate Big Mac — I playfully called him Gregory, and he answered without a blink, though giving me a wary smile. Everyone in surprisingly good humour, appropriate to the home of Mark Twain. Anne is wearing her make-up during the day now. At times her face looks like a Halloween mask, but I go out of my way to compliment her — the oils in those lurid old cosmetics will protect her skin (sorry to say that when she wipes off the make-up she isn't the only one to get a shock). I can't help feeling that there's an ironic element somewhere, that she's deliberately modelling herself on that blue-rinsed Divorcee, and for my benefit in particular.

Ricci has started to use a little of the face-cream against the sun, and I've suggested that we all follow suit. The lipstick makes a surprisingly good skin-guard. We must have looked an odd troupe when we climbed down from the camels and stood on the levee. Together we gazed out over the drained bed of the Mississippi, at the great showboats stranded there on the dry sand, hundreds of cars and shacks abandoned around them. It must have taken a long time to drain, it's odd to see the fortified landing stages, the fierce barbed wire fences and sandbagged forts set up along the banks of the last little creek. People defended this greasy stream to the last drop.

Strangely, none of us was too disappointed, I think we were almost relieved to find that the Mississippi was dry. We move on tomorrow, following the footsteps of Daniel Boone!

August 19. Kansas City, Kansas. Interstate 70

Moving through a kind of dream, an embalmed yellow world of sand and amber-like air. We have entered the area of deepest desert, an almost abstract landscape. We must be somewhere near the centre of a vast Sahara that stretches across the American continent. A terrain of opalised trees and sandy palm-gardens set among endless suburbs and factories, shopping malls and theme parks, all silent and forgotten under a mantle of glazed light.

When we arrived in Kansas City this morning a sleepy quarrel broke out over where exactly we were. I kept pointing to the route indicators, but Gregor, who is feverish again, insisted that this is San Clemente, Nixon's old seaside haunt. He rambled away about the bracing effects of the brine and the ozone. Meanwhile Ricci and Anne agreed that we had reached Lake Tahoe, they were ready to strip off and swim in the nearest dune. To stop them I pretended to walk on the water, they were really amazed, stared at me as if I was some kind of hickory stick messiah, even Steiner was impressed and gave me a cool salute.

Obviously the desert has at last got inside our heads, we're seeing everything in terms of ash and sand. The landscape of Kansas is an elaborate kit of internal ciphers, a set of psychological counters of a mysterious kind. You could kill someone here as an abstract gesture, see your own divinity confirmed in the contours of a dune.

Hard to tell what anyone is thinking, we all sit on our camels shrouded in white robes, sun-blistered faces smeared with rouge and lipstick. Anne stays very close to me now, painted like a harpy. Of course, I control the water ration, but she knows I hold the fate of this expedition. I don't trust Ricci — this morning, when I helped him off his tottering camel, I discovered that he wears a concealed Derringer in a wrist holster, as well as his pearl-handled Colts.

Steiner has surrendered completely to the desert. He keeps apart, hardly ever talks now, sometimes goes off without warning for two or three days, then appears at the camp fire in the evening with a jerrican of rusty water. Is he aware of the urban landscape around him, the sun-filled museum of the USA? An hour ago Steiner rode into Kansas City, an empty metropolis of giant car plants, stockyards and skyscrapers, but I'm sure all Steiner could see was the old frontier town. He's waiting for that final shoot-out in the O.K. Corral, to settle for once and for all his grievance against the human race.

August 28. Topeka, Kansas. Interstate 70

An unhappy day. Things are starting to fall apart, we're spending almost all our time hunting for water. Everything is arid here, an endless thirstland, I've never seen so many drained swimming-pools. Orlowski's camel died. While Steiner and I were transferring his gear Ricci secretly raided the 6 jerricans I'd painfully collected. I caught him literally red-handed, chin and hands stained with rust. Hiding in the motel bathroom, gangster suit covered with white dust, jerrican clutched to his chest, he looked quite mad. Steiner was ready to gun him down there and then, in Cabin 6 of the Skyline Park Motel, but I let him go. Orlowski is a dead weight, his fever goes and comes again. Anne lies exhausted on her bed, drawn up alongside mine, unwashed face covered with blisters and smudged mascara, staring at the dials of her seismograph and complaining to me about the San Francisco earthquake, as if it was my fault. Sounds like a special kind of twentieth-century marriage. Have we come too far?

September 8. Abilene, Kansas. Interstate 70

Letting myself get overtired.

We're camping in the bus depot. Apart from Steiner, who's gone off looking for the ghost of Wild Bill Hickock, everyone is sitting on the floor under the tables, too exhausted to search for water. Orlowski is ill, for the last three days we've been pulling him on a makeshift litter. We're down to the last four camels, and whoever loses the next one will have to walk. I drained a precious 5 gallons from the heating system of the Eisenhower Memorial Library. Strange to think of Ike being raised in this small desert town. Tried to talk to Ricci about the real purpose of the expedition

— the attempt to find that special 'America' inside each one of us, that golden coast McNair saw from the deck of the *Apollo* a few weeks before he died. But Ricci just sat back against an old juke box, staring at me glassily. The only thing that keeps him going is the fires he lights. Each small town we pass through he sets ablaze, in seconds the tinder-dry wooden buildings send up huge flames. We leave behind us an apocalyptic sky filled with immense swaying columns of black smoke.

Breaking off to look after Gregor. His mouth is full of blood.

September 21. Dodge City, Kansas. Route 56

11.45 a.m. Out of water here. This was the end of the old Texas Trail, and it looks like it might be ours. Steiner has finally abandoned us. One moment he was leaning against a pump in a filling station forecourt, the next he had gone. Since the camels died we've been forced to walk. Most of the time I've been dragging Gregor by myself, and trying to keep Anne and Ricci on the move. They sit down whenever I'm not looking, in the back seats of empty cars, as if they're waiting for their chauffeur to collect them.

We're lying on the floor of the old Long Branch Saloon, in the middle of a Wild West theme park, trying to recover enough strength to look for water. Outside the temperature must be up to 120° F., for days we've been moving across a vast ash-tip.

2.38 p.m. Orlowski died half an hour ago — he looked twenty years older and half the weight he was when we set out. I did my best for him, but he didn't appreciate it. The last few days have been a nightmare, dragging this deranged commissar along, listening to him curse away, blaming *me*. It was *his* expedition. Still, I'm sorry to see him go, in his own way he was a real American.

Ricci has disappeared somewhere —

Wayne broke off, and let the diary fall on to the plank floor of the saloon. He drew his rifle towards him. From the street a shot had rung out. After a pause, as he climbed to his feet, it was followed by three more in rapid succession, and a clatter of metal cans and bursting glass.

'Target practice, Wayne. Take care . . . ' Sitting in the dim light against the bar, Anne Summers raised a warning hand. Through the heat sores and streaked make-up Wayne could see the last flicker of concern before she sank back into herself, too dehydrated to move. Above them, Orlowski lay on the green baize of the roulette table, hands outstretched across the circle of numbers, as if hoping to clutch some winning play. Were they all part of a theme park tableau, the last reel of a western?

The can-can girls had gone now. Wayne listened to the last of the shots echo down the Wild West street, with its replica stage coach, its dry goods store, tonsorial palace and haberdashers. The harsh sunlight beyond the swing doors steadied him. While he lay in an exhausted doze over his diary, someone had taken the last jerrican of water which he had been guarding with his rifle.

Ricci . . . ? Or had Steiner slipped back, realising that he needed Wayne more than he had ever admitted?

Wayne slapped his cheeks. For days now he had felt light-headed, both from hunger and from the effort of steering Anne Summers along the dusty highway. As the swing doors rocked behind him he stepped into the sun-filled street, swaying like a drunken gunfighter about to be shot down into the dust.

Light flashed from the heels of a small, bearded man standing in the centre of the street a hundred yards away. He had thrown away his white burnouse, and now wore a wide-brimmed hat trimmed with silver, hard leather chaps, narrow vest and tartan shirt. In his left hand he carried the last jerrican of water. He holstered his pearl-handled revolver with a professional flourish, and kicked at the glitter of broken bottles he had used for target practice.

'Ricci − !' Wayne shouted hoarsely. He gripped the cool

trigger and barrel of his Winchester. 'Ricci, I want the water!'

The physicist glanced back at Wayne, shaking his head as if no longer interested in the young stowaway and his dying expedition. Fever had returned to his once-handsome face all its former sharp profiles. He gazed up at the wooden façades of the hotels and saloons, scanning the rooflines for any waiting gunman with a shotgun aimed at his heart.

'Paul! That's my water, Paul . . . ' Angrily, Wayne rapped the butt of his rifle against the door panel of the replica Boot Hill stage-coach parked outside the Long Branch Saloon. He realised that the whole secret logic of their journey across America had been ·leading them to this absurd and childish confrontation in a theme park frontier street, in a make-believe world already overtaken by a second arid West far wilder than anything those vacationing suburbanites of the late twentieth century could ever have imagined.

But it *was* his water!

'Paul!'

As the first of Ricci's bullets struck the plastic sign of the Long Branch Saloon above his head, Wayne ran forward through the overheated air.

15 | Giants in the Sky

Later that afternoon Wayne at last reached the entrance to the Boot Hill cemetery, his rifle and the jerrican of water clasped to his chest. For hours he had been trying to return to Anne Summers, but he had lost his bearings in the theme park. Somewhere among the stage-coaches and collapsed hamburger stands he saw Steiner watching him. The Captain pursued Wayne around the town, staring from the window of the sheriff's office, strolling past the Wells Fargo building, standing on the dusty footplate of the antique locomotive in the replica railroad station. He had thrown away his burnouse, and once again wore his black mariner's jacket and peaked cap. He watched Wayne's wandering progress in a pensive but detached way, as if Wayne were a weary animal in a laboratory maze.

For his part, Wayne no longer felt any anger towards the Captain, even though he knew that he had let himself be used by Steiner, who had casually exploited his determination and will to survive. In many ways he had been no more than a beast of burden, like the mules and camels, eager to carry the others on his back.

Wayne entered the old cemetery and climbed the low rise towards the nearest group of graves. Carefully placing the rifle and jerrican on the ground, he sat down and rested against a now indecipherable headstone. He looked at the town below, at the rooftops almost hidden by the glaring sunlight of the surrounding dunes. He might make his own end here, but he would not be alone. Holding the Winchester as firmly as he could, he waited patiently for Steiner to appear. And sure enough, within a few minutes, the Captain approached the cemetery, crossing the half-empty car park by the entrance. He had already seen Wayne, and climbed the hill towards him with his head down, eyes hidden below the peak of his cap.

Calming himself, Wayne raised the Winchester, fixing its sights on the bright anchor above the tattered braid.

At this moment, as he prepared to shoot the Captain, Wayne saw his second mirage of the Great American Desert.

High above him, almost filling the cloudless, cobalt sky, was the enormous figure of a cowboy. Two huge spurred boots, each the height of a ten-storey building, rested on the hills above the town, while the immense legs, clad in worn leather chaps and as tall as skyscrapers, reached up to the gunbelt a thousand feet in the air. The silver-tipped bullets pointed down at Wayne like a row of aircraft fuselages. Beyond them rose the cliff wall of the cowboy's check shirt, and then the towering shoulders that seemed to carry the sky.

Wayne lay back weakly, staring up at this titanic figure that had materialised like a genie out of the afternoon sky. One of the giant legs moved forward, stepping from one hill crest to another. Wayne feebly raised a hand, frightened that the giant would turn and casually step on him. Looking up at the craggy face under the broad-brimmed hat, he recognised the figure.

'John Wayne . . . !'

He listened to his own cry. Had his dying mind conjured the image of his namesake out of this frontier town and the ghosts of its theme park, the film actor he had first seen in *Stagecoach*?

Unaware of the exhausted youth slumped against the gravestone far below him, the giant hitched his gunbelt a notch and leaned sideways, making room in the sky.

Wayne gasped as another vast cowboy appeared beside him, a lanky man with wistful eyes and gentle hands never far from his guns.

'Henry Fonda . . . ' Dressed as Wyatt Earp in the old western Wayne had seen so many times, *My Darling Clementine*.

Yet another figure joined them, again in sheriff's garb, Gary Cooper with the tired, stoical expression he had worn in *High Noon*. Behind him, advancing calmly across the distant mountains, came a smaller, neatly built man, Alan Ladd as the mysterious stranger in *Shane*. They stood together, an aerial Mount Rushmore, heroes resurrected from the tombs of Boot Hill and the theme park saloons of Dodge City.

Wayne lay back against the gravestone, certain that he was kept alive by his vision of these immense mythological figures. They stepped forward, shoulder to shoulder, ready to fight a last gun-fight across the streets of this Tombstone of the sky. Wayne searched for his rifle, hoping to fire a shot into the air and bring the giants back to save him. They passed above his head, moving in vast strides that darkened the land, across the dusty stage-coaches and deadwood saloons of their own dream, and set off together towards the mountains in the west.

The air had cleared, and a dome of unstressed blue porcelain hung over Wayne, like the ceiling of a calm and well-lit mausoleum. He drifted in and out of a shallow delirium, through brief spells of complete clarity when he saw green hills and mountains, the wooded slopes of the Rockies beckoning to him along the Cimarron trail, jungle-bedecked valleys moist with fast-running streams. Then as abruptly, he would see only the dust and sand of the white dunes around Boot Hill.

Steiner had gone, following the great gods in the sky. When Wayne last saw the Captain he was moving among the tombstones, hands raised to shield his eyes as he stared up at the immense figures. But Wayne found that his shirt was soaked with moisture, and he assumed that Steiner had made him drink from the jerrican.

Some time later, as the evening came on, he noticed a curious machine soaring through the air above the town, an aircraft of gossamer foil with a small erratic propeller that modestly beat the faint wind. There were two slender dragonfly wings, and a transparent fuselage inside which a bearded man pedalled energetically.

Idly, Wayne looked up at this demented cyclist trapped inside his gentle glider. He realised that he could distinctly hear the sounds of a steam-whistle hooting. Was the *Apollo* about to sail up across the evening desert, converted perhaps into a steam-powered land-yacht, its cutwater sending up a graceful bow-wave of white dust? He watched the aircraft circle the silent streets of Dodge City, turn elegantly inside its own length and head towards the Boot Hill cemetery, following the footsteps he and Steiner had left in the sand. The pilot pedalled furiously to climb the slight gradient, then opened a plastic window and peered down at the exhausted young man slumped against his tombstone.

No longer surprised by anything he saw, Wayne casually recognised the bearded man shouting to him. The pilot pedalled away, soaring and swerving as if to attract the attention of a search party below.

'McNair . . . ' Smiling to himself, Wayne waved at the filmy wings dipping above his head. 'McNair, it's the *Gossamer Albatross*. You've brought it all the way from Washington for me . . . '

'Wayne, you're still a damned fool!' Above the wild beard the perspiring face of the *Apollo*'s chief engineer grimaced at him. 'Why the hell are you painted up like a woman? And where are the others − Orlowski, the Captain, Professor Summers?'

Realising that Wayne was too weak to shout back, McNair reversed his pedals and brought the frail craft down in the car park a hundred yards away. As he climbed from the cockpit there was the approaching sound of steam-whistles. A convoy of three antiquated but still magnificent steam-cars turned into the parking lot. Funnels hissed and shuddered, spumes of steam spurted from the pistons and driving gear, their lovingly burnished brass gleamed in the sunset. They pulled up in clouds of steam and a clatter of connecting rods, the hoop-like wheels shedding sand from their untreaded tyres. The third vehicle towed a green water tanker with 'New York Fire Department' emblazoned in gold letters on its side and a spare set of glider wings lashed to its roof. The drivers dismounted, pulling off their goggles and Edwardian dustcoats, and Wayne recognised the Executives he had last seen at the motel by the New Jersey Turnpike. The young woman even carried a papoose on her hip, a handsome baby wearing a miniature aviator's helmet.

Wayne managed to climb to his knees as they ran towards him.

'GM!' he called through cracked lips, wiping the lipstick on to his wrist. 'Heinz, Pepsodent, Xerox — you've just missed John Wayne and Gary Cooper!'

16 | Rescue

Speed, steam, a throbbing firebox and straining valves – for Wayne this was excitement beyond anything even the Mercury astronauts could have known. After a week's rest they had left Dodge City and were racing westwards along Route 50, GM, Heinz and Pepsodent at the controls of the three steam-cars. As they moved through the west Kansas hill country towards the rising mountain peaks that marked the approaches to the Rockies, Wayne sat back comfortably beside Anne Summers in the rear seat of the lead car. Long plumes of silver steam flared from the jabbering pistons. The spray cooled his forehead, and with each mouthful of surging air Wayne felt his confidence return, pumping up every nerve and blood-vessel.

They were travelling in more than mere style. The three steam-cars – a Buick Roadmaster, a Ford Galaxy and a Chrysler Imperial – had been specially built for the mayor of Detroit in the closing years of the twentieth century. Upholstered like Pullman cars, and fitted with bullet-proof glass and brackets for riot-control weapons, they were the most comfortable vehicles Wayne had ever known, far swifter and more powerful than the cautious, battery-driven Dublin ambulances. They sped along at over thirty miles an hour, and by noon on the first day had covered eighty miles – a distance that would have taken a week by camel.

The desert landscape swept by, a blur of cactus and dust-dry wadis that linked the derelict farms and grain-elevators, ramshackle towns each clustered around its fortified filling station. There were few abandoned vehicles on Route 50, and they kept up an exhilarating pace. Crouched over the Chrysler's large steering wheel in his goggles and driving cape, Heinz floored the accelerator, pausing only when McNair, beside him in the bunker seat, shovelled another spade of coal through the glowing doorway of the firebox.

A hundred miles from Dodge City, as they took the steep gradients without any effort, McNair pointed to the healthy pressure dials.

'Heinz, they could really build engines in Detroit – those old car firms knew their stuff!' He propped his goggles on to his sun-reddened forehead and shouted back at Wayne: 'Not too fast for you, Wayne? If you want, we can slow down to twenty.'

Wayne lay back in the rear seat, letting the damp slipstream cool his face.

'Full ahead, Heinz! Full ahead!' he called out grandly. Beside him Anne Summers clung to a machine-gun bracket, her skin almost green with vertigo. Wayne glanced over his shoulder at the following cars. GM's Buick was behind them, its huge wheels charioting through the dust, twin plumes of steam venting across the highway like furious moustachios. GM sat forward over the wheel, while his strong-wristed young wife shovelled coal in the engineer's seat, their infant son asleep in his goggles against her breast. Pepsodent's powerful Ford Galaxy brought up the rear, towing the water tanker and the dismantled glider roped securely to its roof. The nomads had taken to the cars with surprising flair and enthusiasm, but as Wayne reminded himself, they were true Americans.

After the prospect of total disaster, the expedition had come alive again. Their rescue by McNair marked another turning point, another proving of the dream. The nomads had carried Wayne from the Boot Hill cemetery to their cars, collected a barely conscious Anne Summers from the Long Branch Saloon, and driven them both to the nearby

Holiday Inn.

As Wayne and Anne recovered, resting under a shaded awning beside the drained swimming-pool, McNair described his own escape, along with all but two of the *Apollo*'s crew, from the cloud of radioactive fall-out that had drifted across New York. During their last week of work on the *Apollo*, McNair had discovered the three steam-cars in a Brooklyn warehouse.

'They were ready to be shipped to Europe for the personal use of President Brown. Magnificent beasts, it was a treat to work on them. Luckily, I'd just finished reconditioning the engines when the seismograph fell off the wall. That was the Boston quake. Before we rode out to investigate I recorded that last message to you. We reached Kennedy Airport, and of course found nothing. I decided to check the monitoring equipment atop the Pan Am Building in case there had been any release of radiation. Well, the Geiger counters were screaming blue Fermis. We dropped all work on the *Apollo*, stoked up the steam-cars with coal from the ship's bunkers and set off at top speed down the New Jersey Turnpike . . .'

Two off-duty stokers sampling the Harlem nightclubs had ignored McNair's last warning blasts on the *Apollo*'s siren, and had presumably been trapped by the fall-out cloud, but everyone else had escaped. Ten miles from Washington they overtook the four nomad Executives, plodding along on their camels. Although McNair's warnings about the cloud of ionised gas meant nothing to them, their minds were already well stocked with lurid tales of death from the sky. They abandoned their camels on the spot and climbed into the back of the ancient Buick.

Once in Washington they joined the anxious concourse of the Indian nations, all driven from their hunting grounds by the portents in the sky, the same vision of a vast space-ship that was invariably followed by the mysterious earthquakes and exploding nuclear power stations. Many of the nomads from the Gangster tribe, McNair discovered, were suffering from leukaemia and radiation burns sustained in the quakes that had destroyed Cincinnati and Cleveland.

All these events had baffled McNair, as they did Wayne and Anne Summers, resting now in the Holiday Inn at Dodge City.

'There were some three hundred atomic power stations in the United States,' McNair pointed out. 'Were they all timed to detonate a century ahead, like some kind of insane doomsday weapon? Impossible, Anne. Wayne, think about it.'

Anne gestured weakly with her hand-mirror as she scanned the last of her exposure blisters. Without her make-up, and with the blonde hair in a towel, she resembled a pale-faced, ravaged nun. 'I know . . . But some pretty deranged Presidential orders must have been given during those last days of panic in the White House.'

'True enough, Anne. But why the weird pattern of earthquakes striking the United States at random? They follow none of the known tectonic lines. The San Andreas fault does not run through Chappaquiddick Island. They have high Richter values, but extremely short durations, and an uncanny ability to destroy the reactor core of a nearby nuclear plant.'

For all these conundrums, it began to seem probable that the entire mantle of the United States was cracking like an enormous biscuit. As for the mysterious visions in the sky reported by the Indians, they were clearly the group fantasy of these superstitious and ignorant proto-Americans whose imaginations, fuelled by cactus wine and kef, were projecting their own fears on to every Joshua tree and creosote bush.

'But, McNair,' Wayne protested from his poolside couch, 'I saw those visions too — not the space-ship, but John Wayne and Henry Fonda, Gary Cooper and Alan Ladd, each about a mile high. And they weren't visions, they were real. Steiner saw them.'

'Of course, Wayne. But Steiner, well . . . '

Both Anne and McNair remained sceptical, regarding the vision of the film actors as a product of Wayne's desert sickness. But Wayne worried about the nomads' reports. Many of them contained bizarre and sinister elements, in particular the image of a bald-headed young man, with a bruised face and a fanatic's staring eyes, a strange psychopath among the Mickey Mouse paraphernalia. There had also been a gloomy blue-suited man with the face of a lonely undertaker, perhaps the tribal deity of the Executives, the unrequited spirit of all those commuting Manhattanites . . .

However, for the time being Wayne was only relieved that McNair had found them on their last legs in Dodge City. He had left the crew of the *Apollo* behind in Washington. None of the sailors, all deep-water salt and spray men, had relished the prospect of the American desert. In Washington they would set up a base, administer the Indians (the bosun suggested that the whole state of New Jersey would make a suitable reservation, arid enough for these aboriginal nomads with their hankering after turnpikes, gaudy jewellery stores and drive-ins) and hunt for radio equipment to contact whatever rescue ship Moscow sent out over the next months.

McNair left them there to get on with it, and set off in the steam-cars with Heinz, Pepsodent, GM, Xerox and her new baby — promptly named WTOP after the call-sign of the local radio station in whose lobby the delivery safely occurred. The Executives had developed a taste for cars and the open road, and McNair himself was eager to explore the length and breadth of America, visit its silent factories and engineering plants, its coal mines and shipyards, to test his own ambition of putting this huge clockwork dream together again. He was cautious now about confiding in Wayne, and even in Anne Summers — the deaths of Orlowski and Ricci, Steiner's defection, the grotesque painted masks clearly intended for more than protection against the sun, whatever Wayne and Anne maintained, together warned him to keep a little apart from them.

Tracking them down had been less due to luck than to the long plumes of black smoke left behind at each of the incinerated towns. After zigzagging across the Middle West, finding and then losing the camels' spoor, they at last came across one of the dead beasts in a filling-station forecourt outside St Louis. McNair had spotted the rotting carcase from the *Gossamer Albatross*, which he had dismantled from its exhibition stand in the Smithsonian. Every fifty miles they stopped to bunker the cars – each carried a ton of anthracite in its ample boot – and McNair pedalled the man-powered plane into the air to scan the surrounding desert. It was on one of these flights, outside Topeka, that he had seen the first tell-tale column of smoke, a black finger pointing down to the bone-white desert and some very strange goings-on.

'We arrived literally in the last minute of the final reel,' he told the two survivors. 'The 4.10 to Yuma was one train you were not going to catch. Though God knows where you were heading – you were all painted up like a troupe of drag queens . . . ' Standing by the drained pool of the Holiday Inn, McNair glanced sharply at Wayne and Anne. For all their slight unease with each other, something had bonded them together. 'Too bad about Ricci – I never trusted him myself. His cabin aboard the *Apollo* was packed with weapons, he must have raided every gun-store in Manhattan. But it's a shame we couldn't save Orlowski. As for the Captain, he'll be out there somewhere. He'll come back, Wayne, when he's ready. I always felt that he was carrying out some sort of experiment on himself . . . '

Wayne nodded sagely at this. McNair's evident suspicion persuaded him not to describe the real character of Steiner's betrayal. Curiously, he felt no resentment, almost as if Steiner's callous abandonment of the expedition had been justified by profound inner needs, part of the same private mythology that had sent them all on their journey to the New World. The United States had based itself on the proposition that everyone should be able to live out his furthest fantasies, wherever they might lead, explore every opportunity, however bizarre.

At the same time, he could still not free his mind of the death of Orlowski. He remembered the dying commissar, painted cheeks covered with dust, head bumping in the sand as Wayne dragged his wooden litter along the highway. Orlowski had ranted away, mile after mile: 'It's your fault, Wayne, you brought us here, I should have put you ashore at the Azores . . . *you*, yes, little stowaway, you want to be President more than I do . . . ' And then, at the end: 'You're Nixon, Wayne. One term for you, one very short term . . . '

As for Ricci, whose body had been found by Pepsodent lying in the dust of the Wild West theme park – Wayne had told McNair and Anne Summers that he had been forced to shoot the physicist as he absconded with the last of their water. But in fact the bullet which entered the back of Ricci's head had not come from Wayne's Winchester. By the time Wayne crawled on his knees to reach the precious jerrican the physicist was already dead in the dust. For reasons of his own, Steiner had interceded, this strange guardian angel who had allowed Wayne to make all the running since they first left Plymouth Sound.

But Wayne said nothing of this, aware of the status which Ricci's death had given him, an authority he might need to use in the days ahead. Anne Summers knew this. Clearly she was well aware that Wayne had exploited her weakness for beauty parlours and old movie magazines, her dream of being a film star. But in the streets of Dodge City he had fought to defend her. As they recovered together beside the empty swimming-pool Anne had suddenly taken his hand.

'You kept me alive, Wayne . . . but I won't forgive you.'

Sitting back in the steam-wreathed rear seat of the Chrysler, Wayne thought of her words. He listened to the pounding of the pistons, the squeal of the valves, as they drove up the steepening gradient of the Rockies, ever nearer the source of his lost America.

17 | Across the Rockies

Higher ground now, and cooler dust-free air in which they all breathed more freely. They were moving along an empty highway that switchbacked through the Sangre de Cristo Mountains of southern Colorado, transformed by the climatic reversal into a landscape more like the Utah that Wayne remembered from the library slides in Dublin. Over the side of the Chrysler he looked down at steep rock walls etched like the façades of gothic cathedrals by the harsh winds of a century. There were miles of grit-blasted canyons and vermilion cliffs, then valleys of dunes and flats strewn with western-film locations. On either side of the road, six thousand feet above sea level, rose flame-coloured walls with serrated rims, a labyrinth of miniature Grand Canyons. As the steam-cars laboured up the gradient, pistons flagging in the thinner air, everyone stared at the opalised trees that climbed the mountain slopes, the fossilised remains of dense pine forests. Everywhere nature had come to an abrupt dead stop.

Two hours later they passed through the last col, and descended towards the drained basin of the Rio Grande. Wayne searched for any signs of freshwater springs and seeps, but the river was a burnt-out cicatrice that ran through a painted desert of small mesas, isolated hoodoos and crumbling pinnacles of rock that stood on either side of the cracked basin like forgotten chess pieces.

They stopped for the night at Alamosa, banked the engines of the three cars with wet slack and slept under the stars in the cool mountain air with its scent of amber and pyrites and death. The next morning they took the high road into the San Juan Mountains, the great divide between the eastern and western halves of the American continent. The deep-hearted engines pulled at the gradient with the guts of old Pacific locos, up into the mountains past abandoned ski-lodges like the villa-fortresses of some race of latterday Incas. As the air grew even colder, their breath shorter, they stopped at a resort lodge to break down the door and help themselves to blankets, ski-gloves, heavy tweed coats for the men and coonskins for Anne Summers, Xerox and the baby.

At Wolf Creek Pass, nearly eleven thousand feet or three OPEC Towers above sea level, Wayne leaned forward over the rear windshield and pounded Heinz on the shoulder.

'Heinz, hold it for a second!' He stood up and signalled the cars behind to halt. In the cold, thin air the steam from the panting engines condensed in a wet mist that soaked the ancient road.

'Anne, what are they? McNair, can you see them? They look like signals . . .'

Wayne pointed to the ragged white aprons that were draped against the steep ridges cutting the roof of the sky a thousand feet above them. Small fragments of these bright tatters lay on the hard ground beside the road like the flags of a discarded semaphore.

Wayne jumped down from the Chrysler and approached the nearest patch. He fell to his knees and scooped the frozen white crystals into his hands, pressed them to his cheeks.

'Anne — it's *snow!*'

Everyone leapt from the cars, tossed away their gloves and goggles. Laughing happily, GM and Heinz rolled in the snow, Pepsodent kicked up vivid sprays and crammed the crystals into his mouth, Xerox tobogganed with her delighted baby down the nursery slopes. Snowball fights rampaged around the cars, Anne Summers's excited face was

109

bright with exploding frost as she chased Wayne and McNair.

They were still laughing over all this ten minutes later as they left the pass and coasted down the long winding gradient towards Durango. On either side were snow-capped ridges, alpine meadows like the elegantly landscaped greens of mossy golf-courses.

Everyone leaned forward, peering down at the strange white haze, an immense mist of white talc, that covered the valley of the San Juan River. A thousand feet below them, its flocculent canopy lay against the waists of the mountains, and stretched across Utah and Arizona, south into New Mexico.

As they moved towards it Wayne felt a moment's panic, wondering how they could breathe this vapour of milled bone, presumably ash distilled from the potash lakes of Death Valley, so hot that even the rocks had begun to evaporate.

But as they rounded the last bend the dust-lake seemed to grow thinner. A faint steam surrounded them, a wet vapour like the spumes of moisture from the pistons of the Chrysler.

He was drenched! Wayne looked down at the wet, gleaming surface of his leather cape. Moisture rilled across the windshields, ran off Heinz's goggles, glinted in Anne's eyebrows, dripped from the sunburnt end of McNair's nose.

'Clouds! McNair, my God, it's raining!'

Shouting at each other, they careened down the mountain road. Already through the wet mist they could see the vivid lime-green foliage of young pines growing on the slopes. They were descending into a dripping forest world. It was warmer now, a temperate, humid air. They passed a giant tropical oak beside a small stream, then the crystal sluice of a narrow waterfall. A forest of pines and silver birch packed the mossy slopes, a dozen mountain burns ran their quick-water together into a gushing torrent. The stream detoured across the road and washed the dust from

110

their wheels, then joined a wide cascade that funnelled through a smooth rock-spout and fell into a small valley lake three hundred feet below them.

The air cleared. The quilted cloud-base, a soft upholstered ceiling, lifted above them, the roof of a huge green boudoir. The air was thicker here, hot and damp, the humid atmosphere of a tropical jungle on which the engines feasted. Everywhere they saw heavy forest oaks and sycamores. Vivid lilies spilled ruffs of white bells from the roadside branches, sinewy lianas vined themselves around the birch trees. The first well-nourished palms appeared, sharp-bladed parasols raised to the incessant drip of moist air swirling across them, there were tamarinds and groves of forest bamboo, gaudy orchids and veils of Spanish moss that hung misty tapestries from the stately arms of the oaks. The saturated air leaked moisture on to everything it touched, a glimmer of emerald light.

They paused to edge through another cascade that sluiced across the road. Anne pointed towards the jungle valley below them. A small lake, half a mile long, reached between the forest slopes. Dark clouds were massing only a hundred feet above the black water. A violent gust thrashed the surface of the lake, a discharge of shot that raced across the water towards them. At the last moment there was a bright blue flash, and a kingfisher fled from the heart of the squall. Already the first heavy drops were hitting the hot metal hood of the Chrysler, spitting like angry insects against the furnace door. McNair pulled out the glowing fire-box shovel and caught dozens of the boiling drops. Everyone cheered and peeled off their winter coats, Xerox dandled her naked baby, still wearing his goggles, in the happy deluge, a squealing cherub in the dark forest. Reducing the car's speed to a crawl, Heinz fumbled with the instrument panel, then let out a triumphant cry as the ancient windshield wipers, as yet never called upon, magnificently cleaved two fanlight windows through the opaque torrent.

Followed by this monsoon downpour, they descended

through the mountains, surrounded on all sides by the dense tropical forest. The wayside filling stations and cafeterias, hunting lodges and motel cabins had long been overrun by vegetation, forecourts cracked by ground ivy and waist-high ferns, by vines that wreathed the fuel pumps and sprung through the wooden roofs.

Durango was a jungle town. They sped down the empty streets, along a rain-washed pavement lined by a forest wall three storeys high, a mass of tropical oaks that had shouldered aside the ramshackle houses. Palm trees split the store-fronts, lifted through the plate-glass windows into the leaning sky and jostled with the rusty neon signs. In the centre of Durango the shells of abandoned cars formed a line of curbside bowers for bouquets of flame-tipped cannas and wild roses.

'Heinz, watch it!' As the Chrysler swerved erratically, McNair reached over and steadied the steering-wheel. Heinz was sitting back helplessly, hands raised from the controls, goggles askew on his forehead. He pointed at a tall, long-legged creature crossing the empty street, an elegant pedestrian in a dappled yellow coat.

'It's a giraffe!' Wayne and Anne Summers stood up in the rear seat as the Chrysler slewed to a steaming halt. They waited as the creature sauntered off along the store-fronts, nibbling at the delicious fruits that dangled from the overhead telephone wires.

As they soon discovered, wildlife of every kind filled the forest, descendants of the birds and mammals turned loose a century earlier by the emigrating zoo-keepers. A moody leopard eyed them from the portico of the police station, two cheetahs sat on their haunches by the steps of the mayor's office. Alarmed by the pounding engines and flashing pistons of the steam-cars, a cloud of golden orioles rose from the jungle canopy. Gaudy macaws flashed their plumage as they sailed over the deserted parking lots, a frantic parrot skittered out of the Chrysler's way, screeched reproachfully as it clambered for a footing on the roof of an automobile showroom.

Two days later, as they drove through the late afternoon towards Las Vegas, their senses had been flooded by the endless waves of heat and jungle that had followed them down from the mountains, their bodies drenched like mannequins in the scents of tropical flowers. An immense Mato Grosso covered the west of the United States, transforming the desert states into a forest world of fast-running jungle rivers, hundreds of lakes glutted by monsoon rain. The warm south Pacific current had ousted the cold Humboldt, and for a century had been sending hot, moisture-laden winds across the Sierra Nevada. California, the Mojave Desert, Death Valley itself, were now provinces of the great Amazon forest that had crossed the Panama Isthmus and reached up through Mexico and Baja California to colonise the empty desert.

'Wayne . . . ! I can see Las Vegas . . . !'

Two hundred feet above Wayne's head, in the narrow interval of sky visible between the forest walls, the man-powered glider circled the air. They had stopped to change a tyre on the Galaxy. Heinz and Anne Summers were helping Pepsodent crank up the massive jack, leaving Wayne to relax in the rear seat of the Chrysler. McNair waved excitedly from the cockpit of the *Gossamer Albatross*. His voice was lost in the chittering of thousands of tropical birds, tenants of a demented aviary confined behind their green bars, tribes of perpetually irritated parakeets, macaws squawking over some complex dispute like the inmates of a roadside asylum, delicate humming-birds mesmerised in mid-air by their own beauty.

Watching the lazy glider, its wings drugged by the sun, Wayne shut the raucous noise out of his mind. For some reason he had found himself thinking of the desert again, of the endless white world of the Kansas plain, with its bone-like towns and grain silos, abstract elements of a private dream waiting for him to act out anything he wished. He had gained control there, of Steiner, Anne Summers and the others. Here, in this raucous madhouse, one could never be alone, the noise and activity cracked his head like a coconut.

'Wayne! Wake up!'

McNair was coming in to land, the glider's fragile wing-tips only an arm's length from the forest wall. His excited beard poked from the plastic cabin, and for a moment he resembled one of the demented birds, drunk on the air.

Wayne jumped from the Chrysler and ran towards the glider. The delicate craft soared along the road, its reversed propeller churning the hot air. As Wayne and Anne caught the wingtips, McNair was already clambering from the cockpit.

'Anne, I saw Las Vegas . . . !' McNair stumbled forward on weak legs, breathlessly leaning on Anne's shoulder. 'Do you realise, Wayne . . . ?'

'Good.' Wayne helped to steady the engineer. 'It's only twenty miles away.'

'No!' McNair vigorously shook his head, driving drops of sweat from his beard. 'It's all lit up! The neon signs are full on! Anne, there must be people there, thousands of them!'

18 | The Electrographic Dream

And so they arrived at the electric paradise. Dusk had fallen as they drove the last miles, down through the mountains to Las Vegas. Wayne sat forward, hands gripping the rear windshield of the Chrysler, listening to the beat of pistons and valve-gear echo among the dark trees. He was gazing across the forest canopy below them, when a huge crown of pink and golden light blazed through the trees as if from an open furnace hatch. A lake of neon signs formed a shimmering corona, miles of strip-lighting raced along the porticos of the casinos, zipped up the illuminated curtain-walling of the hotels and spilled over into mushy cascades. Under the ultramarine sky, so dark now that the tone had left their faces, the spectacle of this sometime gambling capital seemed as unreal as an electrographic dream.

Wayne stood up in the rear seat, letting the blaze of light illustrate his shirt and hands, emboss his forehead with its crystal glimmer. Anne reached forward to hold his arm. Her face flickered anxiously in the first reflections from the skyline signs of the big hotels. He pressed her hand, trying to reassure himself as much as her.

'Wayne, it's wonderful – but who are they . . . ?'

'Anne, I don't know yet. Perhaps the Gamblers. Whoever they are, they've certainly struck it rich.'

Heinz had cautiously cut the Chrysler's speed to walking pace. The old nomad peered with evident suspicion at the neon signs, now and then reaching across to brush the reflected light from McNair's shoulder. Pepsodent's Galaxy and GM's Buick were bumper to bumper behind them, the awed faces of the Indians pressed against their windshields like those of beggars at a banquet.

'Come on, Heinz,' Wayne urged. 'Pour on the steam. Let's show them we're here. Anne, can you see the hotels? Caesar's Palace and the Desert Inn. They're all there along the Strip, the Dunes, the Flamingo, the Sahara. Heinz, those are your star-ships in the sky . . . '

'But, Wayne, who's staying in them? The whole place looks empty.' Anne touched her hair, peering at her reflection in the rear windshield. 'And why hasn't anyone known about them before?'

'Because we're the first to cross the Rockies.' Wayne felt his confidence return. 'No one else has ever crossed America. McNair, think of that!'

'Wayne, I am . . . You've told us a hundred times a day.'

McNair laughed good-humouredly, openly admiring Wayne as the latter stood proudly in the rear of the Chrysler, the last of the pioneers to drive his wagon train across the continent. They had reached the northern outskirts of the city, an illuminated but silent terrain of parking lots, motels, bars and highway junctions. Wayne waited for someone to look out of a gas station window and catch sight of them. At any moment the first excited crowds would gather and cheer them on their way to the city centre.

But for all its brilliant lights, Las Vegas seemed strangely silent. The street lamps shone down on the empty car parks, yet there were no cars or people about, no one was playing the countless slot-machines in the stores and arcades. The façades of the casinos in Fremont Street glowed with an almost hallucinatory intensity, but below the Golden Nugget, the Mint and the Horseshoe the sidewalks were deserted. Large sections of the city had been invaded by the jungle, and the neon signs on the Dunes and the Desert Inn shone through a tangle of vines and giant ferns. The southern half of the city, to the east of the Strip, was partly submerged under a large lake fed by the moun-

116

tain rivers, and a second Las Vegas, a drowned city as incandescent as the first, glimmered at them from a sea of light.

They stopped outside the Golden Nugget. Wayne peered up and down the deserted street, an overheated gulch more vivid than the fire-box of the Chrysler. He waited uneasily for something to happen. GM's Buick pulled alongside, an anxious Xerox tucked under her young husband's arm, the baby inside her shirt. Pepsodent joined them, large white eyes roving like alarmed searchlights. A wing of the glider flapped loose in its ropes, and it suddenly occurred to Wayne that they were just a shabby circus troupe, arriving with their modest aviation spectacle at this long out-of-season resort. Las Vegas effortlessly outstared even his ambitious dreams. Perhaps the pit bosses, gangsters and casino operators who had abandoned the city a century earlier had casually left the lights on, and these neon ravines had comfortably powered themselves from a vast invisible battery charged by the excitements of generations of high rollers . . .

'Wayne − ' Anne shook her blonde hair fretfully as they moved slowly towards the Strip. 'We can't stay here, it's all mad. Perhaps everyone's asleep?'

Wayne was counting the silent hotel balconies. Had something moved? 'Anne, no one slept here. This was a town without any clocks.' He drummed his fist on the windshield. 'Listen!'

From somewhere nearby, a little further up the Strip, came the sounds of music, a ripple of applause and a man's voice. A band was playing, an elegant hotel orchestra. The singer's voice rose on the night air, crooning in a relaxed but showy baritone half-familiar to them all.

Five minutes later they stepped down from the cars and walked cautiously up to the entrance of the Sahara Hotel. Through the well-lit but deserted foyer they could now hear clearly the sounds of the stage show, the eager clapping of the audience, the confident and teasing voice of the entertainer moving through his patter between songs. Wayne

117

waved reassuringly to the frightened nomads sitting in the steam-cars, and then entered the hotel. He led Anne and McNair through the silent roulette wheels and blackjack tables. Everywhere piles of chips glittered in the unbroken light, stacked neatly on the immaculate green baize.

As they stepped through the rear doors of the auditorium Anne held Wayne's arm. She stared at him with sudden concern, trying to wake him from a dangerous dream.

'Wayne, it's — You remember him!'

They paused in the heavily draped shadows, looking down at the illuminated stage. The theatre was filled by a well-dressed and middle-aged audience sitting at the supper tables. A male vocalist in a sleek black tuxedo swayed under the spotlight, microphone held to his lips, head thrown back as he reached the climax of his song.

'And more, much more than this, I did it . . . '

The audience burst into applause, their cheers overwhelming the last words of the song. Even the waiters joined in, several musicians lowered their violins to clap. A large, florid man in a plaid suit stood up in the audience, cigar in hand, and doffed his Stetson as the vocalist bowed. Women in blue rinses dabbed their eyes.

'Good God!' McNair pushed past Wayne, shocked to recognise the singer. 'It's Sinatra!'

Wayne had already identified the man with the microphone, the portly but powerful build, the balding head and iron-like thatch. This was the Sinatra of the later period, the Sinatra of the endless farewell appearances and testimonial concerts, when America had clung to its last great icons, its emblems of self-confidence, forcing them to return again and again to the stage. As the applause continued the waiters moved swiftly, serving drinks to the tables. The orchestra struck up once more.

'Wayne . . . ' Anne Summers was looking uncertainly for the exit. 'Where are we . . . ?'

'Wait!' Wayne pointed to the swinging spotlight. 'Watch this, Anne.'

Sinatra had turned and gestured to the wings with a

flourish of his microphone cable, left hand beating to the music. A handsome tuxedo-draped figure strolled on at an elegant pace, a cigarette in one hand, a glass in the other.

'Ladies and gentlemen . . . ' Sinatra raised a hand to calm the audience. 'I'd like to present an old pal of mine, a guy Bogie once called the drinking man's drinking man — Dean Martin!'

Wayne stared at the scene below him, excited by the applause and music. The spotlight swung across the stage. The orchestra leader raised his baton, and a crescendo greeted a third figure who had appeared shyly in the wings, a pretty, fresh-faced girl in a gingham dress and crimson shoes, a pair of engaging pigtails. She allowed Sinatra to kiss her, glancing at her shoes as if to make sure that they were still there, and gave a characteristic skip.

Once again Wayne had recognised her — Judy Garland. The audience applauded wildly, the Texan in the plaid coat doffed his Stetson and waved his cigar, the blue rinses dabbed. Sinatra replaced his microphone in its stand. He took the others by the hands, and together they began the last chorus.

Holding Anne tightly around the shoulders, Wayne gazed down at the spangled stage. He felt elated but calm, even though McNair seemed momentarily deranged, shaking his watch like a mad hatter trying to hide inside his own beard.

Anne pulled herself away from him. 'Wayne, what's happening? Have we gone back in time?'

'I don't think so, Anne. It's clever, though . . . '

Wayne smiled at the thought. Going back in time, to 1976, say, a happy notion, the fulfilment of all his dreams that somewhere on this continent a piece of America was preserved intact. Even in this jungle-infested Las Vegas . . . Sinatra and Dean Martin — why not? But Judy Garland? Her daughter should have been here with the mature Sinatra and Martin, the mother had been dead of drugs and alcohol for too many years to be singing as this straw-haired teenager from *The Wizard of Oz*. Apart from anything else, the wistful young Judy Garland would never have sung this brassy, self-congratulatory song. She was his own generation, the girl from Kansas City, a sweet stowaway of a kind. He too had come from Kansas, though a very different one.

Releasing Anne, he looked around, suddenly sensing that the whole thing might be a sinister joke on himself, a less than kind judgment. In a way they were singing his song, and he was as pleased with himself as the elderly Sinatra . . .

'You know, Anne, I've always wanted to meet Sinatra.'

'Wayne, you can't — '

Ignoring her, Wayne ran down the carpeted steps of the central aisle. The waiters made no attempt to stop him, and none of the audience noticed as he climbed the narrow bridge across the orchestra pit. The three singers were well into the climax of their song, and a deafening volume of sound freighted every molecule in the air. But as he hesitated in the glare of the spotlight neither Sinatra nor Dean Martin was aware of him, although they were staring straight at Wayne. Their sun-tanned, immaculately made-up faces were exactly as he remembered them from the movie magazines.

'Mr Sinatra . . . ' Wayne held out his hand, shouting over the music. 'Can I introduce myself . . . ?'

Sinatra stepped forward, his hard eyes not noticing Wayne. As his hands beat out the last bars of the music his elbow caught Wayne on the shoulder. Before Wayne could stop him Sinatra spun round, and lost his balance on his stiffly jointed legs. He collided into Dean Martin, upsetting his drink, and kicked Judy Garland smartly in the ankle. He then fell backwards on to the floor, where he lay still singing and gesturing, eyes showing no emotion at this surprising change of posture.

The spotlights faltered, their beams blurring. As befitted this luxury hotel, everything was moving into a well-carpeted pandemonium. The players in the orchestra had lost their scores, the violinists were calmly breaking their bows and ripping the strings from their instruments, a trombonist swallowed his mouth-piece, the conductor stab-

120

bed himself in the eye with his baton. Sinatra lay on his back, legs kicking, gesturing at the ceiling.

'*My way may way may way my wayeee* . . . !' he crooned in falsetto.

Beside him Dean Martin compulsively puffed on his cigarette, splashing the whiskey into his face. The amber drops streamed down his nose across his amiable, leering smile. Meanwhile Judy Garland was moving into an epileptic seizure. She glanced down at her magic shoes, then gave a tic-like smile, launched into an ever-more rapid set of skips that sent her vibrating across the stage.

'*Did it did it did it did it did it did it* . . . ' jabbered Sinatra, then came to a stop like a dead doll.

As the music trailed away into a painful see-saw the spotlights swerved across the auditorium. Waiters dashed about like maniacs, one of the blue rinses poked out her right eye, the huge Texan in the plaid jacket stood up, jammed his cigar down his throat with one hand and knocked his head off with the other. When Dean Martin splashed the last drops of whiskey into his face the audience applauded so vigorously that their hands came off. Judy Garland's winsome skipping had become a St Vitus-like blur, she moved to the edge of the stage and fell into the woodwind section, where the musicians were calmly stabbing themselves in the face.

After a last whine, everything fell silent. Within the space of a second, as if a plug had been pulled, the audience froze. The spotlights withdrew, an uneasy silence moved across the tiers of diners, the headless waiters lying among their trays and glasses.

'Wayne . . . maybe it's time to stop laughing.'

The auditorium lights came on as McNair called out his warning. Through the dim glow Wayne could see a group of olive-uniformed figures by the rear doors, peaked fatigue caps hiding their faces. Six of them surrounded McNair and Anne Summers. They were small and slim-shouldered, little more than children, but there were pistols in their hands.

The leader came forward and beckoned to Wayne. He was at least eighteen, but he seemed far younger than Wayne, his stern face almost hidden under the huge vizor of a helicopter pilot's yellow helmet.

'The show's not over, Mr Wayne,' he said in a flat, Spanish-accented voice. 'But Mr Manson would like you to take the finale outside.'

His tone was so matter-of-fact that at first Wayne assumed that these olive-suited youngsters were themselves robots, like the rest of the audience, and the animatronic Garland, Sinatra and Martin. Had they strayed into a Las Vegas populated by automatons, machines to keep the slots warm until the real gamblers returned? But as he hesitated the youth in the yellow helmet pointed to him in a way Wayne had seen too many times before, the bored, warning gesture of the European security police. This young Mexican looked at him with the suspicious gaze no robot-builder could simulate.

When Wayne reached the balcony the leader raised Wayne's arms and expertly frisked his jacket. 'Quite a stage-show, Mr Wayne, the kind of cybernetic expertise you Old World Americans haven't seen in a long time. So, where are your weapons?'

Wayne shrugged, and the Mexican snapped: 'Come on, we have film of you using a Winchester, shooting snakes and . . . vermin. Right, Wayne?' He peered into Wayne's eyes with a look of remarkable maturity, as if fully aware of Wayne's motives for crossing America. He had the strong but sensitive face of the young Mexican students Wayne had watched in the refectory of the American University in Dublin, brooding by themselves, as Wayne wrongly guessed, over their dreams of tequila, bullfights and mañana. But this young man was a tougher proposition, a slow temper was burning at the end of its fuse. Wayne thought of trying to hit him . . .

The second-in-command stepped forward, a handsome seventeen-year-old girl with a motor-biker's goggles in a bandeau around her thick black hair. She gestured warningly with a silver hand-radio.

'Paco, the President told us to leave them alone. He wants to see them tonight. Paco . . . '

Paco's eyes retreated behind his vizor, into the intense and private world of his helmet. 'All right, Ursula, if that's what the President wants.'

McNair pushed forward, fending off an armed youngster who was stroking his beard. 'The President? Wait a minute.'

'Yes, what President?' Anne Summers repeated. She shook herself free of two uniformed teenagers, staring at this circle of armed and curious adolescents like a schoolteacher caught up in an elaborate classroom prank. 'Which President are you talking about?'

'The President of the United States,' Paco replied quietly. 'President Manson.'

19 | The Hughes Suite

Later, after a brief struggle, Wayne remembered being man-handled out of the hotel by the group of teenagers, past the silent roulette and blackjack tables into the brilliant, sudden night. Countless neon signs glowed through the jungle foliage that clustered around the great casinos of the Strip, lighting up the undersides of millions of leaves. A trio of black sedans were parked outside the Sahara, radiator grilles like chromed harmonicas. Wayne recognised them immediately, sleek and wide-bodied vehicles from the last great age of the automobile, a real Buick, Pontiac and Dodge of the 1960s.

An armed squad of uniformed youths waited by the cars, talking in a friendly way to the four frightened nomads. A white-doored police car roared at speed down the Strip, followed by Pepsodent's astonished eyes. GM protected his wife and baby from the wailing siren, arms around them as they crouched over the fading warmth of the fire-box, while a nervous Heinz tried to answer the young Mexicans' questions about the pistons and valve-gear of the steam-cars.

'Right, we'll pick your friends up later.' Paco pushed Wayne into the front passenger seat of the Pontiac, then climbed into the back as Ursula took the wheel. Without any need to steam up, the engine kicked instantly into life. Wayne caught a last glimpse of Anne Summers and McNair being bundled through the open doors of the Dodge. Then they were away into the night, speeding along the shores of an illuminated jungle lake. A mushy light dissolved in the water, reefs of sugar candy that flowed from the façades of vast night-clubs like lurid cathedrals.

As the spray struck the windshield Ursula switched on the dashboard radio. There was a buzz of static and inter-com chatter. A flight controller with a child's voice discus-sed the cloud cover above the Rockies, then recited a list of fuelling points in Flagstaff and Phoenix. Ursula touched a tab, and immediately Elvis Presley filled the car with his powerful beat. An old-style disc jockey cut in, his commen-tary a high-pitched gabble of show-business gossip, airline information and plugs for a local automobile dealer.

'Ursula, for God's sake . . . ' Paco gripped the reverberat-ing bowl of his helmet. 'We're supposed to be on duty.'

Ursula grudgingly reduced the volume, her vivid eye-brows raised for Wayne's benefit. 'Paco, you're too serious . . . all the time that Stravinsky, Stockhausen and John Cage. When are you going to come dancing? Wayne, I'll show you my jive steps. Or maybe you're the tango type?'

'Maybe,' Wayne agreed promptly. He was eager to please this broad-shouldered beauty in her goggles and combat gear. 'A radio station — that's impressive. How many of you are there here?'

'Not enough,' Paco replied with some gloom. 'A hun-dred, maybe more. We need new recruits, but nobody likes America. I'm not surprised. That headache music is a cen-tury old, a tape we found of a local radio programme. How did they stand it?'

'Well, it has vitality,' Wayne pointed out. It had never occurred to him to criticise the United States, and Paco's moody appraisals unsettled him. 'Are you all from the same tribe — the Gamblers?'

'No!' As Ursula laughed, slapping Wayne's shoulder in a cheerful way, Paco snorted scornfully. 'Ursula and I come from Chavez, the Chicano freeport in Baja California. You're the gringo, friend, you're the American. Remember, Mexican backs built these hotels. Oh, relax . . . I don't intend to claim them for Montezuma. But this time we won't just be waiters and busboys.'

'You're right, I had to stow away myself to get to America.' Wayne stared out at the hotels flashing past, each surrounded by acres of deserted parking lots. A hundred of these teenagers, and someone who called himself President. He felt relieved, the number was manageable. Despite the screaming squad-car and the blaze of lights, Las Vegas was almost empty. 'Still, you've made a start. Already you have an air force.'

It was a clever guess. Paco gestured dismissively. 'Just the President's Sea-King and a few Hueys. There's plenty of aviation fuel in government storage tanks – enough for a couple of years. But it takes time to train mechanics. Your friend McNair, he's a good engineer. We can use him. And the lady professor.'

Thinking of the great Kansas desert, of Orlowski's death and his own near disaster at Boot Hill, Wayne asked sharply: 'You saw everything? Why didn't you help us?'

'Take it easy . . . ' Paco eyed Wayne defensively, unsure about the wisdom of admitting this volatile newcomer to their private teenage domain. 'I only saw you on film – we have a few robot cameras on the other side of the Rockies, with trip-zooms that focus on anything that moves. It's bad about your two friends, though.'

'Two? Did you see Steiner? The Captain?'

Paco's face retreated into his helmet. 'We didn't see him. He must have died very quickly, Wayne. If he moved, the President has him on film.'

The Pontiac was turning into the car park beside a huge hotel. They stepped out and walked to the doors of a private elevator emblazoned with the Presidential seal.

'The Desert Inn Hotel,' Paco commented as they rode upwards. 'Mean anything to you? A man's name, perhaps?'

'Of course – Howard Hughes.'

'That's very good, Wayne. Too good. But Mr Manson will like that . . . '

They reached the penthouse level, and emerged into a quiet, carpeted corridor. A toneless light shone down on to a chromium desk where a white-coated youth sat reading a comic.

'Hi, Paco — the old man's been sweating.'

'We're here.' Paco glanced at the comic — Batman and Robin against the Cat-woman — and tossed it into the waste basket. 'What happened to that maintenance manual I gave you?'

'Oh, Paco . . . '

With a theatrical groan, the boy pressed a wall switch. The doors parted into the vestibule of a large but plainly furnished hotel suite. Here a second young technician in a laboratory coat was checking a line of steel-blue electronic consoles set up against one wall. Although the windows looked out on the lights of the evening city, the air in the suite tasted curiously sterile. An elaborate secondary air-conditioning system had been built inside the rooms, over-head pipes ran from the adjacent bedroom to a nest of fan-powered filters in the window. The blades fluttered continuously, a devoted fingertip response to minute fluctuations in humidity and temperature.

Beckoning Wayne to follow him, Paco opened the bed-room door. A metallic blue light, as if in some hospital intensive care unit, shone down on the marble-skinned body of a middle-aged man lying on a surgical couch in front of a battery of television screens. He was naked except for the towel around his waist, and held an aerosol inhaler in one hand, a remote-control TV unit in the other. The blue light trembled against his white skin, and gave it a look of engorged, unhealthy activity, that of trapped venous blood struggling to return to an over-active heart. His eyes were fixed on the tiers of screens, as if his real existence resided in this ionised flow of flickering images rather than in his own restless musculature.

'President Manson . . . ' While Ursula perused the Bat-man comic in the anteroom, Paco ushered Wayne forward. He pointed to the white line painted inside the door at their feet, warning Wayne to stop there. 'Mr Wayne — the Presi-dent of the United States.'

Wayne hesitated, trying to recognise this hypermanic figure in his loincloth. The man's strong forehead, fleshy nose and jowls reminded him immediately of the former President Nixon, now sitting out a century's exile in the old Hughes suite in Las Vegas. The resemblance was uncanny, as if the man in front of the television screens was a skilful actor who had made a career out of impersonating Presidents, and found that he could imitate Nixon more convincingly than any other. He had caught the long stares and suddenly lowered eyes, the mixture of idealism and corruption, the deep melancholy and lack of confidence coupled at the same time with a powerful inner conviction.

Above Wayne's head, aligned with the white paint on the floor, was the metal shroud of a ventilation unit. It drummed faintly in the blue light, sucking the air away from his skin, decontaminating the sealed room.

'Come in, Wayne! I've been waiting to meet you since you set out from Washington.' The man on the couch turned, and flashed an eerie smile at Wayne. But when Wayne stepped forward, crossing the white line, he quickly raised his aerosol, fingers working the remote transmitter to prevent Wayne from looming into excessive close-up. Controlling himself, he smiled his strange smile again. 'That was quite a trip, Wayne. I was proud of you . . . Paco, you can leave us. Check out the Sea-King and the gunships, we have a long day tomorrow.'

After Paco saluted and withdrew, Manson gestured with his aerosol at one of the television screens. The picture showed the now silent auditorium at the Sahara Hotel, the robot audience collapsed among the tables.

Manson sadly shook his head. 'What a shambles, the old professor is losing his touch. It's a good thing your friends have arrived, Wayne, I can use them. McNair, in particular, I like his steam-cars and that pedal plane. But I have a bigger job waiting for him, the biggest of all. NASA and Von Braun could have used McNair, if the American public hadn't gone soft on the Space Age – and soft on everything else . . . You have the pioneer spirit, Wayne, I watched you, my boy. In fact, I was concerned for you, maybe you pushed yourself too hard, but that's the kind of iron we need here, if I was younger . . . '

Manson rambled to himself, no longer aware of Wayne. He lay on his couch with the aerosol and TV control unit in either hand, a modern Pharaoh holding the orb and sceptre of his office. The mosaic of images flickered down on his unhealthy face.

Wayne examined each of the screens in turn. Apart from the jumbled auditorium at the Sahara, these revealed a half-lit airport somewhere near Las Vegas; a lakeside restaurant terrace where Anne Summers and McNair sat alone like stranded tourists; a high-ceilinged room with glass wall-maps, crossed Stars and Stripes behind a huge roulette wheel; the control room of a nuclear generating plant where two teenage technicians were sweeping a tiled floor; an aerial view of the Strip from the roof of a hotel nearby, the illuminated windows of the Desert Inn penthouse clearly visible.

The images glimmered away, lighting up Manson's pallid skin, a ghostly second epidermis. On the walls behind him was a display of framed photographs, old news agency pictures from the middle and late twentieth century. Wayne recognised them all, the Apollo space vehicle, the Titan and Minuteman missiles in their silos, a B-52 strategic bomber, and a tall man with a quiet, lonely face under his snap-brimmed hat, standing in a business suit beside a huge multi-engined sea-plane.

Manson was watching Wayne with his wary eyes, smiling cannily to himself. 'Do you know who that is, Wayne? Whose suite we're in? Of course you do. Howard Hughes, the last of the great Americans. I've taken over his empire, what those pigmies left of it. This was *his* suite, Wayne. It was right where you're standing, on the top floor of the Desert Inn, Las Vegas, that he slammed the door on the world. The most far-sighted decision any American ever took . . . ' Manson's eyes misted over in what was clearly a familiar flux of emotion. 'I'm glad you're here, Wayne, I like

129

the look of you. Hughes would have wanted me to take you on. Anyone who can cross America in three months must have blood that's as clean as the wind.'

On an impulse, Wayne stepped across the white line. He listened to the feverish whir of the ventilator fans, trying to pull him back. But Manson had sat up and was smoothing his dark hair. He smiled in a remarkably innocent way, as if recognising in Wayne a younger version of himself.

'We followed you right across the States, Wayne. I knew you'd make it, from the first moment I saw you walking down Broadway, you had style and swing. Three months – I was your age when I came across, do you know that it took me *two years*? I had to crawl through the dust on my hands and knees. It poisoned me, Wayne, some unknown virus crept into my blood, some bacillus that dying nation left behind made up of failure and second-rate dreams . . . '

Manson stared at his white body, an unhealthy intruder into his mental space. With a grimace of distaste, he went on: 'Stay here for a few weeks, Wayne, you and your friends will need to rest. You might decide to remain longer, and help the Hughes Company put the old USA back on to its feet. But first we've got to stop the virus spreading. Yes, Wayne, the virus. Believe me, there are disease vectors advancing from the east. The boys in the laboratory haven't identified it yet, but it's there all right, and there's only one antidote. Once we stop it there'll be a big future here. Sooner or later I'll need someone to take over from me, I've served seven terms already. You could be Vice-President, Wayne, even President of the United States . . . '

Manson's voice wandered, his arms fell to his sides. The door opened slightly, and Paco beckoned Wayne from the bedroom. His face was without expression, as if he were well used to seeing passing visitors promised the Presidency.

At the door, Wayne looked back. Manson lay half-asleep on the couch, his left hand clutching the aerosol like a baby bottle, his right hand tirelessly switching the television screens into a flickering blur.

Yet for all his quirks, his obsessions with germs and disease, Manson had established the only base of organised power that had existed in north America for a hundred years. The reclamation of this jungle city, the millions of coloured lights that shone through the tangled ferns and palms, the elaborate television and communications gear, the renovation of at least part of the old Hughes empire, together rekindled something of the power of the United States, and hinted at what could be done in the future. However bizarre, Manson had recognised the stamp of Wayne's character in the long journey across the continent, the ambition that had carried the sometime stowaway and bastard son of a Dublin secretary to the leadership of the *Apollo* expedition.

But should he remain here with this strange recluse, or move on into California?

At the door he heard Manson call out for the last time, almost plaintively from the edge of sleep.

'You'll stay, Wayne. Stay with me and become President . . .'

20 | Wayne's Diary: Part Two

November 2. Sands Hotel, Las Vegas

An amazing week. Just back with Anne and McNair after touring the nuclear generating plant at Lake Mead. They were as impressed as I was. The fast breeder reactor supplies all the current that powers Las Vegas, every neon tube, telex and television set. Relaxing now in my tenth-floor suite at the Sands. I have the hotel to myself, except for the two teenage boys, Chavez and Enrico, who share the penthouse and have the job of chauffeuring me around in a brand-new 1956 Cadillac (tail fins, wraparound windshield, pastel body tints). Anne is at the Hilton, McNair at the Stardust.

Seen so much of Manson's whole operation, plus trips along the jungle highways into California. It's a complete miniature United States, set here in the middle of this Amazon rain-forest, kept going by Manson's weird, off-hand genius. He stays in the background, rarely emerges from the Hughes suite at the Desert Inn, but I'm more and more convinced that the future of America, and maybe the world itself, lies here with Manson at Las Vegas. It's a node of intense possibility that could expand to transform the planet, start everything up again. Manson's working towards this, anyway, and in many ways he has every right to call himself the forty-fifth President. Assuming I stay with him here, and become his right-hand man, which seems to be what he wants, I can't stop myself thinking who might be the forty-sixth . . .

November 5. Sands Hotel, Las Vegas

In many ways this is a very strange place. Spent this morning at McCarran International Airport, the main engineering base of the Manson operation, and at the old Hughes Executive Air Terminal, which handles the communications set-up. I noticed that apart from Manson there is no one here over the age of twenty. It means that he did all this himself. He's surrounded by this entourage of enthusiastic teenagers, mostly Mexican runaways he's recruited from the small settlements in Baja California. He's trained them on the teaching machines in the Hughes building to a high level of proficiency in computer maintenance, electrical engineering, signals equipment and so on. There's a fleet of helicopters, used mostly for photo-reconnaissance over southern California, and a little flying school with about ten pupils where Paco is the senior instructor.

Hard to tell exactly how many people there are here. Half of Manson's force is away at any time, either oil-prospecting (all the gasoline comes from secret tanks left behind by government agencies and the big multinationals) or hunting the Los Angeles area for nuclear fuel rods and electronics equipment. Recently they've been spreading further afield, to the old navy base at San Diego and the advanced computer plants near San Francisco.

The rest of the force is here in Vegas, mostly working at the airport, rebuilding the old helicopters in the engineering hangars, reconditioning everything from trucks and automobiles to specialist radio and TV gear. And despite the plentiful supply of Batman comics the atmosphere is quite puritanical. These kids are dedicated, all right. As Enrico showed the three of us around they were none too keen to waste time answering questions.

However, they *were* interested in McNair's heavy engineering know-how and in Anne Summers's nuclear expertise. The brightest of the boys and girls work at the Lake Mead atomic power station — it's an impressive achievement to keep it running, though they're obviously stretched. McNair and Anne are going back there tomorrow to help out. Apparently the lights in Las Vegas are deliberately left blazing, not because anyone is interested in the casinos, but to run the reactor at full stretch. Manson's plan is that once they've mastered the Lake Mead plant they can move on to the reactors in Phoenix and Salt Lake City, launch an eastward drive across America. Risky, of course — according to Anne, a by-product of the fast breeder reactor at Lake Mead is a substantial quantity of weapons grade plutonium!

November 16. Sands Hotel, Las Vegas

A slight unpleasantness. It's now two weeks since I last saw Manson alone, and I've begun to feel that Paco is keeping me away from him. There was an edgy meeting with him three days ago in the lobby of the Desert Inn — we had been waiting for hours to discuss the possibility of a trip to San Francisco to inspect the earthquake damage. Manson suddenly appeared, wearing a strange blue suit and smiling in an uncomfortable way. He welcomed Anne and McNair and wished them luck, then disappeared into his limo. Since then I haven't seen him. McNair and Anne were a little puzzled by him, but they like the kids and the challenge of their work here. Both say they're happy to stay for a couple of months until a rescue mission arrives and negotiations begin about recognising Manson's whole enterprise.

However, they at least have an active role. I'm rather left out with nothing to do. Because I'm restless I'm getting a little too curious for Paco. My well-intentioned efforts to grasp the whole extent of Manson's empire seem to annoy him. I don't think he realises what is at stake here, and how Moscow might react. Obviously Manson has a long-range group with at least two helicopters on the other

134

side of the Rockies, part of the team checking out the de-stabilised power stations on the east coast. They must have spotted the *Apollo* expedition as soon as we docked in New York harbour, keeping in touch with Manson via the old TV station antennae, huge towers with microwave links that span the continent.

Yet this morning, when I casually raised this with Paco, he went very quiet, and I suddenly noticed the Colt 45 he wears on his hip. I pressed him about the nuclear explosion that devastated Boston, but he was rather evasive, started talking about the dangers of disease, eyeing me up and down as if I was one of Manson's vectors. Apparently some new strain of a particularly virulent virus has been incubating for the past century in the old biological warfare labs, and the only safe course is to obliterate the entire urban area affected.

But how? Has Manson laid his hands on some nuclear weapons? The old atomic testing site is only thirty miles to the north of Vegas. I talked about this to Anne and McNair, they're worried too, but no one seems to know. Manson is very secretive, and obviously hasn't told these youngsters too much for fear of frightening them away.

They're all very likeable, but extremely provincial, and I don't think they could cope for long in the real world. An hour ago, when I went out for a breath of evening air, a jeep patrol led by Ursula and two gun-toting girls had stopped in the Strip outside Caesar's Palace, a great overgrown mausoleum. They were harassing Heinz and Pepsodent for trying to break into the lobby, brandishing pistols in the nomads' faces. These young Mexicans have a special contempt for the proto-Americans, black and white, regard them as degenerate aboriginals. Fortunately McNair drove up in his huge Rolls and saved the scene, announced that he had appointed Pepsodent to be his personal driver. Immense gratitude and relief. Xerox, with GM and the baby in tow, has become Anne's maid, but Heinz seems reluctant to attach himself to me. He keeps looking up at the jungle hills, I think the old boy has a

135

touch of Davy Crockett.

November 18. Sands Hotel, Las Vegas

Another piece of the puzzle falls into place. This evening Manson put on a display for us, of a very special kind. He had invited us to dinner at the Desert Inn, though needless to say he didn't appear. As we relaxed on the terrace there was a sudden flare of gaudy light across the lake from some kind of projector, an intense beam as wide as a runway. A dozen rainbows shimmered in the night air, then came together to form an immense three-dimensional figure as high as a skyscraper. We all stared at this creature, a spritely animal from an old nursery wallpaper, with a round smiling face, ears sticking up like black fans, a button nose.

Mickey Mouse, needless to say. Anne and McNair were amazed, but I'd seen something like it before, out in the desert at Boot Hill. We watched two of Manson's boys operating the camera on the roof of the Silver Slipper, throwing up a whole series of these laser-projected holographic images. After Mickey there appeared a huge statue of a bare-legged woman in a pink dress raised provocatively above her thighs. She stood astride Las Vegas, blonde hair thrown back, letting the fountain of casino light cool her legs. Marilyn Monroe, of course.

It was an extraordinary light show. For an hour the whole iconic past of pop Americana moved by in parade, Superman and Donald Duck, Clark Gable and the Incredible Hulk, a Coca Cola bottle twenty stories high, the Starship *Enterprise* like an airborne petroleum refinery, all silver pipes and cylinders, a dollar bill the size of a football field and the colour of purest Astroturf. Last of all came a succession of Presidents, Jefferson, Lincoln, FDR, Eisenhower and Jack Kennedy, immense dignified heads filling the night sky. We faded out on an eerie image of a sombre-faced man in a blue suit, the grey eminence of this once carefree city of a million lights, our host . . .

136

Anyway, I now know the source of the terrifying visions that drove the nomad tribes from their hunting grounds along the east coast, and the space-ship that GM, Heinz and Pepsodent saw in the sky over Boston. Manson's team had been moving from city to city, putting on these laser shows to warn the Indians away. The power of these images is unsettling − I can remember the giant Fonda, Wayne, Ladd and Cooper over Boot Hill. Manson's team must have been there. Was Manson testing me, urging me on towards the West, trying to give me strength to cross the Rockies? I think tonight's display was his subtle way of telling me to ignore Paco and any trivial problems here.

November 23. Beverly Hills Hotel, Los Angeles

Manson finally appeared yesterday! He materialised out of the humid Las Vegas sky like a distracted angel, at the start of an exhilarating three-day trip to California. Soon after breakfast in my suite at the Sands − quails' eggs, truffles, rashers of wild pig (the forests around Vegas teem with game, everything from marmosets and mandrills to snow leopards and scarlet ibis, all escapees from the southern California zoos), there was an enormous racket through the ceiling, as if the whole hotel was rising from its launch pad. Manson's Sea-King had landed on the reinforced roof. An ambulance chopper, with the Presidential seal on the fuselage, piloted by Paco himself, taking a day off from the flying school.

A message came down on the intercom, in Manson's strange, dissociated voice, inviting me to join him on an inspection tour of the reclamation projects in Los Angeles. I promptly rode the elevator to the roof, crouched through a blizzard of orchid petals driven up from the jungle below, and climbed into the front cockpit beside Paco. Manson was sitting behind a glass partition in a peculiar fisherman's chair that pivoted from the port to starboard windows. He looked very Presidential in a fawn safari suit, an eccentric landowner out for a day's shooting. Already waiting for us in the sky above the centre of Vegas was our armed escort, two pilotless helicopter gunships operated by Paco, their control settings matched to the Sea-King's.

We formated up and set off at a fast pace towards the south-west, soon left Vegas behind, an overlit crown burning a hole in the jungle. Paco kept to about 300 feet above the tree-tops, the gunships soaring along on either side. We soon reached the California/Nevada border, headed on towards the Mojave Desert. Below us was the unbroken forest canopy, densely packed trees divided by the concrete highways. Strange to think that this was once an arid desert. An immense Amazon rain-forest now stretches its green shoulders down from the mountains to the coast. Death Valley has bloomed into a horticultural-ist's paradise. As we came off Interstate 15 and descended towards Glendale, I could see the upper floors of the taller office blocks and apartment houses rising above the foliage. Now and then, below the canopy, I caught a glimpse of the dawn world of the forest floor, a shadowy realm of suburban stores and houses split apart by the huge palms and oaks. Everywhere fast jungle rivers carved their way towards the sea, cutting deep ravines through the old shopping malls and private estates, heading for the great new delta of the Los Angeles River at Long Beach, a pan of silt and water-logged channels a mile in diameter. Strange to see the Watts Towers standing on a small jewelled island 300 yards from either shore. The *Queen Mary* sits in a sea of silt, decked in creepers and bougainvilia from its funnels to the Plimsoll line.

The first sight of the Pacific Ocean moved me in a deep sense, this huge, rain-heavy vat steaming like an infinite Java Sea. At last I had crossed America! I looked round and Manson gave me a cheery thumbs up. We tracked the course of the Los Angeles River. It curves down through Burbank and Glendale, then follows the line of the Hollywood and Harbour Freeways towards Long Beach.

Paco pointed out its two main tributaries, the Bel Air River and the Hollywood River, both strong brown channels a hundred feet across, fed by the hot Pacific rain and the thousands of leaking swimming-pools. Most of these are slime-green tanks crammed with water-lilies, roosting places for flocks of cranes and flamingos. As we circled over Bel Air and Beverly Hills I could see alligators sunning themselves beside the swimming-pools, while elegant birds stood on the ends of diving-boards, waiting for some talent scout to film them as they stared nonchalantly at the overgrown gardens of the abandoned mansions.

From the air Los Angeles is a bizarre sight. The great freeways are linear gardens, tapestries of Spanish moss a thousand yards long hanging from the concrete overpasses. A huge colony of spider monkeys has taken over the Hollywood Bowl, an army of them bickered and fought like a bored audience, then sat up together as we soared past. Sloths hang from the loops of Magic Mountain, trapping themselves in the Möbius strips of the scenic railway. Palm trees rise through the crown of the Brown Derby, pumas prowl the corner of Hollywood and Vine, waiting for unwary tourists, hyenas and jackasses have left their footprints in the silt outside Mann's Chinese Theatre.

When we landed in the car park of the Beverly Hills Hotel − now a Manson communications post − a tribe of garrulous baboons was sitting in the old beach furniture around the stagnant pool, gibbering and quarrelling with each other like a crowd of producers. Paco fired a round of buckshot over their heads, and they sidled off in disgust towards the jungle, gnashing their teeth and showing their rumps to us. Manson was tremendously amused, even let me help him from the aircraft, laughing in his harsh, eerie way.

November 24. Beverly Hills Hotel, Los Angeles

We spent the night in this old luxury hotel, where the elite of the film and television worlds once displayed themselves. Nothing has changed, apart from the array of

139

communications gear in the lobby and the 300-foot aerial that pokes through the ferns on the roof. There are several reconnaissance teams at work in the LA area, foraging for specialist aircraft and electronics equipment. When they arrived Manson quizzed them carefully, then retired to his third-floor suite, resting in a chair behind an oxygen mask, the cylinder between his knees. It's hard to tell what is really wrong with him, perhaps some kind of psychosomatic asthma — I almost get the impression he's been alone so long that other people seem a total intrusion into what by rights should be an empty planet.

Paco, I've discovered, is intense but likeable and intelligent. 'We'll find you a car, Wayne, so you can see more of LA. The old freeway system is still there, should last as long as the Pyramids.' With remarkable frankness he told me that he sees Manson's Vegas and Los Angeles operations as the base for a new Mexican kingdom that will occupy the whole of north America to the west of the Rockies. I tried to explain to him my own dreams of a renascent USA, but he clearly thinks I'm crazily impractical, hung up on brand names and a lot of infantile delusions about unlimited growth. In his eyes it was an excess of fantasy that killed the old United States, the whole Mickey Mouse and Marilyn thing, the most brilliant technologies devoted to trivia like instant cameras and space spectaculars that should have stayed in the pages of science fiction. As he put it, some of the last Presidents of the USA seemed to have been recruited straight from Disneyland. Paco reads the Batman comics, but he regards himself as coldly realistic. Oddly enough, I don't think he has as much faith in Manson as I have, sees him as an eccentric Lloyd Wright, Edison or Land.

Paco is right about the freeways, though. When we took off again this morning on a north-east circuit of the city, the freeway system was lying there intact. Apart from the office blocks and hotels, the bridges and highway embankments are the only things that rise above the forest. Everything else, all those dingbats and ticky-tack apartment houses I was so looking forward to seeing, have vanished in a thousand mud-slides.

As we crossed the Hollywood Freeway we spotted a solitary car moving along the empty road, a pink Mark V Continental towing a sizeable trailer with what looked like a huge steel water-tank. 'The second stage of an Atlas satellite launcher,' Paco told me. He talked to the crew on the intercom, Miguel and Diego who have been out here in LA for two months and are going home to Vegas with their trophy. Manson was very excited, I hadn't seen him get so worked up before. He ordered Paco to fly along the freeway only ten feet above the Continental, I thought we might bounce off its roof into the jungle below. Manson was shouting to himself like a child, swinging his chair from one window to the other. Is he planning to put himself into orbit, perhaps even build a space station, where he will be safe at last in that germless, people-free vacuum?

Manson is certainly very interested in some unusual military hardware. The United States has got to be defended, or at least that part of it − California and Nevada (Hughes-land) − that is now viable. No point in handing it over to the Moscow bureaucrats on a plate. We landed at the Lockheed Aircraft plant at Burbank; acres of cracked concrete runways covered with waist-high palmettos, huge gloomy hangars and machine shops. I saw straight away that Manson wasn't interested in any of the wide-bodied passenger jets − TriStars − still half-assembled in the production hangars. Far more to the point, Lockheed was a major government contractor, specialising in advanced missile systems. Paco used oxyacetylene cutting equipment to get us into the top-security compound, we followed fifty feet behind Manson as he prowled the design offices and machining rooms, closely inspecting what seemed to be part-assembled ICBMs and cruise missiles − war-heads and guidance systems.

Seeing all this potential destructive power made Manson

very nervous. When we flew back over the Hollywood hills a huge cloud of frightened flamingos rose from the swimming-pools below. Manson signalled to Paco, who gave me a weary look, then switched on the rear cockpit override that gave Manson manual control of the two gunships. All hell broke loose, suddenly the gunships were veering and banking on either side of us, gatlings blazing, waist-guns pouring fire into the flocks of helpless birds. The air was a whirlwind of noise and bloody feathers, thousands of bits of flamingo spattered on to the forest canopy like pink spray from a gun. But Manson wasn't satisfied, for the next hour we swerved in and out of the hills and valleys, massacring anything that moved — deer grazing peacefully on the Paramount back lot, a herd of llamas quietly eating the vine-leaves above a filling station on Ventura Boulevard, even a bull elephant trying to defend his small herd bathing in a Bel Air hotel pool. The female and her young luckily escaped into the forest, but the bull died in the bloody pool, still trumpeting in the boiling red water as the gunships circled around him like crazed sharks.

Paco and I were both sickened by this. Back at the Beverly Hills Hotel we climbed quietly out of the Sea-King. But Manson looked glutted like a large boa, scribbling some war-head design on his knee-pad, a series of concentric blast-circles. I had the frightened sense that life for him is itself a kind of disease . . .

4 a.m., November 25. Beverly Hills Hotel

A weird but important midnight meeting with Manson. It ended a few minutes ago, leaving me confused but determined to do something. There's an opportunity to be seized here, and perhaps time is shorter than I think. It only needs a single reconnaissance plane from one of the Pacific exploration ships and not only Hughes Enterprises Inc. but my own dreams of becoming the forty-sixth President will be as dead as that elephant.

142

At midnight I was lying awake in my room on the fifth floor, listening to the noisy Beverly Hills wildlife, a crowd of raucous peacocks dazzled by their own eyes. Through the window I could see the shadowy gunships in the car park, still covered with caked blood and flamingo feathers. Just then the intercom buzzed and Manson asked me down to his suite.

He was still wearing the safari suit, and sat in front of his TV consoles — vivid colour pictures of Las Vegas at night taken by a camera on the roof of the Desert Inn. He looked pale but alert, as if he had decided long ago to dispense with sleep by a simple executive decree.

'Come in, Wayne . . . ' He beckoned me to a chair. 'An interesting trip so far, though you probably didn't enjoy the turkey shoot this afternoon. Too bad about that elephant, but target practice is what Paco needs, particularly targets he doesn't like shooting at.' At this point the telex chattered out a message. Manson stared at the strip, winced and sat there for a moment with opaque eyes, staring at some unrealisable dream behind the wall. 'Bad news about the virus, Wayne, it looks like there may be outbreaks soon in Miami and Baltimore. Thank God the west coast has been clear of it so far . . . '

'The virus, sir?' I asked. 'What exactly is this disease?'

I wanted to pin him down, but his eyes drifted away. 'A virulent new strain, Wayne. It likes to come in on an east wind. It's been incubating for a hundred years, waiting to take over those dead old cities.'

'But, Mr President, we landed in New York. Were we exposed to it?'

Manson gazed at me, as if seeing me for the first time. 'You were exposed, Wayne, but I guess you're immune. That's why I want you to join me here. There's a lot to be done. These Mexican kids are bright, and McNair will be a big help on the engineering side, along with Professor Summers. But I need someone to stand in for me. I've worked so hard, Wayne, so many years, I don't want to see it all go.'

A black, heavy rain was hitting the jungle, dancing on the blades of the gunships, washing the blood from the barrels. Manson sat there like an oozing waxwork as the lightning flickered across his tired face. Trying to rally his spirits, I complimented him on all he'd done, establishing this advanced industrial and communications base in the Nevada jungle. 'It's amazing, Mr President, I don't know how you managed on your own.'

Manson stared at me with a sly smile. I could see he liked that 'Mr President', but he's no fool.

'I had a little help, Wayne. My original partner joined me in Las Vegas fifteen years ago. A great engineer, until he cracked up. In fact, he taught Paco to fly the helicopter.'

'Where is he?' I asked. Fifteen years? That could be . . . 'Did he build the robots in the Sahara Hotel?'

Manson waved vaguely. 'One of his minor efforts. He's in Las Vegas, but he's not well . . . the strain of that trip across the continent.' An odd look came into Manson's eyes, a dead dream of all the empty highways and drained swimming-pools of America. 'He takes it easy now, a little occupational therapy with his puppets. Anything more than that excites him.'

The storm continued, the torrent of rain buckshotted into the palms as if a thousand gunships were firing their gatlings at us. I asked Manson when he had first arrived. Was it with an earlier expedition? But he avoided details, referring with marked distaste to Bremen, Antwerp and Liverpool — he must have spent months hanging around harbours and quays, waiting to jump ship. He talked about his youth in the American ghetto in Berlin, mentioned the Spandau district.

'But Europe doesn't exist for me any more, Wayne — except that I see it waking now like an old dog, smelling us here and trying to get its snout into this new America I've built. It was a gamble, Wayne, a gamble with my own life. I put everything on that one spin of the wheel each of us is given, a small stack of dreams and hopes. And now they'll try to steal it from me. And from you too, Wayne.'

What did he have in mind? I decided on a wild guess.

'Mr President — the missiles you're putting together, and the atomic disasters at Boston, Cincinnati and Cleveland — they weren't the old nuclear plants exploding?'

Manson's eyes were fixed on the television screens. Some special activity was taking place in the Vegas control room. 'I had to take them out, Wayne, there was a threat of plague in the east. I used the old cruise missiles. Before his breakdown my partner renovated the war-heads and guidance systems. They're slow but reliable, like homing pigeons going back to a hot supper. Think of it as a necessary prophylactic measure. But we need more missiles, Wayne. There are only two Titans and six cruises left.'

'And the laser shows, sir?'

'A warning to the Indians. A strange people, shabby and degenerate, but at least they stayed behind when the others left. I don't want to harm them, they helped me when I came across. But we've got to stop the plague before it reaches the Rockies. Wayne, we need to activate the Minuteman missiles, they're sitting in silos all over Nevada. Your friends could do it, they have the expertise . . .'

I listened to him as the rain beat steadily against the dark foliage. I knew I was rationalising my doubts, and that Manson was deliberately exposing his real motives, testing me out. Plague . . . ? Mutated pathogens were a possibility, but . . . Presumably Manson wanted to establish a cordon sanitaire, a wilderness of radioactive cities stretching from the Great Lakes to the Gulf of Mexico that would slow down the advance from the east. The Maginot Line mentality, a psychological structure rather than a physical defence. What about his exposed Pacific flank? By rights blockhouses and strongpoints should have been blooming all the way from Malibu to Newport Beach, he should have been ready to defend Marina del Rey to the last antique dealer and real estate operator.

'With your encouragement, Wayne, if you put in a good

word. McNair and Professor Summers will listen to you.'
Manson turned to face me, eyes steady through the distant
lightning. 'The Titans and Minutemen have a 500-kiloton
yield, and a long range. New York, Paris . . . Moscow
. . .'

'And more than that, sir.' I hesitated, remembering my
conversation with Orlowski in the White House. 'Mr
President, we could take out the Bering Dam, reverse the
Arctic current. The Mississippi would flow again, you
could grow enough wheat to feed the world, really have
something to bargain with.'

Manson beamed at me with a cracked smile. 'Wayne,
you're a gambler.' He spoke with real pride. 'And you've
come to the right place.'

November 25. Malibu Beach

A strange night. Did I believe myself when I suggested to
Manson that we should destroy the Bering Straits Dam? Or
was I being infected by his obsessions? Curiously, it's not a
bad idea — after all, it's that dam, the manipulation of a
whole continent's climate, that artificially maintains America's present desert/jungle divide. A piece of exploitation,
by the way, a perversion of the 'natural' America, as brutal
and self-serving as any of the Hollywood and Marvel
Comic fantasies of which Paco disapproves.

I went back to my room as the last of the storm moved
away up the California coast. I was very impressed by
Manson. For all his weirdness, he has the old Yankee
virtues. He wants to see America great again, and
becoming President is little more than decoration on the
cake. On the other hand, there are his obsessions . . .
worrying, to put it mildly. Other people's bodies obviously
make him uneasy, and like Nixon he has this peculiar
distaste for his own flesh. Paco and the boys see him as a
self-immersed eccentric, but so were Hughes and Henry
Ford. Hughes's genius presides over Manson, but so does
someone else I can't identify — I have an image in my mind

146

of staring eyes with a mad, messianic gleam . . .

Thinking about Manson, I fell asleep, woke at 8 a.m. to hear tremendous noise and excitement. Paco warming up the helicopters in the car park, a gabble of adolescent chatter on the intercom. A patrol group of three teenage Mexicans had turned up in a red Buick convertible. I reached the lobby in time to see Manson disappearing into the Sea-King. Paco told me to stay behind, I'd be picked up by car the next day. Obviously they were all on some hush-hush mission, I heard the youngsters yelling 'Edwards' to each other — presumably Edwards Air Force Base. I tried to climb into the cockpit as Manson ignored me from his swivel chair, but Paco slammed the hatch on my fingers, then shouted: 'There's another expedition ship! It landed yesterday in Miami!' Then they were gone, thrashing the jungle to death as they veered away through the Hollywood hills.

Back in the deserted hotel I felt flat and impotent. So a follow-up expedition had arrived. Although they were 3,000 miles away I was convinced that they would reach Las Vegas at any minute, before I had time to organise everything. In Manson's suite the television sets glowed in the bright sunlight. I lowered the blinds and watched for three hours as the airport radars scanned the sky over Las Vegas, waiting for an attack.

When nothing happened I calmed myself and went down to the car park. The red Buick convertible stood in the drive, a family of quarrelling baboons packed into the rear seat like up-country tourists. They whistled and waved when I approached, obviously expecting me to chauffeur them around Los Angeles, then took off in blue cloud as I sounded the horn.

I started the car, and drove down an empty Sunset Boulevard all the way to the Pacific coast highway. A rain-heavy, overcast sky. I finally stopped at Malibu, alone by the ocean on the edge of this huge city. I walked through the groves of palm trees and sat on the beach, a fringe of sand littered with rotting coconuts and the remains of hundreds of stills. A good place to think. I wandered through the shells of the film stars' houses, husks of dreams impaled by the palms. I'm writing the last entry in this diary — from now on there won't be time to keep it up to date.

There's a clear choice to be made — either to back away from Manson, taking McNair and Anne with me, or to throw in my lot with him. Even if he is crazy, that may be a help. It's madness I can probably put to good use. It will be months before a major expedition can reach Vegas, by then we should have established ourselves. Moscow will have to treat with us, they'll tolerate our role here as they do the military and papal regimes in South America.

All I need is ten years to make this country great again.

President Wayne . . . it sounds less strange than it used to.

21 | Crash-landing

The giraffe paused among the pools of water in Fremont Street, raised its delicate muzzle to the rain-washed air and gazed at the glittering façade of the Golden Nugget. As it continued its elegant hobble along the deserted pavement, Wayne rested on the pedals of the *Gossamer Albatross*, three hundred feet above. The previous night's lightning had cut swathes through the jungle to the north of Las Vegas, driving this gentle creature into the suburbs of the city. It now strolled down the deserted streets, inspecting the casinos like a timid tourist, unaware of Wayne gliding silently on the strong thermals above its head.

Deftly banking the filmy glider, its propeller a poised sword behind his back, Wayne followed the giraffe past the Horseshoe and the Mint. Mischievously he crept up on the unsuspecting beast, then edged the aircraft's shadow forward until the animal was at the centre of a huge target sight. The giraffe froze, unable to reach the sunlit pavement a few hoof-steps away. It glanced up at the vast machine of prey, outstretched wings and silver dagger emblazoned against the sun. With a nasal bleat it thrashed itself into life, then broke into a frantic loping canter, a desperate zigzag across the street.

Laughing good-naturedly to himself, Wayne began to pedal again. He followed the giraffe in and out of the deserted streets, steering it with the aircraft's shadow until it at last reached the safety of the forest to the west of the city.

Glad to see it go, Wayne made a wide turn over the centre of downtown Las Vegas, soaring on a carpet of warm air that rose from the thousands of illuminated signs below. He had chased the giraffe without any malice — left to itself the beast would soon have been run down by some speeding teenager at the wheel of his Cadillac.

However, as he paused above the Circus Circus, he noticed the clear disapproval in the faces of the two gun-toting girls exchanging gossip and spare cosmetics outside the entrance. Ursula was shaking her handsome head, once again pretending to be shocked by Wayne. It was two months now since he had made his decision on that empty beach at Malibu. Yet for all Wayne's closeness to the President he had never really penetrated the wall of reserve that Paco and the young Hispanics had built between them.

Only the previous evening, during an unexpected visit to the Lady Luck Casino, Manson had openly referred to Wayne as the 'Vice-President'. Taking their cue from the old man, and trying to break the oddly uncomfortable atmosphere, McNair and Anne Summers had applauded generously, throwing silver dollars at Wayne's feet as he stood bowing on the roulette table. But the armed entourage of youths and girls who had driven Manson along the Strip for this uneasy outing had conspicuously failed to join in. They accepted Anne and McNair, and not only because they were lending their skills to the nuclear engineering project at Lake Mead.

For his part, Wayne had done everything to open Las Vegas up and give the young Mexicans a taste of real American life. The USA was not just about computers and high-tech industries. With Paco's grudging help Wayne had renovated a drug-store and a hamburger bar near the old Greyhound Bus terminal, the first of a chain of fast-food outlets that he hoped to see spring up all around the town. They would be needed when the flood of youngsters began to arrive from the new recruitment centres he was urging Manson to set up in Baja California. There was a derelict Coca Cola bottling plant in north Las Vegas, and Wayne was trying to persuade McNair to spare a brief moment from his work on the Hoover Dam and start it up again, using the abundant supplies of old syrup.

Drug-stores and discos were what the youngsters needed above all else. At present they spent their spare time lying around in their suites in the big hotels, dozing, watching old porno films and smoking pot, like a lot of middle-aged vacationers. Wayne and two reluctant fifteen-year-old volunteers had reconditioned the projection cameras at a drive-in movie theatre off the Boulder Highway, but hardly anyone had bothered to turn up to the first performance, a gala double bill of *The Sands of Iwo Jima* and *Star Wars*, which these dedicated young Mexicans clearly regarded as colonialist propaganda put out by a corrupt capitalist regime on its last legs. As for the hot-rod race meeting Wayne had organised — that had been a total fiasco, Wayne found himself strapped helplessly into an exploding car, laughed at by a crowd of bemused youngsters leaning on their rifles. But at least he had tried.

No, Wayne reflected as he waved to the girls outside the Circus Circus, in some way he made them uneasy. Perhaps they saw the selfless ambition in Wayne's eyes, his continental dream of a new America. They resented the fact that Manson had picked him out precisely because he was the only one with a large enough vision to remake the nation. They knew, too, that Wayne thought them all a little limited and provincial, and that they would lose their now dominant place in the Hughes Company once the recruitment of new personnel was under way. Wayne had been pushing this for the past month.

'We'll literally be recruiting a nation, sir,' he had emphasised at the first board meeting in Manson's suite at the Desert Inn. Trying to inject some excitement into his fellow directors, McNair, Paco and Anne Summers, he stood up and gestured expansively at the Vegas skyline. 'We need people with the highest skills — computer specialists, systems analysts, architects, agronomists. For the first time in history we'll be recruiting an entire nation using the personnel selection techniques perfected by Exxon, IBM and DuPont. We're building a population from scratch, sir. We'll take only the best because America *needs* only the best . . . '

Paco had stared sourly at his pistol on the polished table, but the President sat back dreamily in his high-backed chair fifteen feet away from them, nodding in approval.

Only Anne had objected, frowning with some surprise at this impassioned speech. 'But, Wayne, that's an incredibly elitist viewpoint. What about those tired, huddled masses, yearning to breathe free . . . ?'

Wayne had gestured dismissively, though he was thinking of the drowned Liberty Statue in its watery grave, so like his dead mother. 'Their turn will come later − right now we have a crash programme on our hands, this is like the days after Pearl Harbor, or the Kennedy Moon Project. We need people who can switch America on again, turn on a hundred nuclear power stations, plan and build irrigation schemes, start up whole industries, people with communications and advertising know-how, finance and merchandising expertise. Frankly, I see the optimum population of the United States at about 100,000.'

'Wayne is right, Mr President.' McNair, surprisingly, had agreed. But McNair, with a larger vision than Anne Summers, had been rhapsodising for weeks about the engineering workshops in the Los Angeles aircraft plants, the limitless computerised tooling facilities − one man with a light pencil at a cathode screen could design and build a space-station without ever touching a screwdriver. McNair had a thousand ambitious ideas of his own, and Wayne encouraged him all the way. He was glad to hear the engineer say:

'We'll certainly need new recruits, but only those prepared to work. Particularly when we move our operations base east of the Rockies, to wherever we choose.'

'Omaha, Nebraska,' Manson interjected. He gazed at his

aerosol container, and explained cryptically: 'Headquarters of the Strategic Air Command.'

Wayne nodded in agreement, without knowing why. 'The military aspect is important, sir — when the time comes to deal with Moscow we've got to talk from a position of strength. But I seriously recommend that we move our base of operations to Washington — it's the traditional seat of government, and we need the trappings of power that go with it to legitimise our authority. I suggest that we set up a complete civil administration with all the arms of central government — issue a currency, passports, deeds of property and nationality, then appoint and receive ambassadors. The Miami expedition won't be the last, sir.'

The survey ship, whatever its mission, had abruptly withdrawn, and not been sighted since. None the less, McNair and Anne had agreed with Wayne, accepting that their reclaimed US citizenship might not wholly satisfy the first commissars who stepped ashore. But the President had lost interest — at times, lately, Wayne suspected that his own enthusiasm bored Manson. There were sly smiles at Paco across the boardroom table. Sitting back in his electric blue suit, aerosol raised in his hand like a divining rod, Manson had begun to reminisce about Omaha and the SAC, the huge H-bomber force perpetually patrolling America in the 1970s. He rambled on about 'Fortress USA' and the dangers of germs. He seemed to visualise hordes of bacterially infected European immigrants clambering up the beaches of the eastern seaboard, bearing rabies, polio, cancer and meningitis towards the Rockies at a steady three kilometres per day.

Listening to this endless monologue, Wayne had almost despaired of the President. Manson seemed totally unable to grasp that he would soon have to deal with the outside world, that one day uninvited strangers would enter the Hughes kingdom, as curious as the vagrant giraffes and deer and not so easily scared away. Like a child, in some respects, Manson had begun to display his unease by a compulsive gambling. Almost every evening now, after his return from the nuclear testing grounds in upstate Nevada, Manson would tour the gambling halls and hotels of Las Vegas. After picking up McNair and Anne, they would move in a convoy of limousines from the Golden Nugget to the Horseshoe, from the Fremont to the Lady Luck. Dressed in a tight black tuxedo, piles of silver dollars at his elbow, Manson would stare at the spinning roulette wheels, as if trying to read the future in these sidling numerals. Wayne's ostensible job as Vice-President was to supervise the endless flow of silver dollars stoically carted from the local bank vaults by Paco and his team. In fact, though, Wayne's real duty was to arrange for McNair to fix the wheels so that the President won more often than he lost.

Curiously, Manson loved to play zero, the house's number, and the easiest to select with the croupier's under-the-table trip. The President seemed to realise all this, smiling his silky smile at Wayne as everyone cheered and the silver dollars formed a glittering wall like some kind of jewelled nuclear body-armour.

Anything to keep the old man's spirits up, though McNair was equally worried by Manson's eccentric behaviour, and his growing obsession with the Minuteman missiles sitting in their jungle silos only a few miles from Las Vegas. 'I realise that we have to burn out the plague cities,' he had confided to Wayne after the board meeting. 'As well as defend ourselves. But only from any bandit riff-raff coming up through central America, not from the rest of the world. Those missiles could reach Berlin and Moscow in about twenty minutes. I know Anne is worried. Could you talk to the old man, Wayne? You've got his ear.'

But Wayne had been unsure. 'We need the pretence of overkill,' he temporised. 'It's all display, really, more bark than bite . . . '

Disturbing, nevertheless, and more and more Wayne needed to come up into the sky to think. Looking out at the brilliant air, Wayne pedalled the *Gossamer Albatross* towards the Desert Inn, careful not to impale the aircraft on the communications antennae that bristled from the roof. He had begun to fly the man-powered glider, partly to clear his nagging headaches, but also because of the unique freedom this antique machine gave him to keep an eye on everything. None of the young Mexicans speeding below him in their Lincolns and Cadillacs bothered to look up at the *Gossamer Albatross*, and the plane was remarkably easy to fly. The original twentieth-century pilots had exhausted themselves keeping airborne for more than a few minutes. Wayne could stay aloft for hours on end. But as McNair remarked ironically before towing him in his Rolls along the Strip: 'In the hundred years since the end of the automobile age homo sapiens has developed stronger legs and lungs – our grandparents must have been a collection of breathless paraplegics . . . '

Pedalling confidently, Wayne climbed high into the clear air, an eager Icarus in his acetate wings, and twice as flammable. Sensibly checking himself – after all, he was now only a heart-beat away from the Presidency of the United States – he banked and soared down towards the lake that covered what had once been the golf course of the Desert Inn Country Club. He could see Anne Summers speeding along the lakeside road in her perky red Mustang, heading for a day's work at the Hoover Dam and the nuclear power station. When Wayne dipped his wings she waved back cheerily. Wayne dived down beside the car, and let the miniature undercarriage of the *Gossamer Albatross* cut bright white plumes through the black water. With a smile, Anne gave a last toot on her horn and sped away among the glittering streets.

Legs cycling happily, Wayne mounted the air again. He loved his mild flirtations with Anne, an elaborate courtship between this winged man and the racing woman. On the ground, by contrast, he felt clumsy and uncouth. Did she realise, as he circled her hotel in the evenings, that one day she might become the First Lady?

Impelled by this vision, Wayne rose into the sky,

climbing the staircases of sunlight. The cool air sucked and whispered at the fabric of the plane, tickling its wings with all the indiscretions of the day. Below Wayne was the broad back of the Convention Center, where so many of the later Presidents of the United States had received their parties' nominations. Here, to the south-west of Las Vegas, the jungle was at its thickest, a raucous and vivid realm filled with tropical birds, giant bats and insects. Beyond the Desert Inn the hotels and casinos along the Strip lay gripped by the forest, only their upper floors emerging from the canopy. Caesar's Palace, the Castaways and the Flamingo were barely visible under the giant ferns and tropical oaks.

Something flashed from the roof of the Sands, sunlight trembled in what seemed to be the eye of a strange piece of optical equipment. One corner of a canvas awning flapped loosely in the wind. As he banked the glider, a wingtip away from the roof, Wayne caught a second glimpse of a long metal tube, unmistakably the barrel of an anti-aircraft weapon.

Alert now, Wayne decided to land on the narrow deck beside the awning. Perhaps a disaffected group of young Mexicans was planning a military putsch? From here they could fire at Manson's Sea-King as it took off from the airport.

Wayne was hovering ten feet above the open deck, trying to stall the glider downwards on to the roof, when there was a blare of sound behind and above him. A violent shadow filled the sky, and a huge machine shambled past. As it hurled away, its harsh blades slashed at the sunlight and chopped the air into exploding blocks. A series of tornadoes seized the *Gossamer Albatross*, flung Wayne across the handlebars and snapped the wings above his head. Torn in all directions, the crippled craft fell into the boiling wake of the helicopter. Like a broken dragonfly, it spun backwards across the jungle canopy.

Trapped within the ragged fuselage, Wayne had a last glimpse of the Sands Hotel, and of the patrolling gunship that had whirled him from the sky. Then the crushed remains of the glider fell towards the forest below. The fractured wings rattled the parasols of the date palms, and sliced through a curtain of Spanish moss into the sudden darkness beyond.

Wayne grappled with the limp controls. He tried to steer the craft into a small, shaded car park set out for him among the tree-trunks, but a sombre, magisterial oak strode across the confused air and struck Wayne and his wounded glider to the ground.

22 | The House of Presidents

He was surrounded by Presidents.

Far above him was a remote steel sky fitted with windows that let on to nothing. Was heaven made of metal? He was lying on a narrow hospital cot in an enormous room, whose walls were so far away that Wayne had to turn his head to see them. There were thousands of seats arranged in rows, as if an audience of angelic medical specialists was about to enter and observe him.

And on all sides the Presidents of the United States gazed down at him with their severe and serious eyes.

Nearest to Wayne, sitting in a wheelchair only an arm's length away, was Franklin Delano Roosevelt. His fine lips were pursed in a characteristic pose as he pondered the condition of Wayne's body and mind. Standing beside him, in homburg hat and salt-and-pepper suit, was Harry Truman, sharp eyes taking no nonsense from Wayne. Nixon stood at the foot of the bed, somewhat apart from the others, a weak but not unfriendly smile on his black-jowled face. Then there were a meditative Carter and a grinning Gerry Ford, who seemed to sympathise with Wayne's unexpected fall from grace. The three Kennedys stood together, JFK, Teddy and John-John. Their smiles beamed down at Wayne, urging him from his sick-bed.

As Wayne sat up, aware that his right leg was encased in plaster, he could see that they were all there, the forty-four Presidents, grouped around his cot in this huge room.

There were Jefferson and Washington in their frock coats, a dignified Lincoln in his stove-pipe hat, a choleric Teddy Roosevelt and a thoughtful Woodrow Wilson, a cheerful Eisenhower with a putter in one hand, ready to urge on Wayne the recuperative benefits of a round of golf. There was even a youthful Jerry Brown, about to say a mantra for Wayne.

Then, at a signal, they were all talking aloud, voices raised in the familiar intonations, gesturing courteously to each other like the members of a Presidential college inducting a new recruit.

President Wayne?

FDR sat forward in his wheelchair, agreeing with Wayne on the merits of rearmament.

' . . . tanks, guns, planes . . . we must be the great arsenal of democracy . . . '

Woodrow Wilson concurred: 'There is such a thing as being too proud to fight . . . '

But Lincoln interceded: ' . . . the ballot is stronger than the bullet . . . ' and added sagely, 'This nation, under God, shall have a new birth of freedom . . . '

At which an agitated Nixon stepped forward to the foot of Wayne's bed, pointing out: 'That would be the cowardly thing to do . . . '

Now they were all shouting together, jostling around Wayne as if trying to win his vote, a babel of remonstrating voices that echoed off the thousands of empty seats around the arena.

' . . . tanks, guns, planes . . . '

' . . . hyphenated Americans . . . '

' . . . safe for democracy . . . '

' . . . too proud to fight . . . '

' . . . *Ich bin ein Berliner* . . . '

Pushed forward by the three Kennedys, FDR shouted into Wayne's face, steely finger jabbing at his shoulder.

' . . . the only thing we have to fear is . . . '

Wayne screamed.

159

Everything was silent. The Presidents, all forty-four of them, had frozen in their postures, hands raised in mid-gesture, mouths open as if they had forgotten their favourite homilies. The last echoes of their voices fled along the far-away roof, vanishing through the windows into the calm sky. Wayne sat up, aware now of his fractured knee-cap and torn thigh muscles. He looked at the frozen robots around him, trying to avoid FDR's pointing finger.

'Are you all right, son?' A small, bright-eyed old man in a white laboratory coat had appeared at the foot of the bed. He stepped nimbly among the Presidents, glancing at each in turn. He muttered to himself, like an experienced nurse at an asylum supervising a group of patients with severe Presidential delusions. Sidestepping through the Kennedys, he smiled reassuringly at Wayne. 'Relax, my boy, you're in one piece, *amazingly*. But don't fly any closer to those gunships or even I won't be able to put you together again.'

When he saw Wayne having to avoid FDR's upraised finger the old man pulled a remote transmitter from his pocket and punched the buttons.

With an audible creak, a whirring of pulleys and sliding of ball-joints, FDR withdrew his forefinger, settled back in his wheelchair and assumed his cat-like smile.

'All right now, Wayne?' The old man nodded sympathetically at the bruises on Wayne's shoulders. 'For a future President you seem in reasonable working order. I've teased you, Wayne, arranging this special treat. Paco tells me you're our new Vice-President. But I'm afraid I haven't built any Vice-Presidents yet . . .'

Wayne lay back, realising that his entire body was an atlas of bruises. Yet his head felt cool and empty, as if this impish old man had siphoned off part of his brain and wired it into the circuitry of these robots. He pointed to the distant roof. 'It's the Convention Center — I thought I'd died . . .'

'You nearly did, my boy.' The old man rested his grey

head against Nixon's shoulder, as if comforting his prodigal son. 'It's a good thing that glider is so light, if you'd been trapped inside a rigid air-frame . . . Well, let's not think about it. I've watched you fly — you're good, Wayne, you have a nice feel for the air. A lovely plane for its day, though basically just a still-wind glider. But you've inspired me to work up something better, there are far lighter materials available these days . . . '

He broke off when he saw that Wayne was watching him with unfeigned curiosity. 'Of course, my boy, who am I, that's what you want to know — ?' He bowed his little head, and gave a puckish skip. 'Dr William Fleming, RIP, Emeritus Professor of Computer Sciences at the American University, Dublin, and sometime head of research at the Hughes Aircraft Company.' He beckoned to the Presidents. 'Our friends, I think, you know well.'

He pressed the tabs on his transmitter. There was a shuffle of feet, a swaying of shoulders, the forty-four Presidents about-turned. FDR spun his wheelchair, and the entire Presidential contingent moved off at a confident stride across the floor of the Convention Center and stopped ten feet from the podium.

'That's better.' The old man jumped up on to the end of the bed. He levelled a pair of excited but shrewd eyes at Wayne, as if this injured young man was an ingenious toy to be inspected and played with. 'Well, Wayne, welcome to my far from modest home — Presidents have been made here, in more senses than one. I'm sorry we had to meet so abruptly, but Charles likes to keep me hidden away here, playing my little games.'

'Dr Fleming . . . ' Wayne tried out the name on his tongue, remembering the affectionate message this old man had written to his mother. Amazingly, he had actually thought of him as his natural father. He now rejected the notion as ludicrous — his real blood lines ran closer to men like Manson. 'I was born in Dublin. You knew my mother there, twenty years ago.'

'A fine woman, on her happy days. She'd be proud of

you, Wayne, Vice-President of the United States . . . '

Wayne laughed shyly. 'Well, that was Mr Manson's decision. He's very generous. I believe in him, sir,' he added, making a point of his loyalty. 'He wants to make America great again.'

'And so do you, Wayne. And so do I. Though with everyone agreed as to the ends, we could afford rather more discussion as to the means . . . Or, for that matter, what exactly we signify by the term "America". It's an emotive symbol, Wayne, went out of fashion in the 1980s and 1990s, somehow lost its appeal . . . '

He broke off, annoyed that he was rambling to himself. Wayne was no longer listening, and had begun to sink into a shallow fever. Evening had fallen across the jungle, and panels of dark sky curtained off the windows in the roof of the Convention Center.

Dr Fleming stood up and smoothed Wayne's pillow, then walked over to the Presidents. He flicked his transmitter and quietly slow-marched them through the doorway below the stage, himself pushing Roosevelt's wheelchair, as Wayne slept through a feverish night filled with forests and dreams, gunships and Presidents and fantasies of man-powered flight.

23 | The Sunlight Flier

The next morning Wayne woke to feel refreshed, his fever gone, leg stiff but bearable, the bruises on his chest like a cloudburst of rainbows. A pleasant light filled the Convention Center. On the far side of the floor Dr Fleming was drilling his Presidents. They were drawn up in four ranks and listened impassively as they each took it in turn to stand at the front and speak to the others. Lincoln presented the Gettysburg Address, FDR promised a new deal, Jack Kennedy pledged to put a man on the moon, Nixon rambled evasively about his missing tapes.

'Mr Lincoln, very good,' Dr Fleming complimented the lanky robot. 'FDR, "tanks, guns and planes" needs a little more work, those glottal stops are still too explosive. Mr Nixon, well, yes . . . a brave effort, those missing eighteen minutes always were difficult to explain. Ah, Wayne, you're awake!'

He skipped over to Wayne in his white tennis sneakers. He had trimmed his beard, and seemed even more lively now that Wayne had recovered. 'Well, Wayne — you slept well?'

'No . . . ' Wayne remembered his dreams. 'Strange. I was flying a huge, man-powered aircraft, the size of this building.'

'A flying convention centre, powered by you alone? But that sounds encouraging, Wayne. Wait till you see what I've been building.'

Later, as Wayne hungrily cleared the breakfast tray, Dr Fleming lounged back in a canvas chair beside the cot. He seemed eager to talk. Wayne questioned him between mouthfuls of scrambled quails' eggs, happy to humour this eccentric and lonely old man. Dr Fleming described his arrival in New York harbour with the 2094 expedition, their shocked discovery of the vast Sahara rolling across the deserted cities of the eastern seaboard, the first abortive safaris to Washington and Pittsburgh.

'There was a serious split in the leadership of the expedition,' Dr Fleming reflected. 'The Indians were a lot more aggressive then, protecting their hunting grounds. We were ambushed by tribes of Professors and Bureaucrats, took several casualties before we left New Jersey. The political people in charge of the expedition decided to pack it in and sail back to Europe, but we scientists were determined to press on across the continent. As a result we were badly equipped, by the time we reached Grand Junction we hadn't much more than one pair of legs between the three of us. Manson saved us, all right. I think we would have died if Charles hadn't appeared on his camel . . . '

'He was living here already?'

'Living?' Dr Fleming held up his small, neat hands. 'Like a down-at-heel Robinson Crusoe with a couple of Indian bodyguards, in the same suite at the Desert Inn. How he made it, I don't know, he seems to have crossed the States by himself. Of course, Las Vegas then was totally deserted, none of the lights was on, there was just the dark jungle, thousands of snakes and malarial swamps, a nightmare of screaming birds and reptiles. Charles's happiest period.'

'And you helped him start everything up again?'

'Helped, Wayne? We did it *all*! In fact, for most of the time I was on my own. The two other expedition members both died in unhappy accidents − one was drowned at Lake Mead in a tank of radioactive coolant, and the other was killed testing a helicopter we'd reconditioned. They'd

164

wanted to go, anyway, after a row with Manson. That left me, and I owed it to Charles to stay. At first the whole Las Vegas operation began as a toy for Manson to play with, but now I seem to be the one with the toys . . . '

Wayne listened to a gunship passing overhead to the airport. 'I thought Mr Manson put all this together.'

'Nonsense. Charles is a brilliant man, in his way. He somehow picked up a little about computers at Spandau, but otherwise . . . ' Dr Fleming snapped his fingers dismissively. 'That's why he needs you, my boy, and your friends in particular. McNair and this Professor − ?'

'Anne Summers. She's a nuclear scientist. You must meet them, Dr Fleming, they'd like to see you.'

'No!' The old man sat back, reaching out for the security of the distant walls. He looked alarmed, like a startled patient. 'I haven't taken part in anything for years. I never go out, Wayne, my general health is poor . . . Charles thought it best if I stayed here. I have everything I need, a lavish laboratory, the boys cook for me, now and then I stroll through the forest . . . a nuclear scientist, you say, that's worrying.' He pulled himself together, as if refusing to think of the future. 'Well, now, Wayne, we'll borrow FDR's wheelchair and I'll show you the old toy-maker's workshop.'

For the next hour Dr Fleming took Wayne on a tour of the laboratories built into the reception rooms and offices below the stands. There were hundreds of feet of benches, fitted with lathes and precision welding machines equipped with microscope attachments, and a large autoclave for baking printed circuits. Mechanical arms and legs lay everywhere, alongside exposed thoraxes and faceless heads like the guts of giant watches, eyes protruding eerily on stalks from a mesh of cogs and coloured circuitry.

One section, at the rear of the auditorium, resembled the studio of a demented sculptor. Here the faces and hands were cut and modelled from sheets of flesh-tinted plastic, then moulded on to the metal armatures of the arms and heads. Dozens of familiar figures stood around, a pantheon of popular Americana gathered dust. Huckleberry Finn and Humphrey Bogart, Lindbergh and Walt Disney, Jim Bowie and Joe Di Maggio, lay stiffly across each other on the floor like drunks. Bing Crosby stood golf club in hand, throat exposed to reveal his voice synthesiser. Muhammed Ali posed in boxer shorts, the stumps of his wrists trailing veins of green and yellow wires. Marilyn Monroe smiled at them as they hurried past, her breasts on the floor at her feet, open chest displaying the ball-joints and pneumatic bladders that filled the empty spaces of her heart. And last of all there were the Presidents, a jumble of arms, legs and faces lying on the work-benches as if about to be assembled into one nightmare monster of the White House.

'Impressed, Wayne?' Dr Fleming asked as they paused beside a heap of discarded Nixons. 'More Chief Executives than even you could dream of . . . '

But he seemed bored with these elaborate toys. Wayne followed his tired gaze through the open doors that led into the great entrance hall of the Convention Center. There was a continuous flicker of light from what appeared to be the reflected image of a huge chandelier.

Curious, Wayne rolled the wheels of his chair towards the doors. As the forest light flooded into the entrance, Dr Fleming pointed proudly to an elaborate structure of glass and wire that hung ten feet above the floor. Part sunburst and part dragonfly, the slender fuselage and transparent wings of this glass aeroplane were held together by a cat's cradle of steel wires so fine that only a few points of condensing moisture in the humid air marked out the crystal surfaces of their delicate geometry.

Dr Fleming stared up at the aircraft. For the first time his agitated little body was completely still.

'Wayne, let me introduce the Sunlight Flier. I have you to thank for it, watching you fly around these past few weeks inspired me to start thinking about man-powered flight. It's pointless to use one's legs for anything but

166

steering when the sun is only too keen to do the work for us . . . '

Dr Fleming reached up to the starboard wing above his head. As his fingers splayed against the transparent pane a ripple of stress lines trembled in the air.

'An amazing material, Wayne, one of the hundreds of new glasses developed during the solar energy crisis of the 1990s. This one was designed to heat up the interior of a house even on a cloudy day. There are millions of miniature lasers focused a few millimetres from the inner surface, together they produce an enormous rise in air temperature. You can see I've had to tie her down . . . ' He strummed a weighted guy-rope that tethered the craft to the floor. 'In effect, the plane generates its own cushion of warm air, if we cant the wings like a helicopter's blades they'll surf forwards or backwards along a rising wave front, heliodynamic as opposed to aerodynamic lift. Infinitely silent and manoeuvrable, powered by the economy of the sun, and as mysterious as a snowflake . . . '

Wayne gazed at this glass aeroplane that shimmered in the bright sunlight above him. It tugged gently at its tethering lines, at times almost invisible. In the centre of the thirty-foot wingspan was an open fuselage, two seats in a metal frame. Control lines ran off from the pilot's handles and disappeared into the air.

'It's remarkable, doctor.' The craft quivered as Wayne propelled himself forwards, an aerial creature nervous at the approach of this wounded pilot. 'But have you flown her yet?'

'Of course not – I'm too old to try.' Dr Fleming gestured modestly, then turned a pair of sly eyes on Wayne. 'But that could be your job, you're the test pilot. Yes, Wayne, *you* pilot the Sunlight Flier and I'll be your navigator.' Before Wayne could protest he went on eagerly: 'What's so extraordinary about this material is its utter simplicity. All you need is a diamond cutter and a reel of steel wire and you can turn out one of these a day. A team of forty or fifty men working together could build an air force in next to no

167

time.' Dr Fleming smiled cannily at Wayne. 'In fact, that's what I have in mind − forty-four men, to be exact . . . '

'Forty-four − ?'

'Forty-four Presidents!' Dr Fleming chuckled with excitement, ideas bursting from his eyes like springs from an overwound clock. 'Give me a few days, Wayne, and I'll reprogramme their command packs. Why not, I'm tired of the Gettysburg Address, Wilson moralising, Nixon going on about his tapes. Let's put them to *work*, they can fill the sky with Sunlight Fliers, we'll take the children and go to live on the sun, away from here for ever . . . '

Dr Fleming smiled at the sunbeams soaring down through the windows of the entrance hall, staircases of light that beckoned to the glass aeroplane straining against its guy-ropes. Wayne gripped the arms of his wheelchair, quietly testing the strength in his injured leg. With luck the cast would be strong enough to support him. He could soon make a crutch from a steel rod in the workshops, and then escape from this mad old man. Much as he admired Dr Fleming, he could hear the faint clicking and cracking of the glass machine. With a shudder he tried to visualise himself flying this suicidal craft into the air. It was time to get back to Manson, back to his duties as Vice-President, away from these glass aeroplanes and dreams of the sun.

Later that afternoon, as Dr Fleming dozed in a hammock on the podium, Wayne eased himself from the wheelchair. He hobbled through the silent workshops towards the entrance, supporting himself with Crosby's putter. But as he limped past the Sunlight Flier he discovered that the glass doors, like all the exits from the Convention Center were protected by their own Presidential guard. Lincoln and Truman smiled their most understanding smiles at him, while Washington beckoned Wayne back to the wheelchair which Carter and Ford had pushed together from the auditorium.

Wayne returned to the great chamber, under the calm gaze of the forty-four Presidents. They stood around him when he climbed back into his hospital bed, watching over him as they would do through the night and the following days, while Dr Fleming lay in his hammock, a happy and mischievous Gepetto welcoming another Pinocchio to his magical toyshop.

24 | A Graduate of Spandau

So, for the next week, as events ran their erratic course in Las Vegas, Wayne remained the prisoner of the old scientist and his forty-four Presidents. Each morning he woke to find the dignified figures standing around his cot, their grave faces without expression. Dr Fleming would sit up in his hammock on the podium and tap out his first instructions on the remote transmitter. Then Reagan and Coolidge would bring Wayne his breakfast, while the others marched off to the laboratories, where they worked with a will constructing the growing fleet of glass aeroplanes. A small detachment remained to stand guard over Wayne, three of the Presidents with a military training — Grant, Eisenhower and Washington. As Ford and Carter pushed the wheelchair, smiling their ever-friendly smiles, the others would follow Wayne wherever he went, quietly ignoring him when he asked for the exit doors of the Center to be unlocked.

During these first days, as Wayne recovered the strength in his leg, he assumed that they were protecting him from further injury, bringing him back to health in readiness for his test flight of the Sunlight Flier. He listened to the sounds of Manson's helicopter flying to and from Las Vegas Airport. There was obviously a marked increase in activity, a tension in the air that had nothing to do with any search for Wayne. Several times each night he would be woken by the roar of the gunships' gatlings as they made practice runs over the jungle.

One evening, a week after his arrival, when the continual noise had shaken a cloud of dust from the roof of the auditorium, Wayne wheeled his chair into one of the renovated elevators and rode up to the observation deck. He found Dr Fleming alone at the rail, his back to the lights of downtown Las Vegas. Two miles to the east of the Convention Center an isolated apartment house was being attacked by the gunships. Led by Manson's Sea-King, they clattered in above the Center, racks of air-to-ground rockets at the ready. Wayne could even see Paco in his bright yellow helmet, and Manson behind him, swivelling his gunnery chair like a manic big-game hunter. One after the other the rockets streaked towards the apartment house and impacted against the glass curtain-walling. A flock of agitated birds rose from a jungle lake beside the building, their vivid bodies carrying pieces of the fire.

'War games, Wayne,' Dr Fleming murmured. 'Heaven alone knows what Charles is playing at. Perhaps he's preparing for visitors in his own special way. I've heard there are bands of mercenaries in the Arizona forests, Indians, freebooters and other riff-raff. They and Manson won't mix easily.'

'Dr Fleming . . . ' Wayne felt excited by the violence of the gunships, the pall of black smoke that leaned across the jungle air. 'It's been good of you to look after me, but I ought to get back to the President.'

Dr Fleming stared at Wayne, recognising him with an effort. 'The President? Haven't you got enough Presidents here already?'

'Sir, Mr Manson will need me now.'

'He won't! I need you, Wayne, to test the Fliers. It's our only way of escape. We're all going to fly to the sun!'

That evening the first night-shift began. As Wayne lay in his cot the Presidents worked without rest, building the fleet of Sunlight Fliers. Dr Fleming drove them on, a taskmaster with his remote transmitter, tapping out an endless stream of microwaved instructions. They cut and shaped the panels of solar glass, then wired them together around the slender fuselage frames, fitted the control lines and mooring points. Wayne woke to find these strange creatures tethered like glass dragonflies to the floor around him. There were single-seater monoplanes, two- and three-seater biplanes, triplanes with wing-clusters seventy feet wide and seats for half a dozen passengers. In the pale dawn this ghostly fleet of glass aeroplanes shimmered around him, eager to fly the day. At night, even the moonlight sent shivers of excitement through these delicate machines. They strained at their guy-ropes like imprisoned sylphs, wings ringing the sound of bells. The Presidents stood among them, patient would-be pilots sprung from Wayne's dreams of flight and the White House.

By the end of the second week a dozen aircraft had been constructed. Wayne hobbled through the laboratories on Crosby's putter, watching the aeroplanes take shape. The Presidents worked with an energy few of their originals could have matched in life, pausing only when Dr Fleming put down his transmitter to listen to the helicopters and the gunfire from the weapons range at the airport.

When they stopped briefly for lunch Dr Fleming pointed with his transmitter at Wayne's leg, as if trying to signal it into action.

'That leg is stronger, now, I can see. Wayne, you're almost ready to try out the first of the Fliers.'

'Well . . . I'm not sure.'

Privately, Wayne had no intention of flying these glass contraptions. He could see himself vanishing in a puff of overheated crystals. But he humoured Dr Fleming, biding his time until he was strong enough to outrun the heavy-footed Presidential guard. For all his anger at being imprisoned in the Convention Center, he liked this lonely old man, and only wished he would turn his talents once again towards helping Manson.

Wayne looked up from their lunch tray at the circle of stationary robots. 'Dr Fleming, I meant to ask — there's one President you've left out . . . '

'Which one, Wayne?'

'Mr Manson.'

Dr Fleming gazed at Wayne with a moment's anger. His hands were raw from the days of cutting glass. Small splinters covered his beard and hair with a fine frost, as if he had aged by decades in the anxieties of the past week.

'No . . . Charles did ask, but I turned him down.'

'Why?' Wayne pressed. 'He's done more for the United States than most of the real Presidents. He's trying to protect everything you've built here.'

'Agreed, Wayne.' Dr Fleming flinched as a series of explosions sounded from the airport weapons range. 'But his methods are a little too drastic for me. Cincinnati, Cleveland — I was to blame there. I helped to renovate the war-heads on those cruise and Titan missiles. I should have realised just how Charles planned to protect America. In exactly the way that the suicide protects himself from his own body.'

'But Dr Fleming,' Wayne insisted, 'he was forced to destroy those cities. The plant and animal life in the New World have lost their resistance to Old World bacteria.'

'Is that what Charles told you?' Dr Fleming picked at a painful spur of glass in his left palm. 'Yes, there's certainly a deadly plague on the way now — it's very virulent, and there's no known antidote.'

'You know about it?'

'Of course. It's the most threatening disease of all. It's called "other people". They'll be coming soon, in ever-larger expeditions, eager to colonise this land again . . . '

Wayne tried to stand up, hoping to embrace this furious old man and calm him. Dr Fleming's goatee was hopping and twitching like the pointer of an angry seismograph. 'You're wrong, doctor, Mr Manson said — '

'Wayne!' Dr Fleming struck the keyboard of his transmitter, sending a fearful spasm through the assembled Presidents. The wings of the glass aeroplanes were trembling in sympathy, as if the floor of the Convention

Center was shifting invisibly. Controlling himself, Dr Fleming said: 'Stop calling him "Mr Manson". You might like to know that Manson is not his real name. For reasons of his own Charles adopted Manson when he was released from Spandau.'

'Released? He emigrated,' Wayne pointed out matter-of-factly. 'Spandau is the American district of Berlin. There was a prison there once,' he added for Dr Fleming's information, 'where war-criminals were held – Hess, Speer . . . '

'And later "detainees" of a different kind. When they levelled the ancient fortress a century ago no Germans wanted to build on the ground, so they gave it to the refugee Americans, as an ironic gesture, I suppose. Spandau was the name of the American mental hospital in Berlin, and the alma mater of your forty-fifth President . . . '

Manson? Charles Manson?

Wayne had heard the name somewhere before. A partner of Howard Hughes, or perhaps someone involved in the Watergate scandal? The name had once been as famous as Dillinger's. But where?

Manson, Charles . . .

'What's the matter, Wayne?' There was a look of real concern on the old man's face. 'I'm sorry, I've cut your idol down to his clay heels. But I had to warn you of the dangers here. Yes, Wayne, after a long journey the ghosts of Charles Manson and IBM meet in Caesar's Palace, playing with cruise missiles in place of gold chips . . . '

Manson? Wayne stood up, supporting himself on the putter. He tried to clear his head. The glass aeroplanes around him were shaking with fear, as they picked up a series of approaching tremors.

Dr Fleming was talking to himself. 'Perhaps you can understand now why I decided to come here. But we can leave all this behind –'

There was the rapid sound of explosions. Anti-aircraft shells burst in the sky, and drummed at the roof of the

Convention Center. Alert again, Dr Fleming tapped the buttons on his transmitter. The Presidents spread their legs and steadied themselves. A powerful air-raid siren wailed through the streets of Las Vegas. There was the clattering roar of an engine under strain, and a gunship scrambled overhead, its frantic blades almost vertical in the sky. Hard behind it came a small, fixed-wing plane, striped bars on its fuselage. It flashed past the windows, followed by the harsh explosions of anti-aircraft shells fired down at the intruder from the roof of a nearby hotel. The huge star-bursts sent plumes of incandescent smoke across the forest canopy, fists of air that punched the walls of the Convention Center.

Before Wayne could pull Dr Fleming to the ground a flash of light filled the auditorium. Two hundred feet above their heads the windows of the Center burst inwards. Thrown to his knees, Wayne shielded his face as hot dust scalded the air. A glass biplane disintegrated, its staywires shredding, crystal panes breaking up like a house of windows. Another plane bounced excitedly off its guy-ropes and fell on its back among the staggering Presidents, exploded in a flicker of colliding glass that covered them all with icing sugar.

Dr Fleming stood in the centre of this pandemonium, transmitter in hand, his beard and eyebrows filmed with brittle dust. Around him the Presidents were going down like skittles, the compression chambers in their balance units upset by the explosions. Madison, Coolidge, Adams and Reagan lost their footing and fell to the floor, legs kicking among the collapsing aircraft. Only Gerald Ford had kept his balance, but in a gesture of solidarity he deliberately stumbled and threw himself to the ground. He climbed to his feet and fell to the floor again, rose with an eager smile, as ever keen to please, dusted his shoulders and flung himself backwards, only to bob up again.

'Gerry . . . for heaven's sake.' Dr Fleming waved the transmitter at the clearing smoke. The dust was rising into the funnel of the roof and being vented away through the windows. Meanwhile the air-raid sirens kept up their gloomy wailing.

'Dr Fleming . . . ' Wayne took the old scientist's arm as he counted the damaged aircraft. Half of the glass fleet was intact, a tremulous herd flinching at each of the distant explosions. 'Sir, we must find Mr Manson.'

'No, Wayne, we stay here!'

'Dr Fleming, these planes will never fly – they're a fantasy!'

Wayne waited for some response, but the old man had raised his wand and was tapping out a last instruction. When a tight-mouthed Truman appeared, eyes already turning to the exit doors, Wayne took his chance. He raised the putter and struck the transmitter from Dr Fleming's tender hand, then ducked away under the quivering wings of a glass triplane. As he hobbled and skipped across the auditorium he could hear Dr Fleming shouting and egging on his robots. The Presidents' heavy feet pounded after him, sliding and skidding like drunken skaters on the broken glass.

The warm, sticky air of the jungle poured through the shattered doors of the entrance hall. Wayne thankfully filled his lungs. With a brief salute to the vanished spirit of Bing Crosby, he threw away the putter, ran down the steps and limped through the siren-filled streets towards the centre of the city.

25 | Siege

Las Vegas was a city under siege. Pausing only when he was a safe two hundred yards from the Convention Center, Wayne rested in the rear seat of an abandoned Buick convertible. The Presidents stood in a confused gang outside the entrance, eyes flinching at the sunlit perimeter of their programmed world.

Ignoring them now, Wayne scanned the busy sky. A cluster of explosions burst high above the city. Manned by Manson's young militia, the anti-aircraft guns kept up a sporadic fire from the roofs of the Dunes and Paradise Hotels. Silhouetted like striped fish against the sky, three reconnaissance planes moved from west to east across Las Vegas.

As fragments of the bright air fell around him, Wayne took shelter under the portico of a filling station, then set off in the first lull towards the Desert Inn. Where was Manson? The neon signs of the casinos and hotels seemed garishly overlit. On all sides a festering light stung the retina, as if this old gambling capital was infected by a jungle fever. The streets were deserted, and burnt-out cars smoked along the sidewalks. Along Paradise Road he counted a dozen bombed motels and apartment blocks in their hearths of blackened forest. Manson's remote-controlled gunships patrolled the eastern outskirts of the city. Wayne watched them attack the empty stadium beside the Boulder highway, driving and circling as if directed by a lunatic flight-commander.

Hundreds of slaughtered birds had fallen into the empty streets, the splayed plumage of macaws and parakeets like gaudy paint-blots. A dead bison lay on its side at the junction of Paradise and Desert Inn Roads, legs stiffening in the sunlight. Nearby was the shrapnel-riddled corpse of an unwary panther that had come forward to enjoy this free kill.

As the air-raid klaxons kept up their melancholy wail, Wayne set off along the Desert Inn Road. The three spotter planes flew steadily towards the Arizona border, joined now by the fourth aircraft which had carried out its roof-top reconnaissance of Las Vegas and made possible Wayne's escape. Were they part of an invading mercenary force, those freebooters Manson was convinced would one day emerge from the jungle darknesses of Arizona and New Mexico? The strict formation flying and uniform insignia suggested an organised military expedition, perhaps part of the naval force that had berthed briefly at Miami.

But why this armed resistance? If the President intended to establish his moral and legal authority, his right to be the first pro-consul of the New America, he was going the wrong way about it by playing the eccentric war-lord. And one half of Manson's young militia seemed to be at odds with the other. As Wayne approached the Desert Inn Hotel he came across the first of a series of sand-bagged defence posts set up at the intersections along the Strip. Coils of barbed wire curled across the street, tangled up in the front wheels of a stalled Cadillac.

Two of Manson's militia-girls stood on the roof of the strongpoint. Wayne recognised Ursula, who had driven him to see Manson after his arrival in Las Vegas, now handsomely kitted out in full combat gear, with smart puttees and webbing. She waved her machine-pistol at three confused boys, none more than fifteen years old, who hid behind the windows of the Cadillac. Despite their green uniforms and weapons, they looked lost and bewildered, round faces blunted by the noise of the wailing klaxon.

Wayne ran forward, trying to make his voice heard above the din.

'Let them through! Ursula, what are you playing at? Pull back that wire!'

With a bored glance at Wayne, Ursula beckoned him away. She levelled her weapon at the front tyres of the Cadillac. There was a burst of automatic fire, steam exploded from the punctured radiator as the heavy car slumped forward on to its flattened tyres. Stunned by the violence, the three youngsters sat frozen in their tilting limousine, then with child-like cries scrambled through the doors and fled down the neon-lit street.

Wayne approached the defence post, pointing up to the penthouse suite of the Desert Inn. 'Ursula, what's happened to the President? I need to see him.'

Ursula stared at Wayne with level-eyed hostility. Clearly she assumed that Wayne had abandoned them in their week of crisis. 'He's gone, Wayne — moved his headquarters to the War Room. And he doesn't want to see you. Now run off and join your friends from the east.'

'Ursula . . . ' Wayne was about to climb through the barbed wire wrapped around the steaming Cadillac. But the two girls had retreated into their emplacement. The sights of their machine-pistols followed Wayne as he sidestepped gingerly away from them. He had reached the safety of an abandoned truck when Ursula stood up and shouted at him, nightclub Pasionaria of the jungle Strip: 'Wayne, this time you won't steal our land from us . . . !'

For the next hour Wayne roamed Las Vegas, searching for any sign of Manson's command headquarters — the 'War Room' to which Ursula had cryptically referred. She made it sound like a cocktail bar, beautiful but absurd girl, he could imagine her teaching him to tango with bursts from her machine-gun. Perhaps the President was ill, or had been overthrown in a palace coup, and the defence of Las Vegas against its real and imaginary enemies was being conducted by Paco and other rival factions. The whole

Hughes/Manson operation had moved with one step to the edge of chaos — nervous shooting in the streets, dangerous overflights by the gunships, which were now napalming the undefended drive-in theatre while the anti-aircraft guns kept up their intermittent fire at a blue and empty sky. And through all this the neon façades of the casinos glowed like so many hallucinated Niagaras.

Tired by the ceaseless ducking in and out of bars and hotel lobbies, Wayne plodded along the Strip. Whenever he approached a strongpoint he was brusquely waved away. Clearly no one wanted to see him. He reflected grimly that the post of Vice-President, never exactly coveted or admired, had reached rock-bottom.

Groups of nervous teenagers hid among the fruit machines in the hotel foyers, crouched under the roulette and blackjack tables in the casinos along Fremont Street. Trapped cherubs in an overlit paradise, they stared at Wayne with unfocused eyes as he shouted at them.

'Chico — where's the War Room? Have you seen Mr Manson? Who's in charge now? Pancho, those planes — where did they come from?'

Giving up, Wayne strode into the street, then snatched the ignition keys from a twelve-year-old sitting in the gutter beside his Continental outside the Golden Nugget. Ignoring the gunfire and helicopters, Wayne set off along the Strip. Somehow he had to reach the airport, almost certainly the new operations centre, with luck he would find the President in the old Hughes Executive Terminal. Manson had probably been felled by a stroke or heart attack and was unaware that his jungle principality was being torn apart by his lieutenants.

But as he reached the junction with Sahara Avenue he saw a small convoy of cars speeding towards him, a familiar red Mustang in the lead. Wayne slewed the Continental across the road, pulling the approaching cars to an angry halt in a blare of horns and headlamps. An exhausted Anne Summers stood up in her driver's seat, bruised hands gripping the windshield. Dark bloodstains marked her chin and arms.

'Wayne? We thought you'd gone! Get out of our way!'

Wayne leapt from the Lincoln, searching his pockets for a shred of bandage to stem her bleeding. But Anne waved him off, ignoring the caked blood.

'It's all right, I'm not hurt. It's poor McNair . . . !'

They ran past the next car, a radio-equipped jeep driven by two nervous militia-girls. The third vehicle was a Plymouth estate wagon. A wan-faced Pepsodent sat at the wheel. Lying on a mattress behind him, legs strapped to a chromium stretcher, was McNair. His clothes and beard were stained with red mountain earth, his eyes closed in a colourless face. His right leg was lashed in a crude splint, rags of lint through which a dark blood seeped over the deck of the car.

Anne Summers flinched at the sounds of anti-aircraft fire that had started up again from the roofs of the Sands and Paradise Hotels. She shielded her eyes from the furious light that blazed from the casino façades, then patted Pepsodent's arm. The Indian's clothes and hands were stained with the same red soil, as if he and McNair had been wrestling in a pit filled with rust.

Wayne held Anne's shoulders and hurried her back to his Lincoln. When they set off along Sahara Avenue she sat back limply, shaking her head as if angry with herself.

'Manson's mad − he tried to kill McNair. Wayne, where have you been? You've got to find Manson and somehow take over. He's activated the Titan and cruise missiles hidden out in the jungle, he's ready to use them against the expedition fleet at Malibu.' In a moment of fury, she struck Wayne's arm. 'You knew he was planning this!'

'Malibu . . . ?' Confused, Wayne could only think of the deserted beach where he had decided to commit himself to Manson. 'How many ships are there?'

'Three, with something like five hundred men and six aircraft. They're from the Pacific piracy patrol based at Hawaii, we talked to them on the radio before Manson jammed the transmissions. There's a smaller expedition coming up from Phoenix, they've joined forces with Mexican and Indian mercenaries across the Rio Grande.'

'And they shot McNair?'

'No — ! McNair was on his way to warn them, but Manson's helicopters appeared out of the sky near Flagstaff and attacked them without any warning. They went off the road, but Pepsodent managed to get to the car and telephone me.'

'Manson's gunships . . . ' Doggedly, Wayne shook his head. 'More likely the mercenaries. Manson said — '

'Wayne, he's *mad*!' Anne drummed her bruised fist on the steering wheel. 'He's going to fire those missiles! You fool, I was there! We thought he wanted to put a communications satellite into orbit, but in fact they're armed with nuclear war-heads! When McNair and I refused to help him I thought he was going to shoot us on the spot . . . '

'But, Anne — ' Wayne searched for some way of reassuring her. They were driving along Sahara Avenue, shielded from the narrow traverse of the sky by the forest canopy. As they neared the Sahara Hotel there was an ugly clatter above their heads, and a huge helicopter drifted past. Signalling Pepsodent and the two girls to a halt, Wayne peered up at the Sea-King, the President's personal craft with its familiar intensive-care unit and gatlings. While the gun-barrels prowled the road below, Wayne caught a glimpse through the palm fronds of Paco's yellow helmet in the high cockpit. In the sealed cabin behind him Manson sat in his swing chair, tilting eyes set in an ashen face. He spoke into his microphone, and the Sea-King banked steeply. The gatlings raked the empty cars, tearing open their roofs in a thunderburst of metallised rain.

The gunship clattered away on its ugly patrol, looking for something to kill. Wayne steadied Anne Summers as she gripped the steering wheel, shocked face against her wrists.

'It's gone now — we'll get McNair into the hotel. Then I'll organise an escape party. We'll head for Los Angeles.'

'Wayne, the missiles — you do understand?' Anne sat up, disengaging herself from Wayne. She looked at him with determined calm. 'The missiles are ready, someone armed them for Manson only a year ago. Six cruises and two Titans, all with nuclear war-heads.'

'I know that.' Wayne listened to the fading roar of the Sea-King. For a moment he had felt like the frightened children in the Golden Nugget. He spoke with as much conviction as he could muster. 'Don't worry — before we go I'll arrest Manson and take over the Presidency.'

26 | Titans and Cruises

Their base camp, for the next three days, was the tenth floor of the Sahara. After a first unhappy night of fever McNair began a heartening recovery. Nursed by Anne Summers, he lay in a darkened bedroom, blinds drawn against the ever more livid neon light from the city below. Pepsodent squatted at the foot of the bed, submachine-gun cradled across his knees, scowling at the anti-aircraft fire outside, the incessant racket of gunships and wailing sirens.

The other Indians – Heinz, Xerox and GM – had left the previous day. Led by the canny Heinz, they had bunkered the ancient Galaxy, raised steam and set off for California. With luck, Wayne reflected, the coal-fired vehicle would travel too slowly to be noticed by Manson's gunships. Alone now, Pepsodent stoically guarded McNair, helping Anne to wash the engineer and change his dressings.

Wayne, meanwhile, kept up his own vigil. From the roof of the Sahara he watched the final collapse of Manson's jungle empire, which seemed to take with it so many of his own dreams of a reborn America. Manson's continuous jamming of the radio space above Las Vegas shut out beyond a wall of static almost all the incoming transmissions from the Malibu and Phoenix expeditions. But from the brief bursts of intercom chatter that occasionally penetrated the static it was clear that both expeditions were drawing nearer to Las Vegas. The small fleet of ships at Malibu had unloaded its vehicles and supplies, and then dispersed across the LA basin, setting up a series of scattered enclaves to avoid the threat posed by Manson's missiles.

On their second day at the Sahara a fragmentary bulletin told Wayne and Anne that Manson had fired one of the two Titans, aiming the huge missile, for some inexplicable reason, not at Los Angeles or Phoenix, but at Des Moines, an unpopulated wilderness city in the white desert to the east of the Rockies.

'That leaves six cruises and the Titan,' Wayne said. 'But why Des Moines, of all places? Why not Washington, or New York — he hated the east coast establishment.'

'A last crazy fling. I always knew he was mad. Yet we indulged him, Wayne — why?' Anne shivered in the grey light of McNair's bedroom, watching as their barely conscious patient sipped at the tea-cup held against his singed beard by Pepsodent. 'Perhaps the guidance systems are at fault, and he can't control which contour maps they select. What lunatic armed them for him, anyway?'

Wayne ignored the question. For reasons of his own he had told Anne nothing of his meeting with Dr Fleming in the Convention Center. But the news of the attack on Des Moines was a worrying development. 'Anne, that isn't Manson. Everything about him is calculated. Over-calculated, even. Des Moines will be a piece in his private jigsaw . . .'

With a shudder, Anne gazed through the blinds at the lurid city below them. 'But where is he? And where is this War Room?'

'No one knows. He never talked about it.' Not even Dr Fleming, for all his hatred of Manson, had mentioned the secret headquarters.

Fortunately, during this period of confusion the reconnaissance flights continued. The con-trails of the high-flying planes with their striped livery criss-crossed the sky. Wayne assumed that they were photographing the city and airport, trying to estimate Manson's military resources and troop-deployment. Had they any idea that Las Vegas was defended by a rag-tag army of children? In an attempt to blind their camera lenses, Manson continued to turn up the electric power flowing into the city. The neon façades of the casinos and hotels were now so many cataracts of white lava, walls of incandescent pink and purple that seemed to set alight the surrounding jungle, turning the Strip and the downtown casino centre into an inflamed, shadowless realm through which the occasional armoured car would appear like a spectral dragon on the floor of a furnace.

At dusk, the short-wave transmissions from the approaching expeditions at last rose above Manson's jamming. There was a brief call for everyone in Las Vegas to lay down their arms and cooperate with the incoming forces. Then Manson's flat voice began to rant back at them, a monotonous tirade obsessed with dirt, disease, bureaucracy and death, as if he were some deranged announcer broadcasting not from Las Vegas but from a plague city of a million filing cabinets.

From the roof of the Sahara, in the centre of the Strip, Wayne watched these events with numbed eyes. Anne Summers tried to rally him. On the third morning, as the air-raid sirens wailed the arrival of another reconnaissance flight, she left the now conscious McNair and took the elevator up to the observation deck.

Wayne was staring at the laser-projected image of a car-bine-toting GI, in helmet and flak jacket, that rose a thousand feet into the air above the city. Now that his batteries atop the Sands and Paradise Hotels had run out of ammunition, Manson had turned to these huge illusory figures for the defence of his realm. Heaven alone knew what the pilots of the spotter planes made of the grimacing giants that rose up to smite them, a bizarre succession of soldiers and gunfighters, Joe Louis feinting left and right jabs at the aircraft speeding through his fists, then King Kong, appropriately in his death-throes, and even Manson himself in blue suit and Homburg presiding above the overlit city like a gloomy mortician in an ambitious but tasteless commercial.

'That image is the saddest of all, Anne,' Wayne confided. 'Though it has a certain tragic dignity. In his own way, Manson at least tried.'

'Wayne, come on. Don't give up now.' Standing behind him, Anne held his shoulders in the first show of tenderness he could remember since the *Apollo*. 'You crossed a continent and brought us here. Las Vegas never was more than the largest light bulb in the world. We can make a fresh start somewhere else, in Pasadena or Santa Barbara.'

'Pasadena . . . ?' It was Wayne's turn to shudder. 'Don't you see, Anne, we didn't come to Las Vegas by chance, and nor did Manson − or Hughes.' He pointed to the transparent image of the GI towering above them. His huge feet planted astride the city on the roofs of the Mint and the Circus Circus, he was firing bursts from his carbine at the striped-wing planes that flew through his chest. 'Manson must have put it on for me − that's John Wayne in *The Sands of Iwo Jima*. It looks like a joke to us, but it's the heart of everything. It was here they dreamed the purest dreams of all . . . '

The purest and the most innocent dreams. Yet Wayne knew he was thinking of Dr Fleming and the six cruise missiles he had armed for Manson. Wayne had said nothing to Anne of his meeting with the old scientist, and claimed only that he had been stranded in the orchid forests of Death Valley. For days now dreams of cruise missiles had filled his sleep. There was still time to retarget their contour maps, point them north-west across the Pacific to the dam that subverted the natural balance between the eastern and western hemispheres. If only he could find Manson there was just enough time for a last spin of the wheel . . .

27 | Love and Hate

At three o'clock that afternoon the first signal rockets rose from the jungle to the east and south-west of Las Vegas, marking the arrival of the Phoenix and Malibu expeditions. The pink and blue star-bursts hung inoffensively above the forest canopy, like the timid display of a third-rate travelling circus. But these first visible signs of the approaching plague he had feared for so long seemed to drive Manson into a last frenzy of activity. Within minutes, as Wayne and Anne returned to McNair's bedroom, the klaxons wailed their warnings, and the electrographic façades of the great hotels and casinos blazed in an almost molten fury.

Already, however, the lights were going out. As the power poured into the centre of Las Vegas, the Golden Nugget was in darkness, its neon piping splintered on the sidewalks, the first black tooth in this diamond-filled jaw. When a small spotter plane appeared and made a roof-top sortie across the city Manson's gunships took after it like deranged sharks from the helipads on the Sands and Paradise Hotels. They clattered along the debris-littered streets, shooting up the rotting carcases of the slaughtered giraffes and alligators. Their bearings lost, and erratically directed by Manson from his secret control centre, the robot gunships roamed the perimeter of the city, napalming the jungle on either side of the main routes to the south and west. Palls of smoke leaned across the sky to form the wavering, mile-high columns of a black pavilion that housed Manson's laser genies under its stormy canopy.

When, an hour after dusk, all the lights in Las Vegas went out as if a single switch had been pulled, this barely dimmed the corona of luminous air that hung over the city. Huge fires were burning around the Vegas perimeter, and the exploding gasoline dump at the Greyhound Bus Terminal had set alight dozens of bars and small hotels. Forest fires sped through the jungle, the flames reflected in the silent façades of the downtown hotels and casinos. Already all the exits from the city were closed, the highways blocked by burning tree-trunks bombed out of the roadside forest.

At midnight Wayne left the darkened Sahara on foot, determined somehow to find Manson's headquarters. Above him, in a smoke-stained sky lit by myriads of burning particles, the laser projectors were putting on their last show for the expedition forces camped for the night in the hills around the city. As Wayne set off for the Strip the giant figure of the murdered JFK slumped across the sky over his head like a disembowelled mountain. Then came a series of weird images, of criminals and dead gangsters, Baby Face Nelson, Dillinger and Pretty Boy Floyd riddled with bullets, Lee Harvey Oswald grimacing in the moments before death.

Last of all, Manson's most threatening ju-ju, came the image of a young man little older than Wayne himself, with a shaven skull and glaring eyes. His broad head hung in the night sky, lit by the distant flames that flickered in its empty chambers. Without thinking, Wayne stopped when he reached the Strip and stared up at the eyes. Even within this diffuse and magnified image, as insubstantial as the air, all their resentment and violence emerged clearly. Within the over-large pupils there lay the memories of an ugly childhood followed by a brutal adolescence and an adult life of madness and imprisonment. The eyes glowered at the expeditions bivouacked in the jungle around Las Vegas, warning them away from a terrible retribution.

189

Walking under the huge, bald head, Wayne realised that he had seen the eyes before somewhere, as he sat sleepily over the slide-projector in the library in Dublin, and that the identity of this mad young man had been a puzzle hovering in the corners of his mind since their arrival in Nevada. He remembered the clicking slides, the images of Presidents and film stars, the famous and the infamous . . .

'Charles Manson!' With a shout he stared at the sky, recalling now the nightmare court case from the remote 1960s, the sick mind behind the Hollywood murders, the cult-children under his baleful spell. But the President . . . ? Wayne turned towards the Desert Inn, with its deserted Hughes suite. A century and a half later another sick, sad young man had emerged from the mental hospital at Spandau, in Berlin's American ghetto, and changed his name as the first step in his long-term plan to rule the United States. Las Vegas burned now as the last act of a Presidential reign which the first Manson had dreamed about in his prison cell, the rule of the criminal and psychopath, his happy finger on the launch buttons of his nuclear missiles.

Wayne ran out into the centre of the Strip, exposing himself to the gunships as they prowled the downtown casino centre. Where was Manson, in what secret command post was he waiting for the invaders who had come to arrest him?

Then he remembered Dr Fleming's words:

' . . . after a long journey the ghosts of Charles Manson and IBM meet in Caesar's Palace, playing with cruise missiles . . . '

Caesar's Palace!

Where else?

The roadblocks along the Strip were unmanned. Outside the Desert Inn he stepped through the coil of barbed wire around the strongpoint from which Ursula had ordered him away. A stormlight glowed inside the deserted emplacement, shining down on the old movie magazines, the discarded record albums and flak jackets. Wayne knelt on the metal floor, straightening the photographs that spilled from a forgotten display frame, instant colour snaps showing Ursula posing proudly in front of her little redoubt. There was even a picture of Wayne, with a caption in Ursula's childish scrawl: 'Mr Busy Busy, our new VP – but cute.'

A faint tropical rain fell across the street as Wayne set off for the next strongpoint outside the Castaways. The warm mist washed the parasol blades of the tall palms, reflecting the distant flames of the burning motels. Behind him he heard the sinister clatter of the two robot gunships, these blank angels which Manson moved around the sky. They came down from the night and hung fifty feet above him as he strode along the centre of the Strip, gatlings pointed at his back, camera zooms in their empty cockpits straining to catch Wayne's profile. Manson had named each of them now. Across the nose of the first gunship was stencilled *Hate*, between the gatlings of the second, *Love*. Wayne stared up at them, tempted to seize their landing rails and pull them from the sky. *Love* and *Hate*, the knuckle tattoos on the fists of the psychopath. But after recognising him they swerved away together, careening in and out of the hotels towards the airport.

The last strongpoint, outside Caesar's Palace, came into view. Certain now that Manson was watching him, Wayne stood below the rusting Roman sign. A narrow path ran from the strongpoint into the dense grove of palms and forest oaks that filled the forecourt of the hotel. In a small clearing sat Manson's Sea-King, its blades drooping, fuselage smeared with oil, cordite and smoke stains. No one was guarding the hotel – clearly the young Mexicans had all abandoned Manson, at last seeing the reality behind the gunships and the laser shows.

Wayne strode towards the darkened façade of the hotel, which was almost invisible behind a matted carapace of ferns and lianas. Somewhere in this strange dream survived its sad magician, the mad Merlin whose devoted machines sat in their eyries atop the nearby hotels.

Light flared from a hatchway in the forest, a bell-hop's luggage gate. A thin-faced youth in a camouflage jacket, still wearing the helmet of the Presidential helicopter flight, beckoned Wayne forward with his pistol.

'You're late, Wayne . . . ' Paco's tired eyes watched Wayne with a dogged curiosity. 'The President's impatient. He wants you to join him at the Big Wheel.'

28 | The War Room

At first, as he stepped through the doors of the sports pavilion, it seemed to Wayne that he had entered a set in some long-abandoned film studio. He had followed Paco from the lobby of the empty hotel, through the endless blackjack and roulette tables that stretched across the carpeted floors below a harsh and gloomy light provided by an emergency generator. Then, as they left behind the Imperial bric-à-brac and reached the doors of the sports pavilion, they stepped over an invisible time line and moved forward two thousand years from this good-humoured fantasy of ancient Rome into an ugly corner of the late twentieth century.

In front of Wayne was a replica of the Pentagon War Room. An electronic target wall leaned down from the ceiling, a map of the United States trapped behind its glass grid like the anguished spirit of some long-dead computer. Below the flickering coastlines and state boundaries was a circular table, telephones and memo pads set out for the President, the Joint Chiefs and their operations assistants. In the centre of the table was a huge roulette wheel, its transparent bowl illuminated from below. It was spinning slowly, and the projected light raced across the walls and ceiling, dappling the display map of the USA and everything else in the room with a series of racing letters.

. . . BALTIMORE . . . TAMPA . . . NEW ORLEANS . . .

PORTLAND . . . TOPEKA . . . TRENTON . . . KNOX-
VILLE . . .

As the names circled the room, Wayne felt Paco nudge
him forward. Sitting at the head of the table, in the place
reserved for both President and croupier, was the naked
figure of Manson. Illuminated by the roulette wheel, his
waxy skin glowed like a painted corpse's. He was crouched
over the control consoles of the two gunships, peering with
a suspicious eye at the display screens which gave a cockpit
view of Las Vegas below the Sands and Paradise Hotels.
Reflected from the glass target wall, the names of all the
cities of America rippled across Manson's skin, so that he
resembled an aging harlequin in an alphabet suit. He
glanced at Wayne without recognising him, and turned his
attention to the double deck of television monitors mounted
behind the table below the target wall.
    Wayne could see clearly what so held Manson's interest.
Each framed by a single camera set up in a small forest
clearing, the six cruises and one Titan missile lay on the
launch ramps of their tracked transporters. Their armed
nose-cones pointed through a peaceful background of
jungle foliage filled with moths and flitting insects.
    Manson nodded to himself, evidently reassured by the
presence of the missiles. His left hand scratched absent-
mindedly at the electric names that glimmered across his
skin. The other hand held an ivory ball which he tossed
loosely in the air, ready to flick it like a firework into the
rotating bowl of the roulette wheel.
    'Wayne, come in and join us − Paco and I have been
waiting all week for you. We're about to play the War Game
. . .'
    Wayne hesitated in the doorway. He listened to Paco's
laboured breathing. The young Mexican's eyes flinched
from the bright lights, and his slim, student's face had
shrunk behind the cheek pads of his helmet. He held tight
to the butt of his pistol, as unsure of himself as he was of
Wayne. The tiers of empty seats rose away into the gloom.

194

Here tennis tournaments and boxing championships had been held in the closing years of the twentieth century. But now Manson had something else in mind, the ultimate video game played with real missiles.

'Wake up, Wayne. Take a seat at the War Table.' Manson gestured him forward, smiling in an almost lewd way. The names of cities raced across his lips, as if he were Cyclops devouring the children of America. 'I know you're a betting man, and you'll enjoy this. We're playing for big stakes, Wayne, the biggest ever . . . '

Wiping his hands on his shirt, Wayne sat down in the chair reserved for the Chairman of the Joint Chiefs. Below him the illuminated wheel rotated steadily. Taking the place of each numeral was the name of an American city, one of thirty-six which circled the wheel, from Atlanta, Buffalo and Charleston through Salt Lake City and San Diego to Tampa, Tulsa and Wichita. Looking up at the electronic target map, Wayne saw that the same thirty-six cities were marked on the display. Small stars pulsed above Boston, Cleveland, Cincinnati and Des Moines.

Manson was staring at his body, conscious for the first time of his own nakedness. Dreamily, he watched the cities crossing his thighs and abdomen, smiling as they disappeared briefly into his pallid navel. Wayne guessed that Manson had stripped himself as an infant might do before destroying his nursery, but also to let the names of these hated cities fester pleasurably on his skin.

'I'm glad you're here, Wayne,' he murmured. 'Everyone else has gone. There are just you and me and Paco, and he isn't too happy.'

The young Mexican shivered and made an irritable gesture. He stood back from the roulette table, pressing the pistol against his hip, like an intelligent child who has stayed up too late.

Manson smiled bravely at him, shaking his head as he stared at his monitors. 'It's the plague, Wayne. I tried to stop it, but it's here, at the gates of the city . . . '

'Mr President — ' Wayne shook himself, half-mesmerised

by the ivory ball bobbing in Manson's hand. 'The Malibu expedition, sir, the advance party will be here in an hour.'

'Wayne? Good God, boy, I know!' Manson glared at Wayne as if he were a malfunctioning robot. He fumbled with a set of buttons inlaid into the table top, his fingers scrabbling for the familiar contours like a blind man comforting himself with a rosary. 'Look, Wayne, you can see it! There's your virus!'

The television screens loomed into close-up. The pictures were transmitted from a series of cameras somewhere off Interstate 15. Emerging through the pre-dawn mist were the advance units of the Malibu brigade. A platoon of marines wearing camouflaged helmets moved forward under the shelter of the jungle foliage. Carbines at the ready, they waved on a bulldozer that cleared aside the fallen palm trees. Walkie-talkie aerials whipped and quivered, there were ten, twenty, then a hundred men. A column of jeeps appeared, rolling over the dead birds and bats, a medium tank crushed the carcase of a charred alligator. From the cautious but confident demeanour of the troops it was clear that they formed part of a disciplined military force, their vehicles fuelled from the small gasoline reserves at Pearl Harbor carefully maintained over the decades for just such an emergency.

'Wayne . . . ' With a whisper, Manson reached a dappled arm across the table. For a moment he was a sad old man searching for reassurance. Ignoring his sagging body, Wayne tried to rally himself, and remembered the dream of America they had shared. How could he save Manson before he turned his gunships loose on the incoming force? Without his banks of TV screens Manson would be as blind as King Lear, and as mad.

'Mr President . . . ' Wayne stood up, hoping to calm Manson, then lead him away to some quiet suite in the hotel. 'I'll look after you, sir.'

'Paco!' Manson flinched from Wayne's touch, repelled by his sweat-stained clothes. A grimace of disgust leaked from his mouth as Paco stepped forward and pushed Wayne into

196

his chair. 'Plague, Paco, there's only one way to destroy it. You have to burn it out, using pieces of the sun . . . '

With a flick of his wrist, as if flushing some obscene object down a chute, Manson tossed the ivory ball into the roulette wheel. It raced around the rotating bowl, shadow soaring across the ceiling of the War Room like a missile. For the first time Manson turned his back on the rows of TV monitors. He sat forward over the command keys, fingers hunting the soft depressions. The ball rippled around the bowl, bounced and flicked, then stopped abruptly, snuggling in the hollow of a city's name.

Manson peered short-sightedly into the wheel, a happy smile on his face. His left hand had already keyed an alert button. Somewhere electronic servos were clicking and humming.

'Minneapolis to pay . . . ' Casually, with the quiet pride of a long-scorned inventor, Manson swung round in his chair. One of the six cruise missiles had come to life in its jungle clearing. The stubby wings and tail fins extended themselves, the transporter turned stiffly and aligned its ramp along a steeper gradient in the eastern sky. The fusing arms clamped to the launch rockets around the missile's tail retracted, there was a momentary flare of white light, and in a burst of flame and smoke the vehicle accelerated. It soared into the early morning sky, an immense plume of exhaust vapour behind it. The booster rockets burned out, then detached themselves and tumbled away. Wings fully extended now, the cruise levelled off at two thousand feet. Already the ground-scanning radars in its sensitive nose were reading the contours of the jungle valleys, avoiding a razor-backed escarpment and selecting the silver highway of a forest river.

Wayne watched the cruise with admiration, almost urging it on its way. The missile was altering course, faced with the impenetrable bulk of the Rockies. But it would thread a path through the cols and ravines, follow the drained bed of the Rio Grande and then fly patiently across the great deserts of Kansas and Nebraska, obeying its instructions until it crossed the Iowa border and headed home for the empty city of Minneapolis.

The camera at the launch site tracked it for the last time, a point of gold against the morning. Manson sat back exultantly, nodding to Paco.

'Come on, Paco, your turn to throw!' But the young Mexican shook his head, his creased face retreating into his helmet. Manson gazed hopefully at Wayne, urging him on. 'Wayne, what about you, boy? The fate of America in *your* hands? I can't offer you Duluth or Seattle, but try your luck with Memphis and Chattanooga, and you'll be doing some good, helping to free the world of plague . . . '

Wayne leaned forward over the illuminated wheel, and held the ivory ball in his hand. He followed Paco's nervous eyes to the target map of America. The cruise was steady but slow, and its light, fuel-efficient engine pushed the 100-kiloton war-head along at little more than 500 miles an hour. It would take five or six hours to make its way through the labyrinth of the Rockies and reach Minneapolis. Time, possibly, to send out the recall codes or route the exhausted bird into the Mississippi.

'Wayne — don't lose heart now! Remember, the Hughes Aircraft Company designed these cruises . . . '

'I'll play, Mr President.' Wayne avoided Manson's excited eyes. The monitor cameras on Interstate 15 showed a column of six tanks moving up between lines of infantrymen. The streets in the centre of Vegas were empty. The grey dawn light exposed a shambles of barbed wire, abandoned strongpoints and burnt-out Buicks. The expedition would soon be there, but it would take them for ever to find Manson in his jungle hotel. By then the gunships could destroy the entire force, send the few survivors running pell-mell for the Pacific . . .

A reconnaissance aircraft passed overhead, its engine drumming at the roof of the sports pavilion. Manson seemed unaware of it, intent only on playing his last game in this film-set War Room. Paco hovered in the shadows behind his sometime patron, his loyalty to Manson in doubt but still too undecided for Wayne to test.

Wayne sat up, deliberately brightening his smile. He tossed the ball in his hand, as Manson's canny eyes opened wide with pleasure. He would play the game, get rid of the remaining five cruises, send them off harmlessly to the empty cities of the desert plain before Manson could turn them loose on the expedition ships.

'I'll try St Louis, Mr President,' he called out. 'We had a hard time there. St Louis to play, on the Great Plague Route . . . '

Two minutes later, when the ball had found its niche and the servos had transmitted their signals from Manson's happy fingers to the jungle launch site, the second cruise set off on its long journey to the shores of the Mississippi.

29 | Countdown

Mobile . . . a plume of supersonic exhaust, a violent lurch up a metal ramp, and an ugly bomb transformed itself into an elegant speedboat surfing the sky.

Fort Worth . . . a flurry of angered flame through a cloud of jacaranda petals. As the glowing debris fell back into the jungle clearing Wayne saw another winged messenger bearing its small dream of the sun.

Columbus . . . dead macaws and parakeets tumbled down a smoking launch ramp, while far above a metal bird shook free its boosters and headed hungrily for the Rockies.

Tampa . . . a swift ride over the Arizona rain-forest to Tucson and the Mexican border at El Paso, then the long haul across the great Texan desert to New Orleans, and straight on from there above the steaming sea to that sweaty Gulf city.

The last of the cruises had gone.

Exhausted, Wayne leaned one shoulder against the table and watched the roulette wheel rotate in front of him, dappling his hands with the names of the target cities of America he had once dreamed of restoring to life. He knew now the source of those random 'earthquakes' which had driven the Indians from their hunting grounds. Manson had been flight-testing his War Room. This huge crystal bowl told of death and the past rather than of the future and promise. Miraculously, Wayne had won St Louis with his first throw. But at least the six cities were empty, the 100-kiloton bombs would do modest damage, level a few long-deserted blocks. And the ivory ball had missed both Washington and New York — the tribes of aboriginal Americans would still be safely huddled on the Mall outside the White House.

'Good, Wayne, you've scored well. The house was happy to pay up. St. Louis, Fort Worth, Tampa, they're on their way . . .'

Manson lay back in his chair, head lolling above his harlequin body, gazing down at the names still moving their electric tapestry across his naked chest. For the past hour, as he and Wayne had taken turns to play the ivory ball into the wheel, Manson had moved into an ever-deeper euphoria, eyes fixed on the missiles spurting from their upraised ramps. At the last launch he seemed barely conscious, a voyeur glutted by this excess of televised violence.

Wayne humoured him, all the while watching the monitor screens. A camera mounted on the Mint Hotel steadily traversed across the centre of Las Vegas. Everyone had arrived now. The jeeps and tanks of the Malibu expedition were parked in a column down Fremont Street. The crews stretched their legs, took off their helmets and walkie-talkies, draped belts of machine-gun ammunition across the hoods of their jeeps. They strolled around the sidewalks, kicking away the shattered glass and avoiding the overripe carcases of the bloated giraffes and panthers. They stared through the clear morning light at the unlit faces of the hotels and casinos, obviously unaware that this derelict jungle city had only recently been the western capital of the United States.

The Phoenix expedition arrived soon afterwards, a mixed brigade of uniformed soldiers, Indian auxiliaries and Mexican freebooters in raffish costumes looted from the department stores of the Lake Mojave resort area. The column of jeeps and half-tracks, dusty Pontiacs and

Chryslers, and a commandeered hearse loaded with booty, rolled up Boulder Highway into Fremont Street and parked nose to nose against the Malibu tanks. Cautious, bearded men in caftans and thigh-length boots, crossed cartridge bandoliers under their leather jackets, fraternised amiably with the Malibu men. Women mercenaries, members of the Divorcees wearing red head-scarves and white Palm Beach suits, silver-handled pistols around their trim waists, jumped up on to the tanks and embraced the embarrassed drivers and radio-operators.

Rifle butts knocked out the plate-glass windows, the soldiers thronged like tourists into the bars and casinos. Already the first timid members of Manson's young militia were coming out of their hiding places below the blackjack tables, still too stunned to answer the friendly questions from the puzzled officers. Hands over their mouths, they pointed to the laser image of the first Charles Manson that glowered in the sky above Las Vegas, and to the two gunships sitting quietly on their helipads atop the distant Sands and Paradise Hotels.

Laughingly, one of the freebooters fired a burst of automatic fire at the scowling image above his head. Clearly everyone in the two expeditions assumed that the war-lord or bandit-general in charge of Las Vegas had run for the hills, and was now hiding out with his men somewhere in the orchid-gardens of Death Valley.

None of them realised that Manson was watching them from his War Room at Caesar's Palace, chuckling dreamily like a vampire drained of blood and teasing himself with the prospect of his next victim. But at least the cruises had gone.

'Mr President, wake up! They're going to kill us!'

Paco stepped forward, pointing to the screens. Bewildered by the scene in front of him, he was trembling with anger. He raised his pistol, about to fire at these intruders into his master's electronic domain, the destroyers of his own dream of a pan-Mexican empire.

'Wait, Paco . . . my boy, it's all right.' Manson murmured soothingly, undisturbed by all this activity. A light aircraft was landing on Las Vegas Boulevard. A high-winged monoplane with striped fuselage, it came in from the sky against the wind and touched down in little more than its own length. It taxied forward, weaving in and out of the dead animals and burnt-out cars, then drew to a halt by the opposed columns of vehicles parked in Fremont Street.

A colonel in combat fatigues and flak jacket, apparently the commander of the Phoenix expedition, stepped down from the plane and saluted his motley force. As his bearded officers and the white-suited Divorcees milled around him he looked up at the shattered façades of the Golden Nugget and the Horseshoe. His cool eye passed to the laser image of the long-forgotten psychopath that filled the sky above his head, and then moved quickly to the two gunships sitting like advertising displays on the roof of the Sands and Paradise Hotels. He said nothing as yet to his mercenaries, but Wayne had already recognised the wary, wind-weathered face under the peaked cap.

Steiner!

So the captain of the *Apollo* had survived the desert around Dodge City. Wayne remembered him walking away from Boot Hill, following the mysterious, mile-high heroes that beckoned him into the west, towards death in that white-bone landscape. As Steiner smiled up at the derelict centre of Las Vegas, Wayne felt a surge of hostility, that same sense of challenge that had forced him to take command of the *Apollo* expedition. If only Steiner realised what he and Manson had achieved, what they had brought to life again in these desolate Nevada jungles, and that he himself had been appointed Vice-President. Perhaps he could use his authority with Steiner to save what was left, conclude an armistice with the invading expeditions . . . ?

'Wayne, my boy . . . ' Manson was watching him with flat eyes. 'Time for the last throw, I think.'

'But, Mr President — ' Wayne gestured to the six empty

launch ramps framed within their monitor screens. 'We've played all the cruises.'

Smirking to himself, Manson pointed over his shoulder. The pallid skin was marked with a hatchwork of weals where his fingers had tried to scratch away the names of the cities. For a moment he resembled an Aztec priest ready to dismember himself. 'There's one left, Wayne, the biggest one of all. The Titan, and everything to play for.'

Wayne shook his head, staring at the screen behind Manson's shoulder. The Titan sat securely on its transporter. This huge ICBM with its 500-kiloton war-head, a wingless monster so different from the air-breathing cruises, could climb beyond the stratosphere and then plunge down its screaming parabola to level a whole city within three minutes of its launch. Wayne held the ivory ball, aware that Manson was watching him in a curious way. Above the sick, damp mouth were two very alert eyes. The roulette wheel rotated on its death round, casting its net of firefly cities around the walls of the War Room. With luck he could pick San Francisco, that long-ruined city as forgotten as Ur, destroyed again and again by a succession of earthquakes as the San Andreas Fault shrugged its irritant burden into the Pacific.

He threw . . .

Zero.

Wayne watched the ball circle the illuminated bowl, safe and defused in its empty niche. No city was marked against it!

With relief he blurted: 'Mr President, there's nothing there, no city − !'

Manson laughed affably, the chuckle of a conjuror who has just deceived a small child.

'Zero pays the house, Wayne.'

Somewhere servos were clicking, relays snapped, a standby generator throbbed. Manson's fingers had already moved to his command console. There was a faint spume of vapour from a fuelling port in the waist of the Titan. As the transporter shunted and heaved in its forest clearing, the huge rocket was moving into a vertical mode, almost as if targeting itself on . . .

'The house? Which one, sir? The White House?'

Manson chuckled again at this. 'In a way. This house, Wayne. Las Vegas. The house always wins in the end.'

Manson pushed himself from the table, as if the game was over. He gazed round at the War Room, at the monitor screens with their views of downtown Las Vegas – the soldiers posing for one another's cameras outside the Golden Nugget, the young militia scampering around the tanks and jeeps, Steiner surrounded by the white-suited Divorcees but more interested in the laser image of the psychopath that straddled the sky. A blonde-haired woman in a lab coat ran towards him across a leaky tapestry of dead birds. As Manson lay back, he seemed completely at peace for the first time, all tension gone from his puffy face, a tired resort tycoon glad to watch his guests enjoying themselves.

But Wayne could only hear the servos moving through their priming sequences. Gusts of vapour spurted from the Titan as it sat on its launcher. Its tanks were being steam-scoured and vented, fuelling clamps waited ready to pump their lox and kerosene into the beast's violent belly. Instrumentation arms extended from the armature of the launch ramp and clasped the nose cone, delicate fingers slid electric pencils into the contact breakers of the guidance system below the war-head, a stream of coded voltages tripped the priming circuits of the nuclear bomb, selecting – so Wayne guessed – an air-burst a thousand feet above the centre of Las Vegas, over a ground-zero where Steiner and Anne Summers were now embracing below the wing of the parked aircraft.

Stung by this show of affection, Wayne snatched the ivory ball from the roulette wheel, this smug passenger riding its zero.

'Mr Manson! The wheel was fixed! St Louis . . . '

'Wayne, I took it for granted that you knew. We're men of the world – the next world, as it happens . . . '

Manson smiled amiably from his chair, inviting Paco to enjoy his little joke. Paco stood stiffly behind him, eyes averted from the screens, pistol held rigidly across his chest. His face was expressionless, and strangely old as if he had aged himself by a fierce act of will. Wayne guessed that the young Mexican had made his decision to stand by Manson to the end, prepared to see the total destruction of Las Vegas and his dreams of a Pan-American kingdom rather than its occupation by the barbarians from the east.

'Mr President, you mustn't give up, sir.' Wayne touched the target map of the United States. A new sun had risen above Nevada, a nova pulsed in the southern apex of the state. 'You've worked so hard, you can't destroy everything now. Mr Manson, I need the recall and shut-down codes.'

Manson held out his open hands, enjoying the play of fireflies across his naked body. 'There are none, Wayne. The Titan's launch systems are totally self-contained. Don't worry, the countdown will take three hours, we've plenty of time to relax here. We can talk about our great adventure together, all the things we tried to do . . . '

'Mr Manson!' Wayne tried to push past Paco, but the Mexican jostled him back, face like a fraught machine under the flying helmet. Wayne pointed to the happy scenes in downtown Las Vegas, where Steiner and Anne Summers strolled arm in arm through the throngs of soldiers, and the white-suited women mercenaries whistled at McNair as he limped up on a bandaged leg, helped by Pepsodent. Heinz, GM and Xerox were there too, late arrivals dismounting from their huge steam-car, each stuffed into an oversize fur coat, a family of bears on an outing with baby-bear. 'Mr President, we've got to leave, sir, warn everyone to get away. There's just time.'

'My boy, calm yourself.' Manson folded his hands across his stomach and assumed a Buddha-like gaze. 'I don't like to see you panic. Remember where we are, cultivate the Roman virtues − dignity, pride, stoicism in the face of death. We knew the plague would reach here one day, we'll just play our parts in a modest cleansing operation. You can be proud, Wayne, you're a true American − '

'I'm not!' Wayne gripped the back of his metal chair. Hoarsely, he shouted: 'I'm not an American! Not a real one, anyway, and I never have been!'

'Wayne . . . ?' Manson was genuinely puzzled. 'My boy, look at what we've achieved here . . . '

'Mr Manson, it's all been a fantasy! These dreams were dead a hundred years ago! All we've done here is build the biggest Mickey Mouse watch in the world. I'm not a real American, not like GM and Heinz and Pepsodent . . . ' Wayne shuddered at himself, shaking his head at the lost years. 'In fact, if I had to say who I was I'd say − "*Ich bin ein Berliner.*" '

Manson's smile stiffened, a pair of sharp eyes dominated his fleshy face, its confused planes came to a hard focus. 'A Berliner, Wayne? I thought you lived in Dublin?'

'An honorary Berliner.' Wayne nodded firmly, agreeing with his verdict on himself. He leaned across the table, and stopped the rotating bowl of the roulette wheel. 'Yes, I'm a Berliner, all right, of a special kind. And I ought to have been locked up in Spandau with you . . . '

Manson sat up, looking round for Paco. He pointed to the motionless roulette wheel, and began to examine his chest. His skin flickered nervously under its skein of stationary cities. Manson scratched at the festering lights, an atlas of tics driving him mad. Already the pallid flesh was marked with points of blood. Milwaukee bled on his right shoulder, Chattanooga leaked a red smear across his throat, Kalamazoo and South Bend erupted in his armpits, Buffalo twitched in his gory navel.

'Paco! Start the wheel!'

Wayne picked up his steel chair. Manson was leaning across the table, trying to turn the heavy wheel. As the young Mexican hovered over him, unsure how to help his master, Wayne raised the chair and drove the legs at Paco's head. The pistol fell to the floor among the tangle of television cables. Wayne threw aside the chair and ran for the doors. He was fumbling with the ornate locks when he heard a brief volley of shots into the wall beside him. Spurs of plastic stung his face. Wayne turned to grapple with Paco as the Mexican stepped up behind him, the bruise of a chair-leg on his right cheek. Wayne felt the pistol strike him across the neck, and fell to the floor through a flicker of fireflies and the harlequin dance of a crazed America.

30 | Execution Squad

He was kneeling by the locked doors of the War Room, left wrist handcuffed to the legs of the bronze statue of a tennis player that formed the handles. The bowl of the roulette wheel was dark now, and the only light came from the television screens and the target wall above the table. Pistol in hand, Paco stood guard beside Manson, who crouched over the control consoles of the helicopter gunships, Paco's camouflage jacket round his shoulders.

Above them, framed within its monitor screen, the Titan sat on its launch platform in the forest clearing. The missile was wreathed in condensing vapour, its nose cone wrapped in a cat's cradle of contact breakers and fusing lines. Wayne searched the darkness for the master clock. In little more than two hours the Titan would set off on its short journey to the stratosphere, then turn 180° and light up this old gambling capital in a way that not even its gangland founders could ever have imagined.

Manson's fingers moved deftly over the control toggles, like a surgeon adjusting the settings of an intensive care unit. He was calm now, his moment of panic behind him, and watched the invading soldiers with a shrewd and cautious eye, glad to see them busy with their good-humoured looting of the bars and casinos.

But the blades of the gunships were turning against the sky, the prayer wheels of a sinister machine religion. As the first puzzled soldiers looked up from the doorways of the ransacked stores, Manson spoke into a microphone. His voice was inaudible within the War Room, but giant amplified fragments boomed out over the city and drummed at the roof of the sports pavilion. The soldiers and mercenaries stopped to peer at the sky, startled by the threatening drone that seemed to emerge from the laser image of Charles Manson.

'. . . Vegas . . . now a plague zone . . . urgent health measures . . . cleansing operation . . . do not leave . . . cordon sanitaire . . . two hours . . . '

The aerial commentary continued, a rambling ultimatum. Everywhere hundreds of soldiers were looking at their looted watches, like tourists caught by some well-timed fraud. A party of officers emerged from the Golden Nugget, juggling silver dollars in their hands, then let them fall around their feet and stared open-mouthed at the sky. Steiner ran down Fremont Street, waving them back to their vehicles. He bundled Anne Summers and the limping McNair into the shelter of the Mint's lobby.

Already Manson's voice was drowned by the engines of the two gunships lifting from the roofs of the Sands and Paradise Hotels. As Manson lowered his microphone Wayne tugged at the brass ankles of the tennis player. Watching the screens above Manson's head, he saw the gunships approaching. They roared in low along the Strip, landing skids barely clearing the roofs of the casinos. They moved in a rigid tandem, blades scrambling across the air, firing their rockets and gatlings into the unguarded vehicles. Jeeps and half-tracks slumped on their riddled tyres, steam spurted from radiators, windshields exploded like glass targets. Fuel tanks flashed and flared from the blazing vehicles, leaked pools of burning gasoline across the roads. The crews scattered, firing back with pistols and carbines from the hotel doorways.

The gunships soared down the centre of Fremont Street, skids only a few feet from the tank turrets, their sights fixed on the parked reconnaissance plane. The gatlings made short work of the flimsy machine, a burst of fire

210

chopped its wings and fuselage into a thrashing heap of agitated matchwood. Glutted by the success of this first assault, the gunships climbed away on a wide circuit of the city, ready to come round for a second pass at the exposed vehicles.

For the next fifteen minutes sporadic shooting continued, as the gunships circled the centre of Las Vegas, suddenly picking on an isolated jeep, firing their rockets at the tanks that trundled blindly around the downtown streets. Manson sat at his control consoles, watching the destruction of the Malibu and Phoenix expeditions from the cockpit cameras of the gunships. Now and then he paused to make sure that the Titan missile at the jungle launch-site continued its long self-preparation. He squatted comfortably on the edge of his chair, fingers working the gunship controls as if they were flippers on an amusement hall pin-table. He seemed unaware of Paco and Wayne and even the War Room itself. Looking at him, Wayne felt that after his long journey Manson had at last become young again. He was no longer in Las Vegas, and was going home to Spandau. He was the delinquent adolescent in the occupational therapy class, playing an elaborate video game with his gunships, eager to use up all the free plays in the world before the ICBM signalled the ultimate tilt.

When he had temporarily run out of targets, Manson returned the gunships to their arming bays atop the Sands and Paradise Hotels. He picked up the microphone and resumed his commentary, a tour-operator well-satisfied with the reception arrangements provided for his party of visitors to this greatest of all theme parks. Wayne could hear his flat voice boom against the façades of the hotels down the Strip, and see on the monitor screens the baffled soldiers and mercenaries listening behind their weapons in the doorways of bars and cocktail lounges.

' . . . here's an update on the Titan . . . you'll be glad to hear there's just one hour and seventeen minutes left . . . that's the big display, folks, the grand finale brought to you direct from the Big Wheel in the War Room . . . this is one game you all have to play, so don't try to leave town, any of you . . .'

Laughing to himself at this ironic imitation of a television compere, Manson lay back in his chair. He patted Paco on the arm, trying to reassure the young Mexican who stood glassily beside him. Wayne stood up, wrenching his wrist to see the screens over Manson's shoulder. The clock raced on through the Titan's countdown, but nothing was happening. No attempt was being made to send an assault party up the Strip. Obviously Steiner and the Malibu expedition commander realised that they were trapped in Las Vegas, that the robot gunships would shoot up the slow-moving jeeps and half-tracks. Anyone trying to leave on foot could never escape in time from the Titan's lethal radiation zone. The blast of neutrons would cut through the soft jungle within a five-mile radius. They were all trapped here under the laser image of the psychopath in the sky, Manson's tutelary deity, with no idea of the site of this mad war-lord's secret command post.

'Paco — !' Manson sat up, uncannily alert. He peered suspiciously at the monitor screens, beckoning the young Mexican to his side. 'What are they doing, Paco? They're playing a last game of their own . . . '

His hands moved to the control consoles of the gun-ships. There was a guttural snarl of exhaust. The blades spun, and the two robot helicopters rose into the air.

Advancing down the Strip was a curious procession of some forty or so marchers, drawn up three abreast. Although they carried rifles over their shoulders and had a vaguely military bearing, they at first sight seemed to be a brigade of cripples, old men with creaking joints and plodding step, conscripted into this scratch force from their back-porches and balconies. They swayed along together, led by a man wearing a powdered wig and eighteenth-century cutaway coat. The ranks behind him wore costumes that were slightly more up to date, severe wing collars and frock coats, and only those in the rear wore twentieth-century suits, sober pinstripes and dark worsteds. They marched stiffly into Manson's screens, the members of a senile militia which had appeared here to do improbable battle with the waiting gunships.

Wayne recognised them immediately. They were Dr Fleming's robot Presidents, instructed by the old scientist to evacuate Las Vegas before the Titan attack, and now solemnly marching down this long highway out of town. The neutron blast would scorch the antique suits and plastic skin from their metal backs, but they would probably make it to Interstate 15, and follow it all the way to the Hollywood Hills.

The gunships hovered behind them, as Manson's hands hesitated on the controls. Above the Titan monitor screen a time signal had appeared, '59 min 59 sec', the seconds fluttering away with the last countdown of the ICBM. Touching Paco with a sudden show of affection, Manson watched Washington lead his colleagues past the Holiday Inn. There was a warm and almost child-like smile on Manson's face, as if he was aware that these stiff-jointed dolls were all that would survive of his own Presidential dreams.

But the Presidents had come to a halt outside Caesar's Palace. They shambled to a dusty stop, Ford blundering into Carter's heels, then made a right turn to form line abreast. Washington faced the hotel, his back to the squad drawn up behind him, unaware of the gunships circling suspiciously overhead. Together, the Presidents ordered arms and stood heavily to attention.

'Paco . . . ' Manson's head tilted shyly, he seemed bewildered by this display. 'It's a last salute. I'm touched, Paco, really moved. Dr Fleming remembered me. We ought to let them in . . . '

He stood up, motioning Paco to the door. But the Presidents had come to life again. Rifles at the assault, they broke into a run, and followed Washington up the narrow jungle drive towards the hotel entrance. Wigs and ties flying, they lumbered forward, covering the ground with their stamping feet. Behind them a tank had appeared at the junction of the Strip and Flamingo Road. Soldiers in camouflage helmets were darting across the roads on all sides. As Manson screamed with rage, lunging for the controls of the gunships, the first covering machine-gun fire came from the Castaways Hotel.

The scrum of Presidents had reached the entrance to Caesar's Palace, after a confused stampede through the trees. With a harsh blare, the first of the gunships soared in behind them. Its gatlings clattered, cutting a swathe through the frock-coated ranks. Madison, Taft and Buchanan fell across the steps, legs still kicking gamely. A riddled Gerry Ford tottered in circles around the drive, his gyros jammed, and knocked down Jackson and Van Buren. Carter ran head on through a plate-glass window. Picked up by a lobby camera, his startled face was frozen for ever in an immense, dazed smile. But as the second gunship roared in above the jungle canopy, strafing the entrance doors and chopping them into glass jigsaws, a score of the Presidents had fought their way into the hotel. Unaware of their hostile reception, they wrestled past each other like exuberant conventioneers. Heading towards the sports pavilion, they fanned out through the craps and blackjack tables. Washington still led them, antique duelling pistol in hand. Behind him came Truman and Eisenhower, Hoover and Wilson and the three Kennedys.

'Paco! Stop them! Switch them off!' Like an enraged child faced with a set of uncooperative toys, Manson punched the control consoles of his gunships. But the young Mexican was staring limply at the banks of swerving screens. There was an angry blare as the helicopters veered away, their auto-pilots catching them before they stalled into the forest oaks. Manson seized the pistol from the still stunned Paco, then turned to fire at the doors, at the thudding Presidential feet.

Wayne flattened himself against the steps, left hand cuffed to the tennis player's bronze ankles. Gunfire surrounded the hotel, and machine-gun bullets had already fractured the electrographic map of America above Manson's head. There was a stampede of heavy feet, and the doors collapsed, throwing Wayne across the steps. The posse of robots burst into the sports pavilion, a pandemonium of Presidents brandishing their rifles. They paused together, like a middle-aged football pack orienting themselves, while their gyros steadied and they matched the target image in their memory stores with the speechless man cowering naked in front of them.

Manson knelt by his chair, and stared with unfeigned horror at the semi-circle of Presidents shuffling into position around him, a reproving board of elders. There was an aloof Jefferson, a smiling but wan Dwight Eisenhower, a matter-of-fact Truman in a hurry to get everything over, a prim Wilson and even a sweating Nixon embarrassed by their physical resemblance.

Raising the pistol, Manson backed away among the television screens, trying to draw their light on to himself. He looked down at his pallid, blood-flecked body, a trapped adolescent puzzled to find himself in this senile flesh, caught after hours in the therapy room with his broken toys, yet still cunning enough to put on an ingratiating smile. He waved to Paco, who had moved away from him, and now stood behind the line of Presidents, looking down at him with a calm and detached gaze.

'Paco, we can still . . . ' Manson stood up, and slipped against the helicopter control consoles. The cockpit pictures swerved eerily, a rush of rooftops, a swaying vista of tanks and men running towards the besieged hotel. Manson surveyed the banks of television screens, and the whole bullet-riddled stage set of the War Room, a sadness in his eyes of a child at game's end. He turned hopefully to the Presidents, and then let out an angry cry and fired his pistol straight at the solemn figure of Washington.

As the two bullets carried away half his face, Washington flinched and staggered back. A third bullet caught his chest, but he shook himself in a dignified way and raised his antique pistol, calmly signalling to his fellow-Presidents. Together, they raised their rifles.

Bruised and buffeted by the metal feet that had stamped across him, Wayne barely heard the volley of shots. His left wrist was still cuffed to the fragment of the tennis player, but the handle was now free of the door. He rolled out of Carter's way as the last of the Presidents trundled smiling into the War Room. On the floor in the corner Manson was scrambling about like a fish stranded by a bloody pool. Wayne lifted himself to his feet. When the Presidents raised their rifles again, watched by the impassive Paco, Wayne limped up the steps and hobbled away into the casino.

Soldiers in full combat gear moved among the blackjack tables, weapons pointed at Wayne's head. Wayne stumbled forward, too hoarse to tell them not to fire. Then a man in a sailor's peaked cap stepped up to him and held his shoulders in his strong hands.

'Wayne? Dr Fleming said you'd be here.' Steiner listened to the last volley of shots from the War Room. He peered into Wayne's face with a not unfriendly smile. 'Calm down, you're all right. In fact, you've just become President of the United States. Can you walk? Somehow we've all got to get out of Las Vegas – there's less than an hour to go.'

31 | Flight

They stood below the derelict façade of the Golden Nugget. In the now silent streets small flames wandered among the burnt-out jeeps and half-tracks. Las Vegas was deserted, apart from themselves and Manson's missile. The soldiers and mercenaries had left in the serviceable vehicles, taking their wounded with them.

As GM scanned the sky, rifle trained on the roof-tops, Anne Summers and Pepsodent helped the limping McNair from the lobby of the Mint. Steiner steered them towards his command tank, which sat ready to move in the centre of Fremont Street, Heinz at the controls, its heavy engine pumping impatiently. Xerox perched on the turret in her splendid fur coat, her baby in a sable muff propped against the open hatch.

Feet apart, Steiner stood in the empty street, ruefully surveying the charred matchwood of his reconnaissance plane. Despite his flak vest and camouflage jacket, he once more resembled a ship's captain, legs braced against the coming storm. Under the mariner's cap his face had lost its deep tan, and he seemed younger and fresher. He had spent the past months in the shadowy world of the Arizona rain-forest, recuperating after his rescue by Mexican freebooters from across the Rio Grande, coming to terms with his failure to lead the *Apollo* expedition and facing up to the fact that he had not really cared about its fate. He had seen the laser image in the sky above Dodge

City and rightly guessed that the exhausted expedition was being deliberately drawn into the electronic web of Manson's jungle empire. Unwilling to take the risk of trying to save Anne and Wayne, he had watched the arrival of McNair and the steam-cars, and then moved on by himself towards Amarillo, travelling at night to avoid the robot cameras. Somewhere in the endless white deserts of west Texas he had finally run out of luck, but was saved by a party of foraging Mexicans lured northwards by the rumours of Manson's El Dorado.

While recovering in Phoenix, Steiner was approached by emissaries of the Miami survey fleet, and offered weapons, vehicles and spotter aircraft if he would lead a second expeditionary force across the Colorado River. Steiner accepted the command, recognising that his own solitary nature had been partly responsible for the deaths of Ricci and Orlowski, and that his quest for an empty continent was as much a delusion as any of Manson's crippled dreams. Yet now, after the long drive through the tropical rain-forest, he found himself trapped within a lunatic fantasy far more extreme than anything of his own.

Steiner placed an encouraging arm around Anne Summers as she waited nervously beside the tank.

'Thirty minutes left, time to move, Anne. Everyone else has gone. They should be fifteen miles from here. With luck, we'll find a deep shelter somewhere . . . '

Anne embraced Wayne with relief, rubbing his bruised wrist. 'Wayne, we thought you'd joined Manson! Where's Dr Fleming? He was supposed to be rounding up all those pathetic children. You've no idea where the Titan launch site is?'

Wayne shook his head, still too weary to speak. As Anne held his hands he looked round at the streets over which he and Manson had once ruled. He realised that time had begun to leak from Las Vegas like the last music from an antique record player. After the dreams and fantasies which had wound him up to the great adventure of crossing America he was once again becoming the young stowaway, cared for by this capable woman professor whom he had once thought of making his First Lady. But he was glad to see Steiner again, to play the role of second in command to this canny navigator, even though he knew that the Captain had little hope of getting them to safety. At the same time he felt a strange loyalty to Manson, despite the Titan missile counting down to its take-off somewhere in the jungle.

There was a distant roar of gunfire. A mile away, along the northern outskirts of Las Vegas, *Love* and *Hate* flew aimlessly along the empty boulevards. They circled and dived like neurotic toys, now and then swerving to discharge a burst of fire at each other. The face of the long-dead psychopath, Charles Manson, still glowered down at them from the bright sky. But already the projected image was wearing itself out. Scanning lines shimmered below the jaw, a noose tightening around the neck. A narrow interference band crossed the eyes, and the baleful glare gave way to a series of panicky left-to-right glances, as if the decapitated head had realised that it was being abandoned here in the sky above the doomed city.

Wayne looked back for the last time at the Desert Inn, at the now empty Hughes penthouse bristling with radio and television aerials. The two gunships had also spotted the isolated hotel, and homed in angrily, their radars seeing themselves in the dish antennae. The gatlings riddled the windows of the penthouse, and cut a violent swathe through the tottering aerials. Unsatisfied, the gunships turned away in frustration. They soared across the forest canopy, shooting at each other as they set off for the American border, quarrelsome twins lost in the green horizons of the south.

'Wayne, we've twenty-five minutes . . . ' Steiner stood on the tank's turret, helping Anne Summers through the hatch. Heinz sat at the controls, goggles over his eyes, working up the heavy throttles. Black smoke pumped from the exhaust stack.

Steiner jumped into the road and put an arm around Wayne's shoulder. 'Wayne, come on — you'll find other dreams to build on.'

But Wayne was pointing towards the Convention Center. Floating through the morning air was an immense cloud of pale-winged dragonflies. Their delicate membranes quivered and trembled as if they were testing the vivid light for the first time. They approached in convoy, sailing down the Strip, a fleet of glass aeroplanes each borne aloft by the smallest caress of the sun. There were dozens of the craft, Sunlight Fliers released to the benign air from the doorways of the Convention Center. They drew nearer, a huge chandelier of twinkling crystal, a palace of windows carried in the palm of the sun. In the lead Flier a delighted old man sat at the flimsy controls, his precarious saddle suspended in an eccentric web of silver wires. His free legs swung in the air, and now and then launched into a burst of make-believe pedalling. When he saw Wayne he shouted happily to him, voice lost in the whispered tinkling of millions of wing crystals.

Already Wayne had recognised Dr Fleming, the old scientist surfing on his sunbeams. Behind him were fifty other Sunlight Fliers, built to a medley of designs, two-, three- and six-seaters. The pilots were all children, bright faces lit by the morning air, the sometime members of Manson's militia. There was Enrico at the controls of a huge crystal biplane, Chavez and Theresa co-pilots of a six-seater triplane like a diaphanous bus, youngsters of twelve and thirteen expertly steering their glass speed-boats and starting to fool about in the tail of the convoy.

They passed Caesar's Palace, and Enrico detached his Flier from the rest of the fleet and steered it down towards the entrance. As it hovered above the ground Paco darted from the doorway of the hotel. He had lined up the Presidents in three ranks, led now by Eisenhower. At Paco's command they moved stiffly down the drive, some limping and hobbling, Ford's gyros still playing him up, and began their long march down the Strip towards the

Interstate Highway. Paco saluted them, threw away his yellow helmet and ran to the waiting Flier. He climbed through the wire struts into the passenger seat behind Enrico, as the great dragonfly rose steeply into the air.

'They're coming for us! Anne, Wayne — leave the tank!' Steiner was shouting to Heinz, telling him to switch off the engine. 'Everybody out! Pepsodent, help McNair! Xerox, get rid of that coat — we're going to join the sun!'

The convoy approached, a crystal cloud descending over the Golden Nugget. Everyone helped McNair from the turret. They stood beside the tank, shouting into the air as a dozen of the Sunlight Fliers hovered above them. A shimmer of wings filled the street, reflected in the dead façades of the old casinos. A glittering ferris wheel lowered itself from the sky, its gondolas of cut glass rotating in a fountain of light. As they swept down, the young pilots jockeyed their delicate craft among the burnt-out jeeps and half-tracks, careful not to dash the glass aeroplanes to pieces among the silver dollars and cartridge cases. Dr Fleming rode at the head of this happy circus, the lapels of his lab coat clapping like excited semaphores. He seemed even younger than the children around him, a wizened robin released from his cage to the kindly air.

Anne climbed behind Dr Fleming, hands around the old scientist's waist, and gave a cry of alarm when he roguishly let the Flier rise straight up like an elevator. The others clambered aboard the hovering craft as they soared past, pulling themselves through the wires hand over hand. Pepsodent carried McNair in his arms and lifted him into a passenger seat. He hung among the silver wires, plaster leg dangling, and set off into the sky with a cheerful wave. GM, Xerox and the baby soared aloft in the six-seater triplane, a family of young trippers in passage to the sun. Pepsodent and Heinz rose nervously into the air behind a couple of twelve-year-old aces with a minute's flying time. Steiner stood behind Paco in the stern of Enrico's Flier, hands holding the criss-cross of wires. He cheered when the hot wind caught his mariner's cap and

221

carried it away into the street below.

Last of all, Wayne waited his turn. He ducked as the convoy of glass planes swept past his head, aware that he was now the only person left in Las Vegas.

'Say, you there − have you seen the President? A young fellow by the name of Wayne?'

Laughter came down from the air. Ursula's monoplane hung above him, wingtips teasingly out of arms' reach. The handsome militia-girl chuckled with delight at having startled Wayne. She soared along Fremont Street, starboard wing rippling a playful arpeggio across the neon tubes in the Golden Nugget façade. Wayne panted after her, seized the wire struts and pulled himself into the passenger seat. Ursula grinned cheerfully and canted the wings. An instant wave of warm air propelled the Flier towards the sky. The roofs of the hotels and casinos along Fremont Street fell away, and in a blaze of light the convoy climbed on to the generous shoulder of the sun, levelled off at a thousand feet and set sail at a brisk seventy knots for the safety of California and the morning gardens of the west.

32 | California Time

They crossed the Nevada border twenty minutes later, soaring through the clear mountain air. They had spread out soon after leaving Las Vegas, and by now were separated from each other by several hundred yards, the Fliers surfing along on their own warm waves. Together the convoy formed a crystal field laid out below the sun to celebrate its passage across America.

Ahead, still in the lead, was Dr Fleming. He sat happily at his controls, Anne Summers with one hand on his coat. In the craft behind them, Steiner had moved forward beside Enrico to try his skill at the subtle wing-warping that steered the Flier through the air, so like its namesake at Kitty Hawk. Far away to Wayne's right, McNair's plaster cast hung against the sky like a melting icicle that had fallen from the sun.

As they left Las Vegas they had passed the group of Presidents marching steadily down Interstate 15, Truman and Eisenhower in the lead. Ford and Nixon had given up and sat by the roadside, while Carter had wandered off into the forest to commune with himself. But the others were marching on, gyros confidently steering them towards the Pacific. Later, the aerial convoy overtook the column of jeeps carrying the escaping soldiers and mercenaries of the Malibu and Phoenix expeditions, now safely out of range of the Titan. When they crossed Devil's Peak, Dr Fleming signalled them to descend, and Wayne looked back to see a slim pencil of vapour rise at speed from the forest ten miles to the south of Las Vegas. It pierced the sky, the exhaust trail of the Titan, vanishing into the stratosphere before its return to the earth.

Clustering together, like fireflies warming themselves in their own light, the squadron of Fliers hovered above the jungle canopy, safe behind the protective bulk of the mountain. Wayne embraced Ursula's shoulders, reassuring the suddenly panicky young woman. Already his confidence was returning. As he waited for the flash that would signal the death of Manson's empire, Wayne briefly mourned the end of his own short Presidency. Yet the dream remained, he would enter the White House one day and sit in that office he had cleaned, without realising it at the time, in preparation for himself. He would arrive at his inauguration in one of these crystal aeroplanes, be the first President to be sworn in on the wing. The old dreams were dead, Manson and Mickey Mouse and Marilyn Monroe belonged to a past America, to that city of antique gamblers about to be vaporised fifty miles away. It was time for new dreams, worthy of a real tomorrow, the dreams of the first of the Presidents of the Sunlight Fliers.